CW01024126

Praise for Sharon Ward

In this third installment of the Fin Fleming, underwater photographer series, Fin is facing her toughest challenge yet. Her dear friends Gus and Theresa have been kidnapped. The police are stymied; and her parents and her stepbrother Oliver leave the whole mess in her lap to pursue their personal goals; and someone is sabotaging things at RIO, the oceanography institute where she works. Aided by some new friends as well as old favorites, Fin sets out to find her friends before it's too late.

— C. Michele Dorsey, author of the Sabrina Salter Mysteries

Sharon Ward's IN DEEP is a stellar, pulse-pounding debut novel featuring a female underwater photographer. A heady mix of underwater adventure, mystery, and romance.

— Hallie Ephron, New York Times bestselling author

Pack your SCUBA fins for a wild trip to the Cayman Islands. *In Deep* delivers on twists and turns while introducing a phenomenal new protagonist in underwater photographer Fin Fleming, tough, perceptive and fearless.

— Edwin Hill, author of *The Secrets We Share*

How much did I love In Deep? Let me count the ways. Fin Fleming, underwater photographer, is a courageous yet vulnerable protagonist I want to sip Margaritas with. The Cayman Islands are exotic and alluring, yet tinged with danger. The underwater scenes and SCUBA diving details are rendered in stunning detail. Wrap that all into a thrilling mystery and you'll be left as breathless as - well, no spoilers here. You must read it to find out!

— C. Michele Dorsey, Author of the Sabrina Salter Mysteries: No Virgin Island, Permanent Sunset, and Tropical Depression

Breathtaking on two levels, Sharon Ward's debut novel IN DEEP will captivate experienced divers as well as those who've only dreamed of exploring the beauty beneath the sea. The underwater world off the Cayman Islands is stunningly rendered, and the complex mystery involving underwater photographer Fin Fleming, especially the electrifying dive scenes, will have readers holding their breath. Brava!

— Brenda Buchanan Author of the Joe Gale Mystery Series

In Deep is a smart and original story that sucks you in from page one. Edge-of-your-seat suspense, a hauntingly realistic villain, and a jaw-dropping twist make this pacy read unputdownable until the very last word.

— Stephanie Scott-Snyder, Author of When Women Offend: Crime and the Female Perpetrator

Dark Tide

Dark Tide

A Fin Fleming Thriller

Sharon Ward

Covers by Milagraphicartist.com

ISBN eBook: 979-8-9854946-2-4

ISBN Trade Paper: 979-8-9854946-6-2

ISBN B&N Edition Trade Paper: 9798985494686

ISBN Hard Cover: 979-8-9854946-7-9

ISBN B&N Edition Hard Cover: 979-8-9854946-9-3

Printed in USA

First Edition

To Jack, the best husband in the universe.
Thank you for all you do

Contents

Foreword

Thank you to all the readers who have been following the adventures of Fin Fleming, underwater photographer. I appreciate your support.

I have to warn you that Fin is a professional diver, certified in all kinds of technical diving categories well beyond the training and experience of recreational divers. If you're a diver, don't do what Fin does. Stay within the bounds of your training.

Always plan your dive and dive your plan. Don't dive alone. Don't dive too deep. Don't use mixed gases unless you've been trained.

And NEVER, NEVER, let your recreational dive computer go into decompression mode. Fin and her friends use professional dive computers that can handle more complex decompression algorithms.

And if you ever get the chance to visit the Cayman Islands, go. It's a fabulous place, even if you're not a diver.

Chapter 1
Benjamin Arrives at RIO

I WAS SITTING in my office at RIO—the name we called the Madelyn Anderson Russo Institute of Oceanography on Grand Cayman. I'd been engrossed in adding music to my video of the life and times of Harry the stingray. I had been filming him since I was a child, right up until his death a little over a year ago.

Since I needed to submit it to the prestigious Underwater Conservancy video contest this week, my schedule for finishing the short film was tight. I'd been working on it for more than a year, and now I was up against the deadline. I'd been having trouble with the soundtrack. Despite extensive searches, I hadn't found affordable music with the qualities and rhythm I wanted until recently. I was still trying to time the score in a way that built tension right up until the moment the shark pounced. It was delicate work, and I was so deeply absorbed in what I was doing that the rest of the world had receded from my awareness. At least, it had receded until I heard my name, shattering my focus.

"Dr. Fleming." A pause. "Dr. Fleming." By the time the words had pierced my consciousness, the voice was sounding annoyed. Really annoyed.

I pulled off my noise-cancelling earphones. "Maddy's not around. She's out of town." My mother, Madelyn Russo, the world famous oceanographer who had founded RIO, was on a speaking tour of the states, hoping to drum up donations to keep the institute operational. It was a never ending process at RIO.

"That's okay. I'm not looking for Maddy."

"Well then, who are you looking for?" Even to my own ears my voice sounded curt and unwelcoming, and I felt bad. I hadn't meant to be rude.

The man standing in the door of my office looked surprised and took a step back. "I believe I'm looking for you. You are Dr. Finola Fleming, aren't you? At least, her name is on this door. I'm Benjamin Brooks. I thought we had an appointment…"

I rose to shake his hand. "Oh, God. Yes, we do have an appointment. I'm sorry to be late. I got lost in the zone. And I didn't answer right away because I'm not used to being called Doctor yet. I guess it took a few tries for your words to penetrate." After years of work on my thesis with Rosie, the smartest Atlantic Pygmy octopus in the world, I'd finally received my doctorate less than six weeks ago, and I was still getting used to being called doctor.

Benjamin shook my hand, but he didn't smile. "I've been waiting on a bench outside human resources for forty-five minutes. Didn't make me feel very welcome on my first day. Is that the way this place usually runs, Dr. Fleming?"

"Please, call me Fin. And no, it's not how we usually work. We're pretty laid back here at RIO, but we're generally good at keeping our commitments. I apologize again. As I said, I was concentrating on a delicate task and lost track of time, but I promise we'll get back on schedule."

He sniffed. "Good. I have commitments too, you know."

Maddy had recently hired Benjamin Brooks as CFO of RIO. She'd started the search after six months with no word from our former CFO —my ex-boyfriend Liam Lawrie. By now, it seemed apparent to everyone that he wasn't coming back from Australia, despite his promises to return. I swallowed a stab of heartbreak at the thought of never seeing Liam again. Time to move on.

I gave Benjamin's navy blue blazer, white button down collar shirt, blue and silver striped tie, and long grey pants the once over. Nobody at RIO dressed like that, even on their first day of work. It wasn't that kind of place.

He might be overdressed for a day at RIO, but Benjamin Brooks was a very good-looking man, with deep blue eyes, dark brown hair, and a slim build. About my age—mid-twenties—and very accomplished for his age. "What commitments do you have today, Ben? I can work around them, although usually first days are pretty light around here."

He'd noticed me eyeing his clothes and flushed. "I had plans for my day. Things I wanted to learn. Project plans I wanted to make. Now my schedule is out of kilter. It's upsetting." He sniffed again. "And please, call me Benjamin."

Wow. I'd known him for less than ten minutes and I already disliked Benjamin Brooks with a white hot intensity. Maddy had offered me the opportunity to interview him before she hired him, but I'd turned her down. We'd lost our two previous CFOs—my stepfather Ray Russo who'd died, and my ex-boyfriend Liam, who'd just disappeared—in quick succession. I didn't want anything to do with choosing their replacement. But after meeting Benjamin, next time I'd know better than to skip the interview process. To me, he seemed all wrong for RIO.

What could Maddy have been thinking when she hired him? He was tense and rigid, completely unlike any of the other people who worked at RIO, most of whom were cheerful, easy-going, and friendly. Well, it was her decision, and I'd do my best to find a way to work with him.

Even if he wasn't Liam. My heart clenched remembering Liam's easy smile and wry humor.

I stood. "Let's start with a tour. I imagine you're excited to see our facility. Everything here is state of the art, and our labs are amazing."

He looked puzzled. "I'm a numbers guy. Why would I want to see the labs? Aren't they just full of fish?"

Once again, I wondered what Maddy had been thinking when she hired Benjamin Brooks. There had to have been better candidates than him, and once again I regretted my decision not to take her up on the opportunity to interview her top picks. I never would have selected this guy.

"Marine research. That's what we do here. RIO's labs are justifiably famous, and they're one of the most important parts of the business. So, yeah, the labs are full of fish."

He nodded. "We can skip the labs for today if you don't mind. That will help us get back on schedule. But in the meantime, can you find out where that infernal squalling is coming from? I can barely hear myself think."

Now that he mentioned it, I could hear loud wailing coming through my open window along with the soft ocean breeze. The noise sounded like it was coming from the marina. I knew that former RIO employees Gus and Theresa Simmons were planning to moor their boat here this week. That way, Gus could be nearby in case my almost-brother Oliver Russo or I needed help running the business while Maddy was away. The noise must be coming from Angelica, their new baby, crying like her heart was broken.

"That must be Angel," I said. "She's usually pretty quiet. Let's go see if Theresa needs any help. We can start our tour in the marina."

"The marina? That's where you keep the boats, isn't it? I thought I made it clear I don't do operations," he said. "I only do finance. And who is Angel?"

I sighed, hoping Maddy hadn't given this jerk a long-term contract. "The marina is one of the most vital parts of the business," I said. "It's an important profit center as well as a place we keep and maintain essential equipment. You'd do well to learn as much as you can about how it operates."

"I thought you said the lab was the most important part of the business," he said.

I didn't think he'd even tried to hide the snark. Our relationship had gotten off to a bad start. Since in my role as VP of marketing and chief underwater photographer at RIO, we'd be working closely together, I needed to find a way to develop some rapport.

I reached into my desk drawer and pulled out two sets of keys, one to my personal boat, the *Tranquility,* and one to Maddy's boat, the *Sea Princess.* Maybe a tour of the famous dive sites around Grand Cayman would help him get a handle on what we do at RIO. Or at least, I hoped a nice ocean voyage might help him relax a little and not be such a jerk.

"C'mon," I said. "We can kill two birds with one stone. We'll see what's up with Angel and then go for a boat. You can see the island from the water and get to know your new home. You might want to leave your blazer here. You'll swelter out there in the sun."

We stopped by his office, where Benjamin removed his jacket and hung it carefully on a hanger behind his door. When he was finished, I headed toward the rear exit next to Maddy's corner office.

The door opened onto the wide rolling lawn that sloped down to the marina. I thought we could pick up Oliver, my honorary brother, at the dive shop on the way. Maybe he'd have better luck connecting with Benjamin than I was having.

Chapter 2
Finding Angel

As we crunched down the crushed shell walkways that led from the exit over to the dive shop and then down to the marina and the entry point for our shore dives, the crying grew louder. I hoped Theresa wasn't having as bad a day as it sounded like Angel was having.

We stopped at the dive shop, and I leaned an elbow on the bottom half of the Dutch door, peering into the dim interior. Oliver Russo, the young man I thought of as my brother even though we were no blood relation, was inside filling tanks. He wore industrial earphones to protect his hearing from the roar of the compressor used to fill the tanks with air.

I reached inside the door and slipped the lock that kept the bottom half closed and crossed the room until I entered Oliver's visual field. He gave me a quick smile as he shut off the compressor and disconnected the tank he'd been filling.

He pulled off his headphones and dropped them on the counter. "What's up, Boss?" he asked with a laugh. Maddy had left me in charge of RIO while she was away, but I didn't think of myself as Oliver's boss, even for these few weeks. Oliver was a hard worker, a self-starter, and smart as a whip. We all considered ourselves lucky to have him in our lives.

"Hey, Oliver. I wanted to introduce you to Benjamin Brooks, RIO's new CFO. I was going to show him around and thought we'd start here at the dive shop. You want to give him an overview of what goes on here?"

Oliver had been managing RIO's entire diving operation since Gus Simmons, our former head of dive operations, had been forced to retire after a heart attack. With Gus on sick leave, Oliver hadn't had anyone to show him the ropes after my stepfather Ray Russo died, but he'd kept the shop running without missing a beat. He'd even made some improvements, no easy feat considering dive shop owners came from all over the world to study our methods.

Oliver nodded. "Sure thing." Then he frowned. "But first I need to let you know another ten or twelve tanks are missing as of this morning."

For the last few days, we'd come in every morning to find several of our scuba tanks missing. Normally, we might not have noticed, since we stocked over 2000 tanks, but we left around twenty tanks chained together out on the concrete pad beside the dive shop each night for the staff to use if they wanted to go night diving. And lately, each day, the pad was empty by morning. Not a single tank remained, and nobody came by to turn in their empties.

Admittedly, we'd been lax in tracking our tanks, but with more than 2,000 tanks in rotation at RIO, keeping track of all their movements wasn't an easy job.

Our staff numbered well over 300 people, most of whom dove at least once or twice every day as part of their jobs, and we needed tanks ready for them at all times. Many of RIO's staff kept a few of RIO's tanks on their private boats, swapping them out for filled tanks as they used them.

We also kept a large number of tanks in the dive shop for rentals and excursions, and the research vessel *Omega* had hundreds of tanks on board in various states of readiness for diving. In addition, tanks were always coming up for required testing and inspections, either because it was time for the annual visual inspection, or for the more intensive hydrostatic test administered every five years. Sometimes, when renters returned a tank completely empty or in otherwise bad shape, the tanks received extra inspections or were removed from service entirely.

Tanks were pulled out of use for all sorts of reasons, and it could be a few days or a few weeks before they were returned to active duty. Our tanks were in constant motion, and every one of them looked exactly like all the others. It's no wonder we hadn't noticed the problem until the missing tanks reached critical mass.

I frowned. "Wow. Not again. Let's put our heads together and see if we can figure out what's going on. But first we should see what's happening with Angel. I didn't hear her before with my earbuds in, but she never cries like that. She sounds really upset."

Oliver nodded. "I didn't hear her through my headphones either, but she does sound upset. I'll go see what's bothering her. Maybe Theresa needs a hand."

Before Benjamin could protest about Angel putting a crimp in his precious schedule, I said, "I'll go see to Theresa and Angel while you talk to Benjamin. Just bring him to the *Tranquility* when you're done. I'll be taking him for a tour around the island. You're welcome to join us if you'd like."

"We'll see," Oliver said. "I'd need to find someone to cover the shop. Mondays are usually pretty busy. Tourists arrive on Saturday or Sunday, and they can't wait to get in the water. It's time consuming setting up all their rental gear."

Benjamin beamed. He'd finally found something at RIO he approved of. Paying customers.

"Thanks, Oliver," I said. "See you in a few minutes." I walked down the shell path to the dock and out toward Gus and Theresa's boat, the *Sunshine Girl*. As I advanced, Angel's cries grew louder and more distressed.

I stopped at the slip where Gus had moored *Sunshine Girl*. I didn't see anyone on deck. "Gus? Theresa?" I called. "Permission to come aboard."

There was no response. I peered around the upper deck and didn't see anyone, but there was no doubt the crying baby was nearby. I kicked off my flip flops and jumped aboard. "Theresa? Where are you?" Neglecting her baby was very out of character for my best friend, and her husband Gus also doted on baby Angelica. They would never leave her alone like this. Something was very wrong.

I crossed the deck to the cabin, and that's when I saw Angel. She was on the floor, safe in a soft sided pen, but crying with all her might. Her face was red, and her eyes were puffy. She looked hot, sweaty, and miserable. I rushed over and picked up the baby.

"Hush, Sweetie," I whispered, jiggling her the way I'd seen Theresa do. "Everything's fine. Auntie Fin is here." I tried to make my words sound reassuring, but the truth was, without Theresa nearby I had very little idea about how to soothe Angel.

And I was concerned. Where were her parents?

Angel nuzzled her sweaty face into my neck and whimpered. I crooned in her ear. She hiccuped and began to fidget. I was trying to keep my panic down when I heard Benjamin speak.

"She needs to be changed. And I think she's hungry." He left Oliver on the dock and strode across the deck to take the disgruntled baby from my arms. "I assume this is Angel. Do you know how to change her?"

Oliver and I both stared at him blankly. We had no idea.

He grimaced. "I thought not. Where are her things?"

Oliver said "Her crib and all her stuff is below. I'll show you."

He walked past me, and Benjamin fell into step behind him. They went down to the cabin where the Simmons family slept when they were living on the boat.

Benjamin was talking softly to Angel, and she responded with a laugh. I guess he was good for something after all.

Oliver came back on deck and sat across from me at the galley table. "I don't like this at all. It doesn't feel right."

"I agree," I said. "Theresa and Gus would never leave Angel alone this way."

Oliver and I fell silent, racking our brains to figure out what was going on.

In a few moments, Benjamin returned with Angel, who seemed much less angry now that she was clean and dry. He opened the refrigerator door in the galley and pulled out a bottle. Angel eagerly lunged for it, and he laughed as he put the nipple in her mouth. She drank greedily, sucking the milk down in huge gulps.

"Not so fast, Little One," Benjamin said softly. "You'll make yourself sick. There's plenty of milk and plenty of time." He smiled down at her, cradled in his arms. Without lifting his gaze from her face, he backed over to the daybed and sat down, Angel supported gently against his shoulder. He began to hum.

Angel stared up at him, her huge brown eyes rapt. I could see her smile at him, even as she continued working on the bottle with admirable intensity. In a few minutes, Benjamin took the nipple from her mouth and hoisted Angel to his shoulder. He patted her back and rubbed gently between her shoulder blades. She gave a mighty burp, spewing a small stream of vomit down Benjamin's back.

I expected outrage at this latest affront, but he merely smiled.

"Feeling better, Sweetie?" he cooed. "You're a good little Angel. Yes, you are." He returned the bottle to her mouth.

I got up and handed Benjamin a towel. "Sorry about your shirt. I'll get you a new one."

"No matter," he said, flipping the towel over his shoulder with practiced ease. "The important thing is this little sweetheart."

He smiled down at her benevolently. The pair seemed to be besotted with each other, and I wondered what Angel saw in him that I was missing.

"I'll get a shirt for you from the gift shop. Medium?" Oliver asked.

Benjamin nodded, without lifting his gaze from Angel, and Oliver trotted off to find a clean shirt.

"I can't imagine what happened to Gus and Theresa," I said. "It's not like them to leave Angelica alone."

Now that the crisis with Angel was under control, I needed to find Gus and Theresa. I pulled out my cellphone and dialed her number. I heard a muted ringing from the far corner of the daybed, muffled by the piles of plush cushions stacked against the inner hull.

I rose and rummaged behind the pile until I felt the hard plastic of a cellphone. I withdrew it and looked at the screen. It showed a missed call—mine, I assumed. Theresa is my best friend, and I knew her passcode—it was Angel's birthdate—so I keyed it in. The phone sprang to life.

Before I could use the phone's apps to see if they held a clue to Theresa's whereabouts, my own phone buzzed with an incoming text message.

Gus and Theresa taken. Safe for now. Unless you want Angelica to be an orphan, do as I tell you. No police. I'll be in touch.

The sender's picture was an evil-looking clown. The number the message purported to be from was my own. I knew it was possible to spoof phone numbers, but I felt violated that my number had been used for such a vile purpose.

I had to get away from Benjamin so I could call the police. Except the message said no police. My head spun with terror. I needed a moment to think. I was still staring at the phone in horror when Oliver returned with a bag containing clean shirts for Benjamin.

"I brought you a bunch of shirts, in case you don't like some of the colors. There's a couple of tees and a couple of polos. They all have the RIO logo on them."

Benjamin smiled. "Thank you, but it's not necessary. I have plenty of shirts."

Oliver reached into the bag he carried. "It's no big deal. We always give new employees a bunch of shirts anyway. I got you a couple of hats too." He pulled out a ball cap and a bucket hat, both also bearing the RIO logo. "It's best to wear a hat in this sun. You can get a nasty burn before you know it."

"Thanks, Oliver," Benjamin said. "I appreciate it. I'll change my shirt when Angel finishes eating. She's just about done." As if on cue, she pushed the nipple out of her mouth and smiled at him, looking exactly like her namesake—an angel. He put the empty bottle aside and lifted her to his shoulder to burp now that she was done with her meal.

When Angel was finished burping, Benjamin rose. He walked the few paces to me, carrying Angel. He paused, as though he were going to hand her to me, but then he turned abruptly and thrust her at Oliver. "Will you hold her while I change?" he asked.

I wanted to scream at him to leave, to get off the boat, to let me think about what to do to save my best friend. And then I realized we were all hanging out in what was probably a crime scene. The police wouldn't be pleased about that. Except I wasn't supposed to call the police. I took a deep breath to calm down.

"Let's go back inside RIO. You can change in there," I said. "It's more private and you'll be more comfortable."

But Benjamin had already pulled off his tie and was unbuttoning his white shirt. As soon as they were off, he looked more relaxed and approachable. He slipped a baby blue T-shirt on and plunked the bucket hat Oliver had brought him on his head.

Despite my fear for Theresa and Gus, I couldn't help noticing his toned abs and the way the new shirt matched his eyes. I felt a pang of disloyalty to Liam for even noticing, but I tamped it down. Liam's actions had made it clear we were over. Still, my reaction to Benjamin had me confused, especially in this time of crisis. I averted my eyes and shooed everyone off the boat.

"Let's put off the boat tour until we locate Theresa and Gus. They must be around somewhere. Oliver, would you mind showing Benjamin how the dive shop, the café, and the gift shop work? I have a conference call with Newton that I forgot about."

I looked at Oliver, and he got the message. He handed Angel to me and speed walked off the boat to the dock, where he stood waiting for Benjamin to join him.

Benjamin frowned, as though this forgotten appointment was just one more example of my ineptitude, but I didn't care. There was no forgotten call. I was scared, and I wanted my father's advice.

"Let's start in the dive shop," Oliver said, "and then we'll work ourselves around the operation until we end up back at Fin's office. Sound okay?"

Benjamin nodded, and the two men took off along the crushed shell path that led to the dive shop. I trotted along the other branch to the back door of RIO and hurried to my office.

I shut my door and sat at my desk before thinking better of using my own office phone to call Newton. What if it was bugged? I went to Benjamin's office and sat at his desk to dial Newton's number. It rang for quite a while before he answered.

Unlike his usually brisk tones, his voice sounded like he'd been awakened from a deep sleep. "Hello?" he rasped.

"Thanks for picking up. I need your help."

"Maddy knows more about RIO operations than I do. But don't call her yet. We were out late with some donors from Japan, and she's probably exhausted."

"It's not about RIO," I said, my voice cracking. "Gus and Theresa are missing. I found Angel all alone on their boat this morning. Theresa's phone was there, and I got a text from the kidnapper. It looks like it came from my phone, but I never sent it. It said no cops. I don't know what to do."

Newton's voice was instantly crisp. "Keep everyone off the boat. Call DS Scott to come meet with you."

My voice broke. "He said no cops, remember? I can't call him. They could be watching."

"I'll handle that from here then. I'll call the Ritz and rent my old suite if it's available. He'll meet you there. Bring Angel with you and leave her with the concierge. Angel's used to being with the caretakers at the kiddy camp there. She'll be fine. Does Oliver know?"

"Yes," I said. "He was with me on their boat. Benjamin knows they're missing too. But I don't think either of them knows they've been kidnapped."

Kidnapped. Such an ugly word. It seemed to echo through the atmosphere.

There was a pause, as though Newton too was feeling the evil word reverberate. But when at last he spoke, it was a different word.

"Benjamin," he said. "Fine. Make sure they both know not to talk about this to anyone else. And you and Oliver should only discuss it when you're sure you're alone. Not at your house or his place. Who knows whether those sites have been compromised? Just give me a half hour to arrange things before you head to the Ritz. I'll call you back if I have any problems." He hung up without a goodbye.

I drew in a deep breath. I was scared. As my late stepfather's best friend, Gus had been like a second—or actually third—father to me, and I loved him. His wife, Theresa, was much younger than he was. My own age, just a little over twenty-five, and she was my best friend.

Truthfully, my only friend. In my head, I kept repeating. *They'll be fine. They are fine. They have to be fine.*

Now I had to figure out how to make my excuses to Benjamin, who was probably going to consider my inability to meet with him as we'd planned another personal affront. Well, it couldn't be helped. He'd understand when we found Gus and Theresa and I could tell him what had been going on.

Or not. I couldn't make his feelings my concern right now. The Simmons family was my top priority.

I realized I didn't have any of Angel's necessities with me—no diapers, bottles, extra clothes. She'd need all that at the Ritz while I was meeting with DS Scott. I was just about to head back to the marina to gather Angel's things when Stanley Simmons, the junior member of RIO's maintenance team, walked by my office door. He glanced in and smiled.

"Is that Miss Angel, come to visit? Mind if I hold her?"

"Sure," I said. "Can you stay with her a few minutes, please? I need to get her things off the boat."

Stanley was a father several times over, and he well knew that babies don't travel anywhere without a lot of stuff. "Sure thing. I have a few minutes."

He took Angel from my arms and sat in one of my guest chairs. "Don't rush. It's been a long time since I had a baby on my knee, and I don't want to miss out on a minute." He smiled and nuzzled Angel's neck.

I ran back to the marina and boarded the *Sunshine Girl*. I went below and gathered up a pile of diapers, a pink binky, a couple of pretty pink dresses, two pink onesies, a pink bathing suit, a white eyelet lace sunhat, and a pair of pink shortie overalls. I stuffed that all into her capacious pink diaper bag before I could succumb to pink overload.

Next, I checked to be sure that her sunscreen and all her powders, lotions, and potions were already packed in the bag. I grabbed the pink baby sling off a hook on the cabin wall, loaded the insulated side of the baby's bag with bottles of milk from the boat's tiny fridge, and zipped it closed. I debated taking her bouncy baby carrier, but I assumed the daycare program at the Ritz probably had the necessary equipment. I decided to leave it behind. Even without it, I marveled at how much gear a tiny baby required.

I scurried back up the path to my office to pick up Angel; I was just about to take her from Stanley when I realized I didn't have a car seat in my Prius to put her in for the trip to the Ritz. I nearly screamed in frustration.

Before I could ask Stanley to watch Angel for another few minutes, the phone on my desk rang. It was the guard in the lobby. "Package here for you, Dr. Fleming."

"Be right there." I scurried to the lobby and smiled when I saw the box containing a top of the line baby car seat on the floor beside the guards' station. *"Bless you, Newton,"* I thought. *"You always manage to think of everything."*

Carrying the box, I walked back to the office where I'd left Stanley and Angel. He saw the box I was carrying. "Want me to install that for you? They're kind of tricky. With six younger siblings and six babies of my own, I'm kind of an expert by now."

"Thank you, Stanley. That would be wonderful." I took Angel, and he picked up the box containing the car seat and her diaper bag and walked out, whistling a happy tune. If only.

Chapter 3
DS Scott

I HADN'T BEEN BACK to the Ritz since Liam had resigned his valet job to work at RIO, and I couldn't stop myself from looking around for his golden hair and bright blue eyes when I pulled up to the valet station. We'd met here when he parked my car, before I knew about his background as a tech executive, and long before Maddy had hired him as RIO's CFO.

But today the valet on duty was a roly-poly young man whose nametag read Ralph from Peoria. I smiled as I handed him my keys and a few bills.

"Thank you, Ma'am," he said, pocketing the bills. I didn't begrudge him the money, but I missed Liam's cheerful greetings and the way he'd always known my name. To Liam, I'd never been an anonymous "Ma'am." I'd been Miss Fleming, and then Fin. And he'd had a ready smile and a quip, every time he saw me.

Every single time.

I hoped someday I'd stop missing him.

I bit my lip to keep from crying. I wanted to be done crying over Liam. He'd made his choice to go back to Australia to try to make a go of his marriage, and that was that. I reached into the backseat to lift Angel out of her car seat.

"She's a pretty little thing," said Ralph. "Need a hand with anything?" He smiled at Angel, who narrowed her eyes and glared at him.

I laughed at her reaction. "Thanks," I said. "We're fine."

I walked across the cool, sunlit lobby to the concierge's desk. She looked up and smiled. "Hello, Ms. Fleming. Oops. Sorry—I hear you're Dr Fleming now. Congratulations." She stood up and reached out for Angel. "I'll bring Angelica to the day care facility. They're expecting her. Do you remember the way to your father's old suite, or would you like me to send someone with you?"

I smiled my thanks. "I remember the way. I appreciate you taking Angel on such short notice."

She handed me a key to the suite where Newton used to live, and I walked to the elevator bank. When I arrived at the penthouse floor, I unlocked the door. DS Scott, the detective superintendent responsible for the CID—Cayman Islands Detective—unit in our area waited inside. I'd had dealings with DS Scott in the past, and I had never been able to shake the feeling that he disapproved of me.

But today, his greeting couldn't have been warmer. "Fin—or should I say Dr. Fleming now? It's good to see you again."

"Just call me Fin. Thanks for coming on short notice," I said.

He grimaced. "I'm used to it. Crimes don't happen on a schedule. Now, tell me what happened."

Wordlessly, I rummaged in my canvas tote until I found Theresa's phone. I'd stuck it in a plastic zip lock bag before I left RIO to preserve any fingerprints, but I was pretty sure the only prints they'd find now would be mine. I handed the bag and my own phone to him.

He glanced at the screen of my phone. "This text is from you," he said.

I shook my head. "I think whoever has Gus and Theresa spoofed my number. I have no idea how or why."

He nodded and put the phone aside. "Tell me what's been going on."

I started with my meeting with Benjamin and hearing Angel cry, and I added as many details as I could remember. He interrupted me a few times to clarify a point, but even with the interruptions, the entire recitation took no more than a few minutes.

"The only people who know that Gus and Theresa are missing are you, Oliver, this Benjamin Brooks, and Newton, correct?" he asked.

I nodded. "I'm not sure if Benjamin actually knows they've been kidnapped. He was there when I found Angel, but I didn't show him the text. He hasn't asked any questions either. I thought that was odd."

"Well, unless he asks, don't say anything. And even then, the less he knows the better. Please write down your phone's passcode," he said, handing me a notepad and pen. "We're going to need to monitor your calls and texts during the investigation."

I jotted down the code for him.

"Do you have any idea why someone would have targeted Gus and Theresa?" he asked. "I've known Gus for years, and he's never been wealthy. I know the pay scale at Fleming Environmental is very different from RIO's, but I don't imagine the new job made him a rich man."

"No, it hasn't yet," I said. "Although it may someday. Newton is very generous with his employees. But Gus is in for a share of the salvage fee from the sunken treasure we recovered last year near Belize."

"I thought you couldn't keep the treasure. Something to do with the ownership. Government property or something like that?" He looked puzzled.

"Yes, originally, we thought the government had claimed the treasure, but it turns out they made the claim on behalf of a syndicate of multiple jurisdictions. The salvage fee should have been a lot more, but we're still in for a substantial reward. And the money is due this week."

"Who knows about the reward?" he asked, rubbing his chin.

"Pretty much everybody. It was in the newspapers, on TV, and covered extensively in the article published in *Your World*. They may not know the exact amount of the reward, because Newton only recently wrapped up the negotiations, but everybody knows there's a lot of money involved."

I thought a moment. "But Maddy, Liam, Oliver, Newton, and I all donated our shares to the Gibb family because of Dylan Gibb's death during the expedition. We convinced Gus and Stewie to hang on to their shares. Liam and my family already have plenty of money. We don't need the reward money. And the Gibb brothers will be getting millions as it is without asking Gus and Stewie to give up their shares too. Gus planned to buy a bigger house for him and Theresa and also put some of the money aside for Angelica's education."

"Speaking of Stewie," DS Scott continued. "Where is he while all this is going on? Usually if there's a problem at RIO, he's right in the thick of it."

"That's true," I said, "but I think this time he's in the clear. He's at rehab again. Maddy fronted him the money. He's supposed to pay her back out of his share of the salvage fee."

"Do you have any idea how much the rehab costs amount to?" he asked.

"Tens of thousands, but a drop in the bucket compared to the size of the check he'll be getting. Stewie has no reason to be coveting anyone else's good fortune this time."

DS Scott nodded and looked thoughtfully over my shoulder. The silence stretched out, feeling like it had lasted for hours.

"I don't know what to do next," I said at last. "The kidnapper told me not to get the police involved. What should I do?"

"Do nothing yet," he said. "Act normally. Go about your usual business. The next steps are up to me. Just give me a minute to think."

He stared into space while I fidgeted. After a few moments, I stood and paced the length of the suite, but on my return, I saw DS Scott's frown. I sat back down and folded my hands in my lap to keep from twitching. My best friend needed me, and although I hated sitting there doing nothing, I didn't want to ruin DS Scott's concentration.

At last he said, "I need to find a way to get a forensics team on their boat without cluing in the kidnapper that you're involved. Can you get them aboard without anyone noticing?"

I nodded. "Yes. Have your officer join a private RIO tour this afternoon at two. I'll lead the tour myself, and I'll take them on several boats, including Gus and Theresa's. I'll ask Oliver to be on their boat before we arrive, and he'll leave with the group while your officer stays behind."

He frowned. "Good. But better if we could have two or three officers stay behind. Is there anyone else you trust?"

I thought a moment. "Maybe Newton's assistant, Justin Nash, but we should probably check with Newton before you tap him to make sure he's trustworthy for this role," I said. "I don't know him well enough to be sure he's discreet."

"What about Alec Stone?" the detective superintendent said. "I have an officer that's an almost perfect double for him."

My ex-husband, the poisonous snake that popped up in my life whenever he was least wanted. "I wouldn't trust him. He's pretty tight with Cara and Lily Flores, Oliver's bio-family. Who knows what that crew is up to? What if they're behind this?"

"Well, it's probably a long shot to think they're involved," DS Scott said. "But you could be right about not involving Alec. Then how about Eugene, your head of maintenance? His twin brother Roland is one of my officers, and they look exactly alike…"

"Perfect. I'd trust Eugene with my life."

"High praise indeed," said DS Scott, "considering how many attempts to kill you there have been. And I'm only counting the ones I know about."

I shrugged. What could I say? I seemed to attract trouble lately.

We agreed that DS Scott would send three police officers to RIO. Before their arrival, Oliver, Eugene, and Justin would hide out below deck on *Sunshine Girl*. We'd make sure each man was dressed exactly like his "double" from the police. I hoped that if anyone was watching, they wouldn't notice the switchover during the tour.

Using the suite's telephone, I called June, Maddy's assistant, and asked her to put up a welcome sign for a VIP tour. I told her the guests would be executives with my father's company here on a retreat. If she thought it odd that they were holding an executive retreat while Newton was off-island and without Gus in attendance, she was wise enough to say nothing.

Even when I asked her to send Eugene to the hardware store down-town to pick up a hammer, a small chisel, and a pack of AA batteries, and to bring them to me at the Ritz along with three of every color and size of RIO shirt, hat, and sunglasses we had in stock at the gift shop, she never questioned me. Whatever Maddy paid June, her discretion alone probably made her worth twice as much.

"Hammer? Chisel? Batteries?" said DS Scott when I'd disconnected the call. "What do you have in mind?"

"Nothing," I said. "I wanted to give Eugene an errand that would look normal, in case anyone follows him."

He nodded, and I thought I saw a glimmer of newfound respect in his eyes. Then I suggested that he instruct his staff to wear long khaki-colored cargo shorts, the pants of choice at RIO. It would make it easier to make the swap on the boat if everybody was dressed in similar clothes since there would be nothing to distinguish them easily. He agreed.

He called his team and requested that Eugene's brother Roland, and the other two officers he'd selected join us in the suite at the Ritz, while I followed up with Newton to request Justin's assistance for the day. I let the concierge know we were expecting several people to join us and to send up anyone who asked for me without delay.

Next, I called the main switchboard at RIO and dialed Benjamin's extension. I thought he'd still be touring RIO with Oliver. I was surprised when he picked up. He sounded exasperated when he heard it was me.

"Where's Angel?" he asked. "I went by your office to check on her but neither of you was around. Nobody here has any idea where you are. Do you need help taking care of her?"

I thought fast. "No thanks, we're good. I got called into a meeting with the local Divemaster's Association. I couldn't take her to the meeting, so I brought her to her playgroup. She's used to being there, and they know how to take care of her. I do need something from you though. You have fresh eyes. I'd like you to observe the lab and see if you can make suggestions for how we can operate more efficiently. Within the bounds of good laboratory and research protocols, of course."

"Of course," he replied. "I'll get started right away." Now he sounded eager and excited about seeing the lab.

DS Scott raised his eyebrows at me. "Your mother runs a tight operation. I doubt this guy will find anything that isn't up to snuff," he said. "Especially because he isn't a scientist."

"I agree. It's just busywork to keep him out of my hair while you're doing the forensics this afternoon. I won't have time to babysit him, and I don't want him tagging along with me asking questions."

I used the hotel phone again to call the dive shop at RIO. When Oliver answered. I told him Justin would be picking him up in a few minutes and asked him if he could join me. I suggested they take a circuitous route on the way to the Ritz in case they were followed.

"Cloak and dagger," he said. "Who would have thought the dive industry would be this full of intrigue? What's it all about, anyway?"

"I'll fill you in when you get here." I hung up, and the phone rang almost immediately. The concierge let me know that three men were on their way up. The suite's doorbell rang, and DS Scott let his team in. I did a double take when I saw Eugene's twin brother. They did look exactly alike. The other two men were a close match for their doubles —one was about Oliver's height and coloring, and the other was a tall, slender man who would be easy to mistake for Justin Nash from a distance.

DS Scott was filling his team in on the plan. He'd just finished when Oliver, Justin and Eugene all arrived at the same time. I don't see Justin often, and I'd forgotten how attractive he is, with his blonde hair and cobalt blue eyes.

We went back over the plan. The men all changed into their matching outfits while DS Scott cloned Oliver's and my cellphones so he could listen to any calls or read texts as they came in. He gave me a burner phone in case I needed to contact him without the kidnappers hearing.

One of the forensics team flipped open his briefcase, and took DNA samples from Oliver, Eugene, Justin, and me for elimination purposes. Roland handed Eugene a large box that looked like something you'd store tools in. Eugene was to carry it to the boat and leave it aboard when he left. That way the police team would have everything they needed to do their work.

Newton called DS Scott to let him know he'd arranged for a full-time nanny for Angel, She'd be staying at his condo to keep her safe while her parents were missing. He offered his condo as a situation room—a hub for all the police activities. The plan made sense because his condo had plenty of space, several guest bedrooms in case the days got long, the necessary high speed internet connections, multiple phone lines, and a twenty-four hour onsite chef. The kidnappers had warned us not to contact the police, and this way we could all visit Angel at the condo, and it wouldn't look suspicious for us to be there if we needed a group meeting. It was especially convenient because my mother, Maddy Russo, also had a condo in the same building as Newton.

DS Scott turned to me. "Do you have a picture of Gus and Theresa? I want to have some posters made up."

"There's a bunch on my phone," I said.

"Good. I'll share them with my team."

DS Scott called his office, asking for a team to set up a hotline at Newton's condo to field calls and leads. He sent them a photo from my phone and asked for them to print up about a thousand posters asking for information on the missing couple. Oliver, Justin, and I volunteered to distribute the posters after the tour ended. Then he asked me to hang back a few minutes after everyone else left. With all the plans finally in place, we were good to go.

Oliver and Justin left first, followed a few minutes later by Eugene carrying the forensics toolbox. The plan was for them all to get aboard Gus's boat, one at a time, as soon as possible after they arrived at RIO. They were to stay below, out of sight, until I came aboard with the tour group.

When everyone except DS Scott and I had left the condo, he cleared his throat. "I have another favor to ask you. I'll be bringing a team over to the Simmons house, and I'd like you to go with us. You know their place, and you can help us determine if anything seems to be missing. Same for their cars. Can you join us after you get done with your tour?"

I nodded. I'd do anything to help get my friends home safely. "Okay, but what about distributing the posters?" I asked. "Can they wait, or do you want Oliver and Justin to pass them out without me?"

"My team will start the distribution as soon as the posters are ready," he said. "You can finish up later if you have time to pitch in," he said.

"What should I do in the meantime?" I didn't think I could stand sitting around doing nothing.

"I know this is hard, and it will get harder with every hour they're missing. But you need to keep to your normal routine as much as possible. It'll be good for you, and it will help keep the kidnapper from getting stressed out if he realizes you're working with us."

I left a few minutes later, to give myself time to prepare for the make believe tour I was supposed to lead. The police forensics team would follow me shortly, once they were sure I'd had enough time to set things up.

Chapter 4
The Tour

I RUSHED into my office at RIO, happy to see that June had treated this impromptu tour like it was for any other group of VIPs. She'd put several folders on my desk, each filled with RIO brochures, and left stacks of freebies like mugs, pens, and notepads that all bore the RIO logo. She'd also put out tote bags for the people on the tour to carry home their RIO-branded loot.

Perfect. This would help make it look like any of our usual tours. On our regular tours we showered our guests with branded merchandise to ensure they'd remember us when it came time to make donations. In case the kidnapper was familiar with our routines, I didn't want anything to stick out as unusual enough that it might make the kidnapper suspicious. I breathed a sigh of relief.

Until I heard Benjamin at my office door. "Where's Angel? You didn't forget her at her play group, did you?"

I bit back a snarl and smiled with what I hoped looked like a pleasant expression. "She was asleep when I went by to pick her up. I'll go back later after I finish this executive tour. She'll probably be awake by then."

"Executive tour? Shouldn't I be on that with you? As RIO's CFO, I should be greeting important visitors, and you'd kill two birds with one stone because I'd be taking that tour you wanted me to go on."

I groaned. "These are executives from Fleming Environmental Investments. My father asked me to personally handle the tour. They may want to discuss his company's internal business. I'm on his board of directors, and I don't think he'd appreciate an outsider…"

"But don't you see? This is perfect. They're financial guys; I'm RIO's financial guy. We speak the same language."

I thought fast. "I may need you to pick up Angel, depending on how long the tour lasts. She really likes you"

"Well sure, if it's for Angel, I completely understand. Let me know when and where you need me." He smiled and left my office.

As soon as Benjamin was out of sight, I ran down the hall to the ladies' room to call DS Scott on the burner phone because he had warned me my office might be bugged. "Someone needs to take Angel to a different day care center and stay with her until Benjamin Brooks picks her up. I need to keep him away from the Ritz and away from the tour, and the only thing I could think of was a day care center."

"No problem. My niece runs a day care center. I'll call her. She'll pick Angel up herself and keep her safe until Benjamin comes to get her." He paused. "And since we don't know this Brooks guy well, I'll have someone follow him to make sure Angel gets back to you safely." He texted the day care center's address to my burner phone. Now I could text it to Benjamin when I needed to.

I ended the call and hurried back to my office. I'd no sooner entered when my desk phone rang. The receptionist said "Your tour group is here. Do you want me to bring them to you or will you pick them up?"

"I'll pick them up," I said after taking a deep breath. This undercover work was stressful.

I sprinted to the lobby to pick up the police team. Acting like we'd never met, I introduced myself to the three men sitting in the comfortable blue chairs under the skylights. They all wore long khaki cargo shorts, short sleeved t-shirts in various colors, bucket hats pulled low over their foreheads, and big dark sunglasses. Everything they wore carried the RIO logo. They looked totally different without their suits and uniforms. I thought it was possible even their own families would have had trouble recognizing them.

Acting their parts, the police team smiled and introduced themselves to me, using the names of some of the foreign office heads at Fleming Environmental. We all shook hands.

"Shall we start with the marina?" I asked. "Then we can work our way back through the dive operations, the research labs, the aquarium, and the giftshop."

They agreed to this plan since we'd prearranged the itinerary only a few minutes ago. I led them through the sunlit halls of RIO's public areas, back to the office area. We walked down the hall and exited by the door next to Maddy's office.

I strolled nonchalantly down the crushed shell path to the docks, turning to chat with Roland, who walked beside me. I waved my arms around as I spoke, trying to look like I was highly engaged, although my real purpose was to keep anyone from looking too closely at the faces of my companions.

I walked them along the pier, gesturing to the boats moored in the slips. In a loud voice, I explained that some belonged to RIO staff members, some were rentals, and some we used for dive training classes.

We walked onto one of the dive boats, which was the first boat we came to. I showed them how we stored the tanks in the holders along the inner hull, and where we had a foam-lined stainless steel table with a rim set aside for the safety of delicate photography equipment or expensive sunglasses and other breakables. I went over the format of the diver roster form, and showed them the safety siren, the first aid kit, and the emergency oxygen. In case the kidnapper was watching, I presented them with everything I'd have shown on a normal VIP tour.

Next, we went on my personal boat, the *Tranquility*. I told them how I had inherited it from my stepfather, Ray Russo, and pointed out some of the improvements my father had made after the boat had been ransacked more than a year ago. We climbed up to the flying bridge, and I showed them the sonar and fish finder.

Now came the delicate part. I had to take the police team onto *Sunshine Girl* where they would go below and quickly change places with the three men hidden in the hold. This was a tricky point in the deception. If the kidnappers were watching, they would probably wonder why I took them on that particular boat. We'd have to be in and out quickly to allay suspicion, and I'd need to make it look like boarding *Sunshine Girl* had been an innocent mistake.

Luckily, Gus's boat was in the slip next to Maddy's boat, the *Sea Princess*, which would normally have been the next stop on the tour. Once again, I talked a blue streak as we walked, waving my arms exuberantly trying to look like I was engrossed in my conversation and not paying attention to what I was doing. I wanted it to look like I absentmindedly boarded the wrong boat.

I stepped aboard the *Sunshine Girl*, but I froze when I heard Benjamin shouting my name. The police team went below where they were out of sight.

"Dr. Fleming. I mean, Fin. May I speak with you a moment?" He was hurrying toward me across the wide rolling lawn from RIO's parking lot.

I speed walked away from the boat to greet him before he got too close. "What's up?" I asked.

"I wanted to introduce myself to our guests. Is that okay with you? I don't want to step on your toes." He smiled pleasantly.

"Uh, sure. No problem. Let me get them for you." I took a few steps toward the dock. "Would the Fleming Environmental execs please join me on the lawn? There's someone here I'd like you to meet." I hoped the cops realized I meant them. After they'd spent the morning together, Benjamin would surely recognize Oliver if the wrong team came out.

I needn't have worried. The three police exited Gus's boat and came over to introduce themselves and to shake hands with Benjamin.

Benjamin peered at Roland, who was no longer wearing his sunglasses. "You look familiar. Have we met?" Of course, Roland looked exactly like Eugene, and Benjamin would have met Eugene earlier today.

"Don't think so, sir," Roland replied in a very posh upper crust British accent, utterly unlike his and Eugene's usual island lilt. "I must have one of those faces, I guess."

"I guess that must be it." Benjamin smiled and yammered on about nothing much for a few moments before I broke in.

"Sorry, Benjamin. These people are on a tight schedule, and I want them to see everything. We need to get a move on."

"Of course," said Benjamin. "Nice to meet you all." He stuck his hands in the capacious pockets of his cargo shorts and ambled off the dock.

As we passed Gus and Theresa's boat, Roland clapped his head. Still speaking in his posh voice, he said "I think I left my sunglasses on that boat. Help me look, will you please?" He hopped onto the deck, followed by the other two cops. All three went below.

Within seconds, three men returned to the dock. "All set," said Eugene as he slid his sunglasses onto his face. His voice was a perfect imitation of Roland's high class accent.

I led the crew along the dock to the next slip, where the *Sea Princess* was moored. We went aboard and looked around for a few minutes. Then I started the engine on one of the rental Zodiacs moored nearby and ferried the team out to the *Omega*, RIO's state of the art research vessel. We spent at least an hour exploring the ship before we got back in the Zodiac and returned to the dock.

I led my team of imposters up to the main RIO building, where we toured the offices and the public aquarium. I took them into the research lab, and introduced them to Rosie, my Atlantic Pygmy octopus. She blinked at them solemnly, but she stayed in her corner.

Last I took them to the gift shop and told them to pick out a gift for themselves. This was a standard part of our VIP tours, but since Oliver and Eugene worked here, they had a hard time acting excited about the assortment of gift items they saw every day. Oliver finally grabbed a tee shirt with Maddy's picture on the front, and Eugene opted for a stuffed octopus. Justin picked out a poster of my late stepfather, Ray Russo, poised on the ladder as he climbed aboard the *Omega*. I had taken the photo shortly before his death, and I loved it.

I felt the burner phone in my pocket buzz with an incoming text. *Finished* was all it said.

Now I had to find a way to swap the police team with my group again, without giving anything away. My original plan hadn't gotten as far as the second swap when I'd been with DS Scott. I had to pause a moment to think of something. I brought the three men to RIO's café and sat them down at a corner table with iced teas and lemonades to keep them occupied while I thought this through.

"Oliver. Eugene." I whispered. "Go to the men's room. Stay there until I tell you to come out but ditch your hats and glasses before you do. Change your shirts if you can."

"We can do better than that. There's a bunch of lockers in there. These guys can put on one of the spare lab coats hanging there, and I'll put on my overalls. I'll stow all our clothes in one of the empty lockers, and we can all get our stuff later."

"Perfect," I said. "The police team don't need to worry about changing because they arrived in the clothes they have on. Now all I need to do is figure out how to get them off the boat."

"Leave that to me," said Oliver. The men rose to begin their switchover.

I sat at the table and stewed until I heard my name coming through the overhead speakers that normally played music or the soundtracks to our documentaries to keep patrons amused. "Dr. Fleming. Dr. Fin Fleming, report to the dock immediately. Repeat. Please report to the dock."

I bit back a grin as I rose and hurried out the café's side entrance, which put me in the front parking lot. Acting as though I had a real emergency, I ran across the lawn and down the path to the dock. I arrived to find Roland sprawled on his back on the wooden dock.

"He slipped," said the cop who looked like Oliver.

"Are you okay?" I asked. "And what are you guys doing out here? I thought…"

"I wanted to take another look at the marina," said Roland. "I'm thinking of buying a boat." He groaned rather convincingly. "But then I slipped."

I've been trained in medic first aid, so I did a quick check, thorough enough to look real to anyone watching. "I think you're okay," I said when I'd finished. "Can you guys help me get him on his feet, please?"

The other two men and I lifted Roland to his feet. Resting his weight gingerly on his phony injured foot, he limped a few steps before straightening up. "Seems fine," he said. "But I think I'll go see a doctor."

Normally I would have brought him to RIO's infirmary to see Doc, but I wanted these men off our grounds as soon as possible to minimize the chances that anyone would recognize them as part of the local police force. Roland leaned on the other two cops, and they walked across the lawn to their car.

I sagged with relief. I thought sure we'd pulled it off. Then my phone buzzed with an incoming text.

Chapter 5
Scary Text Message

"*T*ʀʏ *something like that again and Angel will be an orphan*," it read. "*No more cops*." Once again, the kidnapper had spoofed my phone number. It looked as though the text had come from my own phone. Tears of fear and frustration sprang to my eyes.

I walked slowly to RIO's main parking lot and got in my car to drive to a nearby coffee shop where I could have some hope of privacy to think. Sitting at a table in the corner, I texted DS Scott from the burner phone, suggesting we meet in the fenced-in backyard at my house where we'd be safe from prying eyes. He countered by suggesting my mother's condo downtown since the kidnappers might be watching my place. He told me to wait at least twenty minutes before leaving to give him enough time to get in position free from any unfriendly eyes.

I sipped my unwanted coffee, checking email and generally wasting time until a shadow fell across the table. I looked up to see Newton's assistant, Justin Nash, standing by my table holding what smelled like a cappuccino.

"Mind if I sit with you?" he asked.

"Sure, although I'm leaving in a few minutes. I have an appointment I can't be late for, but I wouldn't mind the company until then." I smiled up at him, noticing again the depths of his dark blue eyes.

"Just say the word when you're ready to leave," he said, returning my smile. "I won't try to keep you."

"How long have you been with Fleming Environmental Investments, Justin?" I asked when he sat down. He'd moved to Grand Cayman when Newton moved the company's base of operations several months ago, and I hadn't known Justin before that.

"Newton hired me right after I finished grad school, nearly two years ago now. But I've known your father since I was a kid. Your grandparents and mine are friends. They share a summer place at the shore every year. Some of my best memories are of those lazy summer days with the whole family gathered around."

I froze. I hadn't known my paternal grandparents were still alive. I'd never met them or heard from them. I'd always assumed they were dead. My smile was stiff. "Must have been fun," I said.

"I always wondered why you never joined us—until Newton told us you were away on the *Omega* every year. I was so jealous. I devoured those annual documentaries, wishing we could have traded lives."

I raised my eyebrows. "Don't get me wrong—those years were wonderful, and I wouldn't have missed the experience for anything." I sipped my coffee. "But then again, it must have been nice to be surrounded by family all the time." I could only imagine how wonderful it might have been.

He shrugged. "It gets old. The parents start asking when I'm going to settle down, get married, give them grandchildren, buy a house... The list of 'you should' continues forever. I can't see Maddy or Ray ever trying to run your life like that. Even Newton seems to assume you can take care of yourself."

My throat tightened. Justin was right that Maddy and my stepfather Ray had always assumed I was capable of taking care of myself and making my own decisions. If I asked for help, they were always there, but they'd instilled self-reliance into me from an early age.

Nobody had ever tried to run my life. Maybe that's why I would have loved Newton to have taken enough interest in me to try. "I guess the childhood you didn't have always looks better than the one you lived through," I said after a moment's thought.

Justin raised his cappuccino in a toast. "I guess that's true."

We chatted about investment banking for a while. Justin seemed to find the topic fascinating, but I didn't understand a word. I asked a few questions, but he must have sensed my indifference to the subject.

"Enough about that," he said. "I read your thesis on training an octopus to match objects and pictures. Rosie sounds intriguing."

"You read my thesis?" I asked, astonished. "Whatever for?"

"Why not? It was an interesting premise. So—can I meet her? For real. Not simply as part of a fake tour. I'd love to see you put her through her paces."

"Sure, when this is all over, I'd be delighted to show you."

"Awesome," he said. He looked at his watch. "I think I've kept you long enough. Don't you have an appointment to get to?"

I gasped. I'd been so wrapped up in feeling sorry for myself that the meeting with DS Scott had slipped my mind. I could not believe that I had forgotten about Gus and Theresa even for a second. I felt like a heartless wretch. "Thanks for the reminder," I said as I ran out the door.

Maddy and Newton had identical ocean-view penthouse condos in the same complex. The building was convenient to both RIO and Newton's offices downtown. She'd bought her place after Ray's death because she hated living without him in the home where they'd been so happy together.

I parked in a visitor's spot at the complex and rushed through the lobby to the elevator. I expected to see DS Scott waiting impatiently outside the door when I arrived, but he was nowhere in sight. I breathed a sigh of relief. Maybe I wasn't that late after all.

I keyed in the code for the electronic lock and went inside. I started to walk across the room to open the heavy drapes that blocked out the sun and nearly jumped out of my skin when someone said, "Leave them closed please. You never know who might be watching."

When my heart resumed its accustomed rhythm, I said, "DS Scott. You startled me. How did you get in here?"

"Maddy shared the code with me," he said. He patted the arm of the chair next to the one he was sitting in. "Let's talk."

I sat down and told him how I'd handled getting his team off the boat and showed him the text I'd received. "I swear no one was watching us. I don't know how they figured it out."

"They're pros, whoever they are. And maybe they're insiders—someone connected to RIO or Fleming Environmental. Maybe that's how they know what's going on. And whoever they are, they probably knew right from the start what you were doing on that tour. When you think about it, why else would you take a group on a boat where a kidnapping had recently taken place? It's my own fault. I should have gone in openly to do the crime scene forensics. At least that way they'd have known where you stood. Now they won't trust anything you say or do, and it'll be a lot harder for us to get things done."

"But at least you have the forensic evidence you need from the boat, right?"

"Not so far. We've got nothing. We got traces of you, Oliver, Benjamin, Angel, Eugene, and Justin. And Gus and Theresa of course."

Just then the door opened, letting in a triangle of light from the hallway outside. Maddy, all five feet of her, rushed across the room to DS Scott. "Dane," she said. "Have you found them yet?"

DS Scott folded her into his arms. "Not yet, but it'll be okay, Maddy. We'll find them or I'll die trying."

My eyeballs nearly fell out of my head. Maddy and DS Scott, on a first name basis? A hugging basis? How long had this been going on? Now the fact that she'd shared her door code with him made more sense.

Newton walked in then, carrying a small travel bag. He averted his eyes from Maddy and DS Scott. "I'll leave this here."

He walked over and kissed my cheek. I saw the pain in his eyes. Everybody except Maddy knew he still loved her. "Back in a minute." He left Maddy's condo, shutting the door behind him.

Maddy stepped out of the circle of DS Scott's arms and turned to look me in the eye. "So now you know," she said.

I nodded. "Now I know. I'm happy for you."

She flushed. "Neither of us was looking for a relationship. We were working together on a plan to root out the drug distribution problem at RIO—and it just happened. We're taking things slow for now."

"It's not my business," I said, "but like I said, I'm happy for you." I turned to DS Scott. "And for you too." His growing relationship with Maddy must be the reason he'd been acting warmer toward me.

He nodded. "Thank you. That means a lot to me."

Just then the door opened, and Newton walked back in. "Everybody caught up?" He paused. "Good. As I told Dane earlier, I arranged for a full-time nanny for Angelica because we need to be sure she's safe and cared for until we find her parents. They'll be headquartered at my place upstairs. We should each make a point of visiting Angel there a couple of times a day. That way it won't look suspicious if we need to meet to discuss plans or whatever. And we can exchange information without fear of being overheard. Agreed?"

We all nodded. "So, what's next?" I asked.

DS Scott walked over and stood beside Newton. "Fin, I'll need your phone again to have the tech team see if they can trace that new text. As soon as they pick it up, you and I will head out to the Simmons home to see what we can uncover there. Newton, you do whatever it is you usually do. Maddy, you go back to your office at RIO and try to act natural." He shrugged. "All of you should keep your eyes open for anything or anyone suspicious looking."

Maddy's face turned pink. "I don't want to seem uncaring about Theresa and Gus, but I'm supposed to be delivering the keynote on ocean warming at the oceanography conference in Miami tomorrow. Then I'm scheduled on a tour to meet with existing and potential donors. Should I keep to that schedule or am I needed here?"

"No, you should act normal—like you're unaware that there's anything going on. You can go back to the States. Can you get to Miami in time for your presentation?" said DS Scott. "I know it's a pretty big deal for you."

"She can travel on my private jet. She'll be there in plenty of time," said Newton with a proprietary tone in his voice.

DS Scott didn't bat an eye. "OK. Good. Everyone should keep on doing what you normally do. Go on about your daily business as well as you can. I know it'll be tough. You're all worried. But there's nothing you can do while my team and I work on finding them, and it will keep you out of danger."

He paused a moment. "Just in case it is an inside job, I'll want to be at RIO as much as possible. Fin, can you start teaching me to dive. Private lessons. It'll give us a reason to be spending a lot of time together, and another good reason for me to be at RIO."

Newton cleared his throat. "Fin is already busy with private lessons. And her other professional responsibilities, of course."

I knew Newton was referring to the secret swimming lessons I'd been giving him. He'd wanted to surprise Maddy. She'd often teased him about his inability to swim, and she'd been angry when she realized he'd nearly drowned on our recent treasure hunting adventure because of his lack of water skills. In her mind, there was no excuse for not knowing how to swim.

"I have time for both," I said. "Especially now that Benjamin's on board to pick up the slack on the business side of things at RIO. And Oliver's always around if I need help." Oliver was enrolled in college full time, but he was taking all remote classes this semester, so he had a flexible schedule.

"Then it's settled," Maddy said. "I'll leave within the hour. One of you lock up when you're done, please."

Both Newton and DS Scott looked wistful when she said she was leaving, but neither said anything. Maddy kissed my cheek and swept out of her condo, picking up her suitcase from the entryway as she passed. Her focus was once again all on her work.

I admired the way she could compartmentalize her life, although I'd found it difficult as a child. She adored me, but sometimes the adoration came on a schedule. Thank God I'd also had Ray, my stepfather, who'd always been there for whatever I needed no matter what else was going on in his life.

DS Scott and I arranged a time for him to come to RIO to begin his lessons, and I confirmed our usual swim class time with Newton. Newton went up to his home office, and DS Scott and I left together to join the search of Gus and Theresa's house.

Chapter 6
Search of Gus and Theresa's Home

WHEN WE ARRIVED, the search team was assembled in the front yard of the Simmons' house, a small cottage set on a good sized lot across the street from the ocean in Grand Cayman's West Bay section.

We got out of his car, and I started to walk toward the house. Dane stopped me.

"Wait. Look. Absorb. Do you notice anything unusual? Anything seem off?"

Although small, the white house was freshly painted and well kept. The crushed shell walk was a blinding white and neatly raked. The front door was painted a lovely soft blue, as were the storm shutters, which at this time of the year were folded back to let in the light. All the windows were open an inch or two to catch the breeze from the trade winds. Under the windows hung wooden boxes painted the same shade of blue as the shutters and door, and the boxes were filled with a riot of bright flowers

The yard was also filled with colorful flowers, including pink and red hibiscus, and climbing purple clematis. A flowering quango tree shaded the home's roof and the patio. Birds and bees flittered among its vibrant pink blooms.

Several palm trees and two tall pimento trees rounded out the landscaping. Although it wasn't visible from the street, I knew there was a small vegetable garden in the back where Theresa had been growing herbs and vegetables. An old VW Jetta and a newer Chevy Bolt were parked on the cement driveway.

I looked carefully, but the house's exterior seemed normal in every way. I shook my head. "Sorry. Nothing jumps out at me."

"That's all right. Let me know if you notice anything that seems off, no matter how small or innocent it looks, okay?"

I nodded.

"Good. Ready to go inside?"

I squared my shoulders, steeling myself for what we might find. "Ready."

Dane nodded to his team. One brought coveralls, gloves, booties, and goggles to Dane and me. While the nearby crew donned their own gear, we put them on. I was dressed first. I waited quietly for Dane to finish.

He looked surprised when he saw me waiting. "How'd you manage to get dressed that fast?"

"This isn't much different from dive gear, and I'm used to gearing up quickly. That way my students don't get into anything they shouldn't while I'm getting ready."

He laughed. "Your dive training prepares you for all sorts of unexpected situations, doesn't it?" But his laugh died quickly. "I don't know what we're going to see in there but let me know if you notice anything that seems unusual or out of place. And if you see something that makes you feel faint or sick, get outside as fast as you can."

I nodded.

"Once we're inside, stay behind me. Step only where I step, and don't touch anything. Don't go wandering off on your own."

I nodded again and took a deep breath.

Dane signaled his team that he was ready to enter the house. They fanned out around the front door. One went to the back, and another peeked in the windows. The team leader rang the doorbell and knocked. "Mr. Simmons. Mrs. Simmons. It's the Cayman Islands Police. We need to talk to you. Please open the door."

The leader of the team repeated the words a few more times before he decided to escalate the action. He made a hand signal to a member of his team, who trotted to the police van.

The second cop returned with a heavy metallic cylinder. When the team lined up along the device's length, I realized it was a battering ram. They were going to break down the door.

I knew Theresa had recently painted the door that beautiful shade of blue. She'd spent months picking out exactly the right color to harmonize with the nearby ocean water. It would break her heart if they ruined her work. And I knew it was completely unnecessary.

"Wait," I yelled, holding up a hand in the universal halt gesture. I ran toward the door. Dane reached out a hand to try to stop me, but he missed. I tugged on the leader's arm a nanosecond before the battering ram hit the fragile wooden door.

"No need to trash the place," I said. "I know where there's a key." I reached into the nearby window box and rummaged toward the back, finally pulling out a brass key. I brushed the dirt off on my coveralls and handed it to Dane.

I could tell he was annoyed at himself because he hadn't thought to ask if I knew where there was a key, but he said nothing, just passed the key over to the man at the head of the small group in front of the door. He took my arm and pulled me away from the entry. "Let them go in first."

We stood back while the small team checked every room in the cottage. The leader came out. "All clear," he said.

Dane and I entered, and I looked around the familiar home. There weren't any signs of a struggle. Nothing seemed out of place. It might have been a bit neater than usual. On the other hand, it wasn't that odd because I knew Gus and Theresa would have made everything ship-shape before leaving.

"Anything?" Dane eyed me hopefully.

"Nope. Looks normal."

We walked through the rooms one by one. We stood in the center of each room, and I looked around carefully. Each time, after a few minutes, I shook my head. Nothing seemed out of place.

When we finished with the inside of the house, we exited through the back door to check out the small garden shed. Nothing there either.

"Both cars are here. How did they leave?" Dane muttered to himself. Then he signaled to one of his team. "Check Uber, Lyft, taxis, rental cars. Canvas the neighborhood. See if anyone saw them depart."

The cop nodded and hurried away.

"Um, Dane?" I pointed to the small dock where Gus kept the *Sunshine Girl*. "They took their boat. We know it's at RIO. All they had to do was walk across the street to leave."

He nodded. "We know the *Sunshine Girl* is at RIO. But no one saw Gus or Theresa there. Maybe the kidnapper brought it to throw us off the trail."

I hadn't thought of that. Then Gus and Theresa could have still been here.

Somewhere.

I looked at their cars in the driveway with trepidation.

Please, no.

Dane's gaze followed mine. "Right. We need to check their cars." His face looked grim. "Where do they keep the keys?"

They usually had the keys hanging on a hook inside a small closet near the back door. I went inside to retrieve them and handed the rings to Dane.

He peered into the front and back seats of both cars while I huddled against the house. I stood in the hot sunshine, but I was freezing. I crossed my arms to stay warm and to keep my hands from shaking.

Dane went around to the back of Theresa's Jetta and opened the trunk. He took a deep breath and let the lid drop.

"Nothing," he said.

We both sighed with relief.

But the ordeal wasn't over yet.

Next, he walked to the Chevy Bolt that belonged to Gus. I could tell he was steeling himself for what he might find.

He opened the trunk, stepped back, and shut his eyes.

My heart stopped.

Time slowed to a crawl.

After what felt like an eon, Dane opened his eyes, looked up, smiled, and shook his head.

I could breathe again.

Chapter 7
Questioning

I WAS STILL SHAKING, and my teeth were chattering. I'd been terrified that Dane would find Gus and Theresa in the trunk of one of their cars. I guess Dane recognized my fear, because he walked over and took my hand, rubbing it gently to bring some warmth to my bloodless fingers.

"I'm sorry you had to go through this, Fin. But things won't get better until we find them. Let me check in with the team, and then I'll get you a coffee. I have a few questions I need to ask, and I think you're the only one that has the answers." His eyes were dark and bleak.

I sat on the front stoop and waited for Dane. I was sitting in direct sunlight, and I could feel the heat on my skin, but I was still shivering.

In a few minutes, Dane exited through the side door and walked around the house to collect me. "Thanks for helping us out. I know how awful this can be."

"Do you?" I asked. "Has your best friend ever disappeared into thin air?" My voice cracked. I couldn't even bring up Gus and what he meant to me.

Dane didn't reply, but he led me over to his car and gently helped me into the front seat. He got in, and we took off. A few minutes later, we pulled into the parking lot at the Sunshine Grill, the restaurant at the Sunshine Suites resort, right across the street from Seven Mile

Beach. As we passed the hotel's pool, I looked at the happy people floating and swimming in the clear water. I had trouble understanding how people could be that happy and carefree.

Dane waved at the hostess when we entered the restaurant and pointed to a table in the back. She smiled and gave the okay sign. A few minutes later, she brought over two glasses of water and two cups of coffee. She'd already prepped Dane's coffee with lots of cream. I gathered he must be a regular here.

"Can we have a minute, please?" he asked her. "And if you can, please give us some privacy."

She grinned at him. "Again?"

He remained silent until she'd left. "I need to ask you some questions about Gus and Theresa. Every bit of information may help. Please don't hold anything back, okay? Believe me, your friends won't mind whatever you say if it eventually helps us find them."

"Okay." I wrapped my hands around the mug of coffee to keep them warm.

"How long have you known Gus and Theresa?" he asked.

"I've known Gus since I was about three years old. He was Ray's best friend. My stepfather, Ray Russo," I added, in case he'd forgotten who Ray was.

He pulled a pen and small notebook from the pocket of his shirt and started taking notes. "And Theresa?" he asked.

"We met when she started dating Gus a few years ago. She worked on the waitstaff at Sunset House. Once she and Gus were a thing, they spent a lot of time out with Maddy and Ray, and I'd always spent a lot of time with Ray and Maddy. Theresa and I hit it off, and I got to know her pretty well. We started hanging around together, even without Gus and my parents."

My voice broke. "I had a crazy childhood, and I never had a chance to spend time with people my own age. I was extremely happy when Theresa and I became friends." My voice broke, and I swallowed hard. "She's my best friend."

He nodded. "I'll do my best to get her back safe and sound. Tell me, did either Gus or Theresa have any enemies that you know about?"

I thought for a moment. "None that I know of. Everybody loves Gus. He's very kind, and he goes out of his way to help people.

Theresa is more volatile. She sometimes gets angry and upsets people."

I thought back to the day she had come to my office and yelled at me because she didn't feel RIO was as concerned about Gus as we should have been after his accident. "But she always apologizes later. It blows right over, and it's usually okay."

He wrote something in his notebook. "But that sounds more like an occasional short term issue. No real enemies, is that right?"

I nodded.

"Were they having any financial problems that you know of?"

"I don't think so. They were trying to save up for a new house while Gus was working at RIO and Theresa was waitressing. But after Gus had the accident, my father offered him a job as VP at Fleming Environmental, and he got a pretty good salary bump. Theresa was able to quit working. Then they had Angelica. And Gus is due for a large chunk of cash from the treasure salvage reward. Should be here any day now."

Dane leaned forward. "Who else knew about the reward? Think hard."

"Lots of people know about it. It was in the news and in *Your World. Cayman Compass.* Our documentary last year. Anybody could know about it."

"Hmm. How much is Gus's share of the reward?" he asked.

"About $ 3,000,000. Maybe a little more."

"And is the amount common knowledge?" he asked. He lifted his cup and sipped, watching me over the rim.

"I don't think so. Newton's been negotiating with the treasure's owners, and he just finalized the deal. The settlement amount hasn't been publicized."

"Good. Please make sure the amount, especially the share going to Gus, doesn't get out. Can you do that?"

"Sure. It's nobody's business anyway."

He thought for another moment. "Do either of them have any identifying marks—tattoos, scars, birthmarks?"

"Not that I know of."

"Medical conditions we should be aware of?"

My heart froze again. I'd forgotten. "Gus has a heart condition, and

I think he takes medication for it. I don't know what it is. Doc would know, though. We can ask her."

"Would he have it with him?" he asked.

I shook my head, remembering the vial I saw on the table in the *Sunshine Girl*'s galley. "Whatever it is, I don't think he has any with him."

"I'm going to need to talk to everyone one at RIO. Can you make them available?"

"Most everyone will be gone for the day, but there might be a few people still around. Do you want me to ask people to come back tonight for you to talk to?"

"No need. If you can, please send me an employee list as soon as you get back. I'll take care of setting up the appointments myself. Please highlight anyone that stands out to you as a person of interest or someone who knew them especially well, and I'll make them a priority. Otherwise, I think I have all I need from you for now. Thank you."

He dropped some money on the table, and we left the café. He drove me back to RIO and let me off at the front entrance.

Chapter 8
Diving

As soon as I got to my office, I pulled up the RIO employee list on my computer and emailed it to Dane. Other than Stewie, I didn't think anyone on the list was especially close to Gus. I didn't have to spend a lot of time highlighting names.

By now, the workday was over. I decided to call it quits and go diving. To keep my line open for the kidnapper, DS Scott had given me a burner phone. I used the burner to call Oliver. "You up for a dive?"

"Sure thing. Todd is still covering the dive shop, and I'm caught up on schoolwork. I can go whenever you want." Todd was a crew member on the *Omega*, but he helped out around RIO whenever the ship was in port. He and Oliver had become close friends during our recent expedition to Belize. "Where do you want to go?"

"Babylon," I said. "I need some spectacular shots for this month's *Your World* column." After turning in my photo montage chronicling the treasure hunting expedition we'd completed a few months ago, the magazine had given me a monthly column. They'd allowed me total freedom on the topics, the locations, and the photos, making it a dream assignment. I loved it.

"Pick me up on your way by the shop. I'll be ready," he said. "We can talk on the boat."

When I poked my head in through the open door of RIO's dive

shop a few minutes later, Oliver was sitting behind the counter, chatting with Todd.

"I already loaded tanks and my gear on the *Tranquility*. We're good to go whenever you want, Captain. Catch you later, Todd."

We ambled down the dock to my boat. I started the engines and backed smoothly out of the slip. As soon as we were away from the 'No Wake' zone, I gunned it, trying to relieve my frustrations over Theresa and Gus with speed and the crystalline flash of sunlight on the salty spray. It didn't work.

I was still worried about my friends. Even when I saw a school of flying fish joyfully keeping pace with the boat, I couldn't muster a smile. The flying fish took turns with a pod of dolphins, both groups leaping through the water off to the side, a sight that nearly always brought me joy.

Not today.

Today I was too worried about my friends. I was worried about baby Angelica. And I was worried that I'd messed up and let the kidnappers know the police were involved. If anything further happened to Theresa and Gus, I would never forgive myself.

Oliver could see how upset I was. After we'd tied up to the mooring at Babylon, he patted the bench beside him. "Let's sit a while before we dive," he said. "Take a minute to get in the right mindset."

"Good idea," I said. "I can't think straight. I'm frantic with worry about Gus and Theresa."

"We all are," Oliver said. "Don't worry. They'll find them."

We must have heard the whine of an approaching boat at the same time because we both looked up and squinted into the sun. "Looks like one of the RIO rentals." I stood up and shaded my eyes with my hand to reduce the glare off the water. "Maybe they found them." I could hardly contain my excitement.

The sleek black Zodiac spun into a tight curve, coming to rest alongside the *Tranquility*. Benjamin was alone on the boat. "Ahoy, Fin. Mind if I join you?" he called.

I sighed and bit back my disappointment that it was Benjamin and not someone sent to tell me that Gus and Theresa were back. "Sure. We were just about to dive though." I was annoyed that he'd followed us out here. Todd must have told him our dive plan and given him Babylon's coordinates.

"Super," he said. "I've been looking forward to diving with the famous Fin Fleming." His cheeks turned pink. "And you too, of course, Oliver,"

Benjamin threw a line to Oliver, who used it to pull the Zodiac close to the *Tranquility*. When the boats were nearly touching, Benjamin hopped over and landed lightly on my boat's deck. Oliver let out some line and then tied the rope off to one of the boat's cleats to keep them moored together. He dropped a couple of fenders over the side to keep the boats from bumping into each other as the waves moved them around.

"What's the dive plan?" Benjamin asked when Oliver finished tying off.

"First, I need to learn a little about your dive background, your skills, how long you've been diving and when you last dove. That way I can come up with a plan that won't put you in danger. Can you refresh my memory? It's been a while since I saw your resume."

"Sure. PADI certified advanced diver. Ten years of experience, mostly in California waters. So, lots of kelp diving. Cold water. Mostly shore dives. I haven't been diving in about two years."

"Okay. Good enough. I usually have a couple of spare sets of equipment on board, but I dropped them at the dive shop the other day for maintenance. I hope you brought your own gear."

"Drat. I didn't bring my own stuff. It's at home and I thought for sure you'd have something with you I could use."

"I would have made sure I brought spares along if I'd known you were coming. Sorry, Benjamin. I'm afraid you'll have to sit this one out."

He made a face. "Okay. You guys head out on scuba. I'm heavy into freediving nowadays anyway."

Oliver and I both sucked in a breath. Ray had died while freediving, and neither of us had tried it since, at least not the kind of stylized free diving practiced by AIDA and USA Freediving. We still dove without gear sometimes when we wanted to interact naturally with sea life, but we never engaged in formal freediving disciplines. It simply wasn't done anymore at RIO out of respect for Ray.

"Okaaay," I said, drawing out the word. "If you do that, you'll be diving alone. I'm on a deadline and I won't have time to babysit. Are you okay with that?"

He nodded. "I'm used to diving alone."

I wasn't happy to hear that, but he was an adult and not my responsibility. Even so, I could at least give him the layout of the dive site below us, and make sure he had some landmarks. "The reef starts at around forty feet here. I'll be trying to get some shots for my *Your World* column. Oliver and I will be diving on the upper reef along the pinnacle and maybe down the wall, depending on what we see. Will you be going below forty feet?"

Benjamin nodded. "About fifty meters, I think. I'll want to dive along the wall." An underwater wall starts at the point where the reef drops off into deeper water and it may extend vertically or near vertically to the bottom.

"Then enter from the bow, and stay to the left," I told him. That way you should skim right along the edge of the drop-off. I'll drop a guideline for you."

"Thanks for the tip. And the line." He pulled the blue t-shirt over his head, giving me another tantalizing glimpse of his abs. Then he walked to the bow and began doing his breathing warm up routine. I dropped a weighted line off the Tranquility's bow. The rope had florescent markings every ten meters. That way Benjamin would have a visual cue to his depth. It was the best I could do for him.

Oliver and I geared up and prepared to do giant stride entries off the stern. I went first, then Oliver handed me my heavy camera and strobe light before he made his own entry. We sank below the waves, using the mooring line as our guide.

The ocean is my natural element, and as always, as soon as I was under water, I felt all my stress roll off. The headache I'd been fighting all day disappeared, and I felt confident that we'd soon find Gus and Theresa safe and sound. I inhaled deeply, exhaled fully, and sank.

We swam into the current along the reef top, admiring the healthy, vibrant coral. I took several shots of some elkhorn coral, a few brain corals, and some tiny finger corals. A few anemones swayed with the rhythm of the water, and tiny, colorful wrasse darted around them. The powerful strobe lights helped add back the colors that the sea water stole from the surroundings, revealing the true brilliant colors.

Next, I took shots of a few parrot fish pecking at the coral. Everybody loves parrot fish, with their bright azure scales and big teeth, but they're pretty common and I knew I needed something with more star power for my column.

Oliver obligingly went through a swim-through we found along the wall, emerging at about eighty feet. The shot of a diver emerging from the swim-through was a common photo and not special enough to cause a stir for my column. While Oliver swam over the drop off, a tightly packed school of yellowfin tuna swarmed past us. I grabbed that photo too, but as of yet, I hadn't captured anything out of the ordinary.

I was staring at the wall trying to think of what unusual or interesting creatures I might see here, when Oliver pointed behind me. I turned and saw Benjamin streaking through the water out in the blue. A large silky shark had abandoned the schooling tuna and was following him. Benjamin was so intent on monitoring his depth, he didn't even seem to notice the shark. I snapped several pictures of them as they sped by.

The shark looked curious rather than aggressive, and I hoped he stayed that way. Oliver and I swam toward where we'd seen Benjamin descending and looked down. He was already about fifty or sixty feet below us, and the shark was right there with him.

Benjamin looked at the dive computer he wore on his wrist. He must have hit his intended depth because he quickly pivoted from his hips and headed back to the surface. If he noticed the shark circling above him, he gave no indication. He kept swimming upward, his powerful arms and legs working in tandem.

Oliver and I swam near to where the shark circled, directly in Benjamin's path. We didn't approach or try to touch the shark. We did the only thing we could do to let the shark know we weren't prey. We breathed through our regulators, creating lots of bubbles and noise.

When Benjamin reached our depth, Oliver positioned himself to one side of him, and I took the other, surrounding Benjamin in our bubbles. Benjamin seemed surprised to see us until Oliver pointed up at the ominous silhouette of the shark.

By now the shark seemed to have realized that we weren't edible and thus of no interest, because he swam away out into the deep blue. Even so, Oliver and I continued to follow Benjamin up to about sixty feet. He'd have to make the rest of his ascent on his own. Oliver and I needed to go up slowly because we were breathing compressed air and needed time to let our bodies release the excess nitrogen we'd absorbed during the dive. Since Benjamin hadn't been breathing at all during his dive, he could—indeed, he had to—ascend as rapidly as possible.

I watched Benjamin shoot through the water to the surface and climb the *Tranquility*'s ladder with a feeling of uneasiness. I didn't like Benjamin, and I wasn't comfortable with him alone on my boat. There was nothing personal aboard, but I felt like he disapproved of me, and I was irrationally afraid his disapproving presence on board the *Tranquility* might permanently taint my boat's serenity.

Oliver and I swam along the top of the reef, ascending slowly until we reached fifteen feet. We hovered there, doing a final three minute safety stop to let our bodies offgas more nitrogen before we swam to the ladder and climbed aboard.

Benjamin met us at the dive platform and pulled our heavy BCDs with the attached tanks off our shoulders. After stowing the gear in the racks along the side of the boat, he came back to the dive platform with warm towels for us.

I wasn't thrilled that he'd looked around enough to find my towels and the towel heater, but I was really happy to have the towel. Its warmth was comforting after this awful day.

Benjamin smiled at me, excitement shining in his eyes. "What a great dive. I wish I'd had more time to see the sights. And thanks for pointing out that shark to me. Crazy to be that close to him and not even know he was there, huh?"

"Yeah. I got some great shots of the two of you. I'd like to use a few of them for my *Your World* column this month. I'll email you the model release forms."

Benjamin paled. "No. I don't want them published. You can't use them. I won't sign the release. In fact, I want you to destroy them right now. Every one of them." He sounded panic stricken.

"Relax," said Oliver. "It's no big deal. Most people will be focused on the shark, not the diver. We weren't up close enough to get a clear shot of your face, and you were wearing a mask—plus with those abs of yours, nobody will be looking at your face anyway."

Oliver laughed, but Benjamin didn't join in.

I knew Benjamin's face wouldn't be recognizable in the printed pictures, meaning I wouldn't actually need a model release. Even though it didn't matter to me whether he signed the release or not, I was annoyed by his refusal. I'd only asked for the model release to flatter him.

I had the shots I needed for my column, and I was still worried about Gus and Theresa. I was eager to head back to shore. "Either of you want to stay for another dive?" I asked politely, hoping they'd decline.

Benjamin shook his head, his lips tight. "I'm done diving. I didn't realize you'd be taking my picture without my permission."

He'd invited himself along on this excursion, and he'd seen me enter the water holding my camera. I wondered if he'd really expected to go diving with a professional underwater photographer carrying a full camera rig and not have any pictures taken.

"I've got an exam coming up I need to study for. I'd better get back early," Oliver said.

I nodded. "Fine by me. I've got what I came for." I started the engines while he helped Benjamin disconnect from the mooring line.

Chapter 9
Timeline

THE FOLLOWING MORNING, I stopped at Newton's condo to see Angelica on my way to work. She was lying on a blanket in a mesh playpen, under the watchful eyes of the nanny Newton had hired. Angel's eyes lit up, and she smiled when I entered the room.

I introduced myself to Mrs. Bingham, the nanny, a pleasant older woman with a no-nonsense manner.

"Would you like to hold her?" she asked me. Without waiting for an answer, she draped a towel over my shoulder and handed me the sweet warm bundle that was Angel.

I stared into the baby's dark brown eyes, so deep they were like a pathway to all the secrets of the universe. I swore in my heart I would find her parents. It was unfathomable that this magnificent creation would be left alone in the world. I would have to redouble my efforts.

I was jingling a set of plastic keys at the baby, trying to make her smile, when Newton walked in.

"She likes those," he said. "They're her favorite."

I looked around at the room, now stuffed with every toy or device a baby could want or need. "With all this stuff around, she couldn't possibly have had time to pick a favorite yet."

Newton shrugged. "I could tell she like it the best." He held out a finger, and Angel grabbed it and held on tight. He smiled down at her, looking so happy it broke my heart.

"Dane is staying at your mother's place while she's away. That way he can join us here more easily when we need to meet. He's on his way over. Want a coffee or anything before he gets here?"

I heard the melodious chime of Newton's doorbell. I reluctantly handed Angel back to Mrs. Bingham. "That must be him now. Glad he's here early. We need to find Gus and Theresa quickly, before something bad happens."

DS Scott—Dane—stood in Newton's foyer, looking as crisp and professional as ever. He accepted Newton's offer of coffee, and we all went into Newton's office while we waited for it to brew.

"Any news?" Newton asked after his housekeeper dropped off a tray of coffee and muffins.

Dane shook his head. "Nothing. I've gathered all the security tapes from the areas around RIO to see what we could find. Neither Theresa nor Gus—nor any possible kidnappers—appear on anything we've reviewed. As near as we can tell, everyone on the tapes has a valid reason for being there. We're staying on it, but so far—nada."

"You won't find Gus and Theresa on tapes from the front of RIO. I think they were taken by boat, right from the marina. And we still don't have security cameras back there."

I kicked myself for not having insisted we cover every inch of RIO with cameras after we'd endured several incidents of vandalism a few years ago. As a non-profit organization, money was always tight, and since we'd never had a problem with vandalism before, we'd all agreed at the time that putting in a few highly visible cameras in the public areas would be adequate.

When I finished mentally berating myself, I said, "I'll ask Benjamin to get a proposal to cover the whole facility with cameras as soon as I get to work. I only wish I'd done it sooner."

"Good. I'll ask Justin to work with Benjamin on the project. I want to make sure it gets done quickly. He'll let me know what it costs, and I'll cover it with an extra donation this month," Newton said.

He was so down to earth I always forgot how rich he was. I should have asked him for financial help for RIO back when we'd had the initial break in problems, but we were just getting to know each other then. Since I'd never seen him around RIO before then, it hadn't occurred to me that he was deeply involved in RIO's operations.

Dane listened to our conversation without comment. Once we'd disposed of the security camera issue, he said, "Fin, tell me what makes you sure they were taken from the marina?"

I sipped my coffee and thought a minute. "Their boat is there, and their cars are still at their house. I bet your team hasn't found any record of them using a taxi or a ride share, right?"

He nodded. "There's no record of them using a cab or a rideshare service. But they could have been taken from their home and then the kidnapper might have brought the boat to the marina. Although as we saw yesterday, there's no sign of a struggle at their home, either."

I thought back to the boat. "I'm pretty sure Gus moored the *Sunshine Girl*. It's in his usual slip, which doesn't mean anything if someone had been watching him, I know. But it's the way the boat was moored. The lines are carefully wound around the cleats, with the excess line coiled neatly nearby. All the fenders were set out. Angel was on the floor, in the shade, in her travel pen on a clean blanket with lots of toys to play with. Everything very meticulous. It felt to me like Gus did it."

"And you don't think a kidnapper would have been that meticulous?" he asked.

"No, I don't," I said. "Most people who aren't experienced sailors leave the extra line in a pile, not realizing how easy it is to tangle up, especially if you need it in a hurry. And would anyone else have been that careful to make sure Angel was safe?"

"You're right. That's a good observation about the baby—and about the lines being coiled neatly. Kidnappers would probably be nervous, and anxious to get out of the area before anyone saw them. It would have been a rush job. They might not have taken the time to coil the lines. I didn't pick up on that because I'm not a boater. Anything else strike you as odd?"

I shook my head.

"What time were you expecting Gus in to work? Did he have a regular routine?" Dane asked.

"Gus doesn't work at RIO anymore, remember? He works for Newton at Fleming Environmental. He agreed to come in whenever he had time in case either Oliver or I needed help, but there was no set schedule. They could have arrived anytime.

"Was the *Sunshine Girl* there when you came to work?" he asked. "Did you see it?"

"Sorry. I don't know if it was there or not. I do sleep on my boat sometimes, but I was at home the night before. I wasn't on the dock early that morning. And even though my office window was open, I'd put my headphones on to work on the music for my video. I didn't hear anything until Benjamin came by a little before ten AM." I stopped and thought a minute. "You might want to check with Oliver. Maybe he noticed the boat when he opened the dive shop."

He nodded. "Good. I'll do that."

"Oh, and I don't think they could have been gone long before I found Angel, either. She was hungry and wet when we found her, but she wasn't starving—not like she'd been left for hours. And I'm sure I'd have heard her when I first came in to work if she'd been crying then."

"Good. That narrows it down. Now if we're lucky, Oliver may remember seeing either *Sunshine Girl* or an empty slip. If he does, we'll have a good handle on the timeline."

DS Scott pulled out his phone, and I watched his fingers fly as he composed a text. Within a few seconds, his phone buzzed with a reply. "Oliver says he doesn't think the boat was there when he arrived at the dive shop around 8:30. If that's the case, we may have narrowed down the time of the crime. Good work, Fin. Thank Oliver for me when you see him later, will you please?"

He opened his briefcase and pulled out a stack of missing person posters. "My team has been distributing these around town, but if you want to put them up at RIO or anywhere you have connections, we'd appreciate the assistance."

I took half the stack. "Oliver and I will get these out. You can count on us."

Newton took the remainder of the stack. "And I'll put these up at Fleming Environmental and at some of the other investment firms where I have connections. A lot of people in the financial community have gotten to know Gus since he joined the firm, and I'm sure they'll want to help."

"Good. Thank you both." DS Scott rose. "I have to get to the office. I'll touch base with you later today."

Chapter 10
Swimming Lessons

Once DS Scott had departed, Newton and I headed off to RIO for his daily swimming lesson. We'd been working on this together since we returned from the treasure hunt a few months ago. Although Newton had made some progress, it hadn't been easy for him to get past his lifelong fear of water. But now, he was able to put his face under without panicking. Now we were working on swim strokes.

Until today, I'd been conducting Newton's swimming lessons in the pool at my house on Rum Point. He wanted to be sure Maddy wouldn't get wind of them before he was ready to unveil his new skills. But since she was out of town and I needed to train DS Scott in scuba now, I'd asked him if we could relocate our classes to RIO's huge saltwater pool.

The outer dimensions of the pool at RIO were Olympic size, 164 feet long and twenty-five feet wide, but one end was much deeper than a regulation Olympic pool would be. The shallow end was a typical three to four feet, but the other end, where we practiced more advanced dive skills with our scuba classes, was twenty-five feet deep.

The floor of the pool stayed level for the first hundred and twenty feet, then it dropped off to the twenty-five foot depth. The pool's walls were marked with the depth at five foot intervals, and the floor was marked with red tiles at the drop off point, to ensure that swimmers knew they were entering deep water.

Newton and I were in the shallow end. Although he'd made great strides in his swimming abilities, I still had him traveling side to side across the pool rather than doing lengthwise laps that crossed the deep end. I wanted to be sure he felt confident in his skills before I took a chance on him losing control in a depth outside his comfort range.

Today he was swimming with his face in the water because we were working on improving his basic strokes. Later, we'd coordinate his breathing with his strokes, but for now, he was doing great with this basic drill.

Because he'd been teased his whole life about his lack of swimming ability, Newton got nervous practicing his skills in front of an audience —another reason we'd held his lessons at my pool. He'd also discussed learning to scuba dive as soon as I thought he was ready. He claimed he wanted to be able to scuba dive so he could spend more time with Oliver and me.

He hadn't said it in so many words, but by reading between the lines of what he had said, I thought he was hoping learning to dive would bring him closer to Maddy. After seeing her with Dane yesterday, I was pretty sure that ship had sailed once again, but Newton wasn't one to give up.

I was standing in waist deep water watching him swim when I heard the door from the men's locker room slam shut. Newton stopped swimming and popped upright, spluttering, and choking when he heard the noise.

DS Scott had arrived early for his scuba lesson. Newton glowered at him.

"Let's take five, Newton," I said. "We can check in with DS Scott on the search for Gus and Theresa."

Newton climbed up the rungs of the pool ladder and grabbed a towel from the stack piled on a nearby bench.

DS Scott sat on the other end of the bench. "How goes it?" he asked pleasantly.

Newton grimaced. "Getting there. It's not easy to learn a new skill at my age."

"I agree," the detective replied. "But it looked like you were doing fine. Maybe we can learn scuba together if it's okay with Fin."

"We'll see," I said. "This is your first scuba lesson. I need to evaluate your swimming ability before we start with scuba skills. Newton and I aren't quite finished with his class, but since you're here early, why don't you do a couple of laps while you wait."

DS Scott went pale. "Down and back, right?"

"That's one lap. Down and back, twice each way. Any stroke you like. Take as much time as you need. No pressure."

I stood on the pool deck watching as he stepped into the pool and began swimming. He was no better a swimmer than Newton, and he'd been raised on the island. I shook my head. I had my work cut out for me if I were going to make divers out of these two.

I turned to Newton. "Your swimming has improved a lot, and it'll get even better when you're wearing fins. Do you feel ready to start your scuba classes?"

He thought a moment, biting his lip. "I think so. Yeah, I do."

"Good." I smiled at him. "How do you feel about learning to dive at the same time as DS Scott?"

He groaned. "Really? You'd do that to me?"

"No, I wouldn't, if you're not comfortable with it. But it'll be a lot easier for me if I only have to fit in one private class a day rather than two, and you guys are pretty evenly matched in your swimming skills. Think of it this way—if you were taking a public class, you wouldn't have any say over who your class dive buddy ended up being. You could consider it the luck of the draw."

He nodded. "Okay. I'll do it. If it's okay with him then it's okay with me."

We stood shoulder to shoulder and watched DS Scott complete his laps. It was slow going. I could almost see Newton's self-confidence growing as he watched the policeman slowing down as he neared the end of his second lap.

By the time he finished, DS Scott was breathing hard, and I could see his muscles shaking. But he'd done what I asked, and he'd get better at all types of swimming as his scuba training progressed.

Now that Dane had finished his swim, I walked the two men down to the dive shop where Oliver was working. Oliver's friend Todd, who was part of the *Omega*'s crew and Oliver's sometimes roommate when the ship was in port, was there too, busy helping a few tourist divers set up their gear for a shore dive from our dock.

"I need to talk to you in private," Oliver said when I came in.

"Same issue?" I asked. From his voice, I surmised that we were missing more tanks.

He nodded, and we walked outside to speak quietly with our heads close together to make it harder for anyone in the shop to overhear.

"I left twenty out last night. Eight were signed out by staff. That means twelve are gone this time. But I was working late, and a group of teenagers came across the lawn. They hung out at one of the picnic tables, drinking and horsing around for quite a while. They'd been here about an hour when I smelled pot. I came out to shoo them off the property. It was obvious they hadn't known I was in the dive shop until I came out and asked them to leave. They were pretty irate about the party ending."

"Did you get their names?"

"No, but I don't think they were permanent residents on the island. I'll keep an eye on the place after hours from now on because I was thinking they might have something to do with the missing tanks. If that's the case, the missing tank problem may be short term anyway since most tourists are gone within a week or two."

"Okay. That's probably what's been going on. But don't worry about the missing tanks right now. We'll figure it out once Gus and Theresa are back. And by the way, Newton is footing the bill for security cameras back here. I'll ask Benjamin to get a proposal and we'll get them installed right away."

"Good idea," he said. "It will give Benjamin something he likes to do."

We both laughed and then returned to the dive shop. We worked together to help Dane and Newton choose well-fitting masks, snorkels, regulator mouthpieces, gear bags, and full foot fins. Newton also bought a top of the line regulator, a buoyancy control device (BCD), a shorty wetsuit, two 100 cubic foot steel tanks, and a sleek Lycra dive-skin. He'd be ready for anything. He pulled out his Black American Express card to pay for it all.

"Do I need to buy all that equipment today too?" Dane asked.

"No, not at all. You can rent tanks, regulators, and BCDs at most dive shops. You'll want to use your own mouthpiece, mask, snorkel, and fins for sanitary reasons, but you can buy the rest if and when you're ready."

"Good to know," he replied. "But I'll take it all now." Then he fingered a shiny diveskin with an abstract pattern of blue triangles across the shoulders. "I'll take this too."

After Oliver rang up his purchases, Dane pulled out a Black American Express card of his own to pay, and Newton raised his eyebrows at the sight of it.

Dane did a double take and looked at Oliver when he saw the total. "There must be a mistake. This is way too low."

"Nope. No mistake. Police diver discount. Plus a little extra off for friends and family." He grinned at Dane.

Once we'd finished with the shopping, I took the men over to a nearby picnic table. Their open water scuba manuals were already on the seat, and they both grabbed them eagerly, like kids on Christmas morning.

We went over some of the key concepts, like the mammalian dive reflex, multiple ways to clear water from a mask, and methods to equalize the pressure in your ears and sinuses during a dive. They listened attentively, which must have been hard for two men used to being in charge.

After we finished the classroom part of the first lesson, we prepped their equipment and went back inside to the pool for their first in water scuba session. This one was easy. We stayed in the shallow end of the pool for the most part, clearing masks and breathing through our snorkels. We set up regulators on filled tanks and they each took a few breaths through the regulators, but I didn't have them try to use them in the water yet. At the end of the session, I asked them to don their fins and do a lap in the pool, breathing through their snorkels. They both did fine.

When they climbed out of the pool, I said "Read chapter two tonight. Same time tomorrow. Bring your gear, everything except tanks. I'll supply those. That's it for today."

Newton and I had been in the habit of having breakfast or at least a coffee together after his swimming lessons, and I wasn't sure how Dane's presence would affect that. I didn't want to upset Newton by setting a precedent he wasn't comfortable with on our first day with Dane in the class, and I couldn't very well ask him how he felt about it with Dane standing right beside him.

I bit my lip, torn between good manners, not wanting to give the impression I wasn't happy Dane was with my mother, and concern for my always iffy relationship with my father.

I was relieved when Newton spoke up. "Care to join us for breakfast in the café, Dane?" he asked. "My treat."

Dane smiled. "I'd like that. The water is warm, but it can still chill you to the bone after a while."

The café was empty since it was still too early for RIO's aquarium and other public areas to be open yet. We sat at a table in the far corner where no one could hear us, and we could see anyone entering the area.

"Okay," I said. "What have you found out?"

Dane sipped his orange juice. "Your hunch was right. Oliver was certain that *Sunshine Girl* wasn't on the dock when he opened the dive shop because he'd have gone over to say good morning. We can be pretty sure that Gus was the person who docked the boat. Oliver got to work about 8:30, and you found Angel at 10. Gus must have arrived— and been taken—sometime in those ninety minutes. Nobody we've talked to saw him or Theresa. That makes it unlikely that they were brought across the grounds. We think now that somebody pulled up alongside in another boat, somehow got Gus and Theresa on board without making a fuss, and then the boat left quietly by sea. We're thinking it might have been a sailboat because nobody remembers hearing any noise."

"Alec Stone owns a sailboat," I said. My ex-husband was a weasel, but I still felt bad throwing him under the bus.

"Yes, he does. But he was in New York at the time. We've already confirmed it." Dane looked glum.

"You know it might not have been a sailboat anyway. Boats come and go all day around here. Nobody would remember hearing the sound of a motor. They probably wouldn't even have looked up."

"True. I hadn't thought of that." He took another sip of juice.

"We're checking all the boat rental agencies and all the marinas here and on Little Cayman and the Brac. So far, nobody has reported renting a sailboat or seeing any unexpected strangers. We're widening our search."

"How?" I asked. "What are you doing exactly? Because to be honest, it doesn't feel like you're making any progress."

He sighed. "I know. But without a ransom demand, we have nothing to go on. No motive that might help us zero in on a suspect. We're checking the credentials of every stranger who rented or chartered a boat, moored in an unfamiliar marina, or in any way did anything we could consider unusual."

Newton spoke up. "I'm not telling you how to run your business, but they've been gone for a full day now and you've got nothing. Do you need more manpower? Equipment? Name it. If money can buy it, you'll have it. I swear it. Gus…" his voice broke, and he took a deep breath before he went on. "Gus is a good man, and he's a friend. I… we…can't lose him."

"Understood," Dane said. "Fin, I'd like to ask you to spend as much time on your boat moving around the islands as you can. We have the police boats and the Coast Guard on the lookout for anything suspicious, but of course, we're conspicuous. You'll blend in. Maybe you'll see or notice something that we wouldn't see. The way you noticed those men doing needle sticks on unsuspecting patrons at the restaurant that time last year…"

I remembered that day. I'd been there with Liam, a few days before we left on the expedition to recover the sunken treasure. We'd been so happy together.

Newton's voice broke into my reverie, bringing me back to the present. "You're not risking my daughter because you and your team can't do your jobs."

"I wouldn't do anything to put Fin at risk. I don't want her to do anything or confront anyone. I'm only asking her to report anything she sees. She can use the burner phone to let me know if she notices anything. That way, no one can connect her to our later actions."

Newton glared at him while speaking to me. "Don't go anywhere alone. Take Oliver or Justin—I'll let him know he can take off whenever you need him, no matter what's going on at work. Even, heaven help me, take Benjamin if there's no one else around. And no sleeping on the boat until we get to the bottom of this. Understood?"

Just yesterday I'd been thinking wistfully how nice it would have been to have a father try to run my life. Now I understood why Justin had found it stifling. "I can handle myself, Newton. I know what I'm doing."

"He's right, though," said Dane. "You shouldn't be alone. In fact, I think you should stay at your father's condo until we solve this case. Even your own house is too isolated for us to be sure we can keep you safe. Who knows what these people are after, or even what they'd do to you now that they know you're working with us?"

I opened my mouth to protest, but realized they were probably right. And now I'd have a good excuse to call Justin.

Chapter 11
Video Editing

DANE AND NEWTON finished their breakfasts and walked out to the parking lot together, seemingly the best of friends all of a sudden. I shrugged. I'd never understand men.

I was on my way to my office when Stanley Simmons stopped me in the hall.

"Morning, Fin. How's little Angel doing today? Is she missing her Mommy and Daddy?"

I smiled at him. "I'm sure she does, Stanley. But she's a good baby. An angel, just like her name."

"Good. Well, if you need any help with her, please let me know. I'll be glad to pitch in taking care of her until her parents come home. She's family, after all."

I'd forgotten that Stanley and Gus were related, and I still couldn't remember exactly how. Cousins maybe? "Thanks, Stanley. Much appreciated, but I think she's fine." I waved as I rushed off to my office. "Gotta go. Thanks again."

I sat down at my desk and reopened the file for my video of Harry the stingray. The Underwater Conservancy contest deadline was coming up fast and I needed to finish it. The break from working on it seemed to have been good for my concentration, because within a few minutes, I had found the perfect background music and it synced right up to the scene with Harry and the hammerhead. I saved the file and sighed with relief.

I called Oliver. "Got a minute to review a video with me? I want to be sure it's as perfect as I think it is. I value your opinion."

"Sure thing," he said. "I'll be right up."

While I waited for Oliver to arrive, I proofread my entry form one last time. I had finished rereading it for the third time when Oliver walked in.

"Let's see what you've got," he said smiling.

I turned my computer around and hit play. Oliver stared at the screen, watching the entire fifteen minute film without comment while I fidgeted.

When it ended, he said nothing. He silently pushed the button and played it again.

I couldn't stand the stress of wondering what he thought, so I rose and walked down to the café to get a couple of lemonades for Oliver and me.

Stanley was polishing the hall floor outside Benjamin's office. He looked up when I walked by. I didn't have a free hand to wave, so I merely nodded and smiled.

Oliver was gazing out my window when I reentered my office.

"What did you think?" I asked, handing him the icy cup.

He paused a moment, and I nearly died inside, sure he was looking for a way to let me down easy. I bit my lip to keep it from trembling.

He took a sip from his cup. "I don't know what to say…"

"Never mind. You don't have to say anything. I knew it was a long shot."

He looked at me like I'd sprouted another head. "Don't be daft. It's brilliant. I loved everything about it. I could see the love and respect you felt for Harry in the early minutes, and I learned a lot about stingrays and reef life in the middle. I felt your terror and sorrow when the hammerhead came on the scene. I loved every frame. Every word. Every note of the music. It's flawless."

I took a deep breath, but before I could say anything, he said, "Truth. Send it in. Right now. Just as it is."

I was stunned by his praise. I smiled and sat at my desk to send in my entry. It took a few minutes for the large video file to send. When it was done, I smiled at Oliver. "I feel bad saying this because of what's going on with Gus and Theresa, but I've been working on that video entry for over a year. Do you have time to celebrate with me?"

He shook his head. "No, sorry. I have a timed exam this afternoon. I have to find a place to hole up where I won't be disturbed."

Chapter 12
Diving with Justin

THERE WAS a knock on my door then, and I looked up to see Justin Nash in the doorframe. "I'd like to celebrate with you if you'll have me. Let's go diving, then we can grab some lunch."

One of the perks of my job as chief underwater photographer at RIO is that I'm required to dive every day, at whatever time or location works for me. And Newton had told me to take Justin with me if I went anywhere when Oliver wasn't available.

"Perfect," I said. "Oliver, you can use my office to take your exam while I'm gone."

He grinned. "Thanks. Have fun. Todd is running the dive shop today, and he'll get you set up with whatever you need, Justin."

"Thanks, but I brought my own gear. I think we're good to go." He smiled and held out his arm. "Shall we?"

We walked down the hall past Stanley, now polishing the floors outside my office, and let ourselves out the door beside my mother's corner office. Since Justin had already dropped his gear at the dive shop, we stopped by to pick it up. Todd handed him some weights and signed out four tanks for us to use. We loaded everything on the *Tranquility*, and I started the engine.

"Where do you want to dive?" I asked him.

"Eagle Ray Rock?" he said. "If that's okay with you."

I shrugged. "Why not?" I put the boat in gear and backed out of my slip for the short trip to the dive site, located nearby on the south side of Grand Cayman.

I pulled up next to the mooring ball and Justin tied the boat off. When he signaled that the boat was secure, I shut down *Tranquility*'s engines and climbed down from the flying bridge. Justin was already setting up his buoyancy control device and regulator on one of the tanks. His movements were practiced and efficient. It was easy to tell he'd had plenty of experience. I pulled my gear bag out from under the bench and started setting up on the opposite side of the boat. When everything was ready, I slipped into one of my old RIO branded dive-skins. Justin was already suited up waiting for me.

We did quick checks of each other's gear and then did giant stride entries off the dive platform on *Tranquility*'s stern. We followed the mooring line down to just above the tops of the scattered coral—about 50 feet below the surface. The reef sloped down from there, with a sandy bottom populated by hundreds of garden eels. Row by row, they ducked into their burrows at our approach, and I noticed Justin smile with delight at the little creatures. They were one of my favorites too.

Thousands of colorful reef fish darted about the corals, making a continuously changing mosaic of bright blues, reds, and yellows. A little further down, I noticed a trumpet fish, barely visible as he hovered upside down, swaying gracefully in the current, hidden in a clump of sea grass that was nearly the same color as his body.

We hit the drop off at about 130 feet and looked down into the abyss. The bottom was far enough away it wasn't even visible, and I felt the same thrill I always feel at the hidden mysteries of the ocean.

Justin checked for current, and he made the hand signal for swimming to the left. I gave the okay sign, and we dropped over the edge and swam slowly along the vertical wall, peering into crevices to see what we could see. Every few kicks, we turned to look out into the blue, and the third time we turned, we saw a pair of spotted eagle rays gliding serenely by. We hovered in place, watching them depart. Spotted eagle rays are a good luck omen, and I hoped their presence meant we'd find Gus and Theresa soon.

We were so enthralled by the eagle rays that we almost missed the green sea turtle coming up behind us until he veered sharply to pass us by, just a few centimeters out of reach. Not that I would ever have tried to touch him, but he had no way of knowing that, and he'd apparently learned to be wary of divers.

We started drifting up the wall, still moving slowly, peering into the small tunnels and crevices we passed until we reached the turnaround point. We swam back the way we had come, rising slowly, only a foot or two with each kick until we were back at around seventy feet. We made our way up the sand chute, enjoying the busy reef life until we reached the mooring line.

We ascended slowly until we reached fifteen feet, then we did our safety stop. I signaled to Justin that I wanted to do five minutes rather than the standard three, because we had spent a large chunk of our dive time at about one hundred fifty feet. He flashed the okay sign and we hovered together until it was time to finish our ascent.

I signaled for him to climb the ladder first. When I was sure he was safely aboard and not likely to fall back in on top of me, I swam to the ladder, removed my fins, and climbed up.

Justin had already stowed his gear when I came up the ladder. As soon as I broke the surface he reached down and took my fins, so I'd have my hands free. Once on board, I removed my regulator from my mouth and walked over to the bench along the side of the boat. I sat down, sliding my empty tank, still strapped in my BCD, into the tank holders that lined the inner hull and gave a deep sigh.

"That was a great dive. Thank you for taking me," Justin said. "Now let me take you to lunch."

"It's still a little early for lunch. Let's go a little way around the island and see if we see anything suspicious. Have you seen the blow holes?"

Chapter 13
Blow Holes

JUSTIN LAUGHED. "No, actually I haven't seen them, or at least, not while they're putting on a show. What are they anyway?"

"They're a natural phenomenon created by the combination of the island's geology and the force of the ocean," I told him. "The Cayman Islands are formed by the tops of an underwater mountain range that was created during the eruption of volcanoes. The base layer of the islands is a stone called granodiorite. The middle layer is basalt, and the layer nearest the surface is carbonates."

He nodded.

"Too much detail?" I asked.

"Nope. I'm always impressed by how much technical stuff you know. Go on." He leaned back against the gunwale.

"Well, carbonates are composed of the bodies of coral, algae, and shells. Geologists believe the carbonate layer built up over the course of 30 million years. One of the defining characteristics of carbonate is that it's extremely porous, providing hundreds of paths for water to flow. Crystal Caverns is one example of how it works, but one of the most striking places to see it is at the Cayman Blow Holes."

"Go on," he said.

"The wind and tides force ocean water into the underwater caverns and crevices, and the water erupts onto the surface in a stunning display of power and beauty. The blow holes are a popular tourist destination. And today, we're going to play tourist. Except we'll stay on the *Tranquility* instead of driving on the road. DS Scott wanted me to spend time patrolling around the island to see if I noticed anything unusual. This is as good a time as any."

I started the engines, and we took off, heading toward Grand Cayman's East End. As we approached the blow holes, we could see the waves frothing against the iron shore. With each set of waves, the sea water was forced through the porous rock. Sea water geysered into the air, sometimes cresting ten to twenty feet into the air.

I held the *Tranquility* steady in the water, far enough out from shore that we weren't at risk of crashing onto the iron shore. Justin and I watched enthralled as thousands of gallons of seawater were thrust through pores in the rock and then pulsed into the air under tremendous force.

The sunlight caught the glistening water droplets and prismed each one into a sparkling jewel. Tiny rainbows were born and died as the water rose into the air and fell back to rejoin the sea. It was an impressive display, and we stared, rapt, for several minutes.

At last Justin broke the spell. "Wow. You don't realize the power and beauty of the ocean until you see something like that."

"I realize it every day. No matter how often I dive, there's always more to discover. The ocean is an endless mystery."

"I wouldn't want to be caught in the current here. It's obvious a person wouldn't have a chance against the tide."

"The current is pretty rough right along here, but there are caves and crevices all over the island that fill up with water at high tide and empty when the water recedes. They're just not as dramatic about it as these blowholes here."

He laughed. "I never thought of the ocean as a diva before."

"The ocean always gets its own way." I looked at the sun, which was almost directly overhead. "Looks like it's time for lunch. I'll get us back to RIO."

Chapter 14
Lunch at Nelsons

I FINISHED TYING the *Tranquility* in her slip in the marina while Justin brought our empty tanks back to the dive shop. I met him on the shell path when we'd finished our tasks.

"I'm starving," he said. "And lunch is on me today."

"Thanks," I said. "I'm starving too. But I can pay for my own lunch." I smiled at him, nearly drowning in those deep blue eyes of his. Thoughts of Liam intruded, but I pushed them aside. He'd obviously moved on.

"I'm sure you can," he said. "But it's only fair. We used your boat for the dive, so let me treat you to lunch."

I shrugged. "Okay. Let's get dressed and go."

We used the locker rooms at RIO to change, and then left through the front entrance to make the short walk to Justin's car. He drove a dark blue Mercedes electric car. I knew from listening to Oliver's lustful musings over pictures of the vehicle that it cost well over $100,000.

"Nice car," I said, as I slid into the passenger seat.

Justin smiled. "Do you like it? I hoped you would. I picked it up yesterday. Fleming Environmental is a huge proponent of electric vehicles, and Newton told me you like blue cars."

I can't tell one car from another, but I sensed he was expecting me to be impressed. I had no idea about cars, so I settled for saying, "I certainly like this one. Where are we going?"

"If you don't mind, I'll surprise you." He grinned and slipped the car into gear. We glided away soundlessly.

I stifled my groan when Justin pulled into the parking lot at Nelson's.

"I think you'll love this place," he said. "It's called Nelson's after Mike Nelson, the lead character in the old Sea Hunt TV series. They play all the episodes of the show, one after the other. I forget how many episodes there are, but well over a hundred. You never have a chance to get bored. And sometimes," he added," they show RIO documentaries for a change of pace. Pretty cool, huh?'

I nodded without enthusiasm. "Pretty cool."

The valet opened my door and I slid out of the car, but I wasn't happy. The last time I'd been here I'd been celebrating Liam's new job as RIO's CEO. That day turned into a nightmare. He and I had uncovered a drug ring preying on unaccompanied young women, and also, the bartender, Stefan Gibb, was an old enemy of mine. He'd done his best to humiliate me that day by playing a blooper reel from the annual RIO documentaries dating from my earliest childhood. Although Stefan and I struck an uneasy truce after that, I hadn't been back to Nelson's since that awful day.

But Justin couldn't have known any of this, so I went inside with him without a word. We crossed the bar area to sit at a small round table along the sandy beach. The huge red market umbrella provided shade from the hot sun, and the ocean breeze was cool and refreshing. I swallowed my anxiety.

The waiter brought menus and took our drink orders. After our dives, we were both thirsty. We ordered iced fruit juice.

"May I have an umbrella in mine?" Justin asked with a laugh.

"Sure thing, Mate." The waiter's Aussie accent reminded me of Liam, and I bit my lip and stared down at my menu. I had to forget about Liam.

I thought things couldn't get much worse until a shadow fell across the table.

"Chris, this table is on the house. Anything they want. Any time they want."

I shut my eyes. That voice sounded like Stefan Gibb. I looked up and frowned. This was indeed a nightmare.

"Justin, maybe we should leave…"

"Please don't leave," said Stefan. "I owe you a lot, and I'm sorry for the harm I've caused you in the past. I own this place now—or I will as soon as I get that check for my share of the treasure we recovered—and I have you to thank for my good fortune. Please let me make it up to you, even if it's only by comping you when you come in here."

I tried to be gracious. "Thank you, Stefan. That's very nice of you, but it's not necessary."

He crossed his arms over his chest. "Yes, it is necessary. For me. And you are doing me a favor by coming here. Who doesn't want to come to a place where they might bump into the world famous diver Fin Fleming? Please stay today, and please come back as often as you like."

He turned and walked away without another word, leaving the decision to stay or go in my hands.

"I'm sorry. I should have known you'd have been here before since you've lived on this island all your life. But I didn't know you had a history with the owner. You should have said something. We can leave if you want."

I thought for a minute. "No, we can stay. Stefan sounded sincere, and the food here is really great." I picked up my juice in a mock salute. "To new beginnings."

Justin nodded gravely. After removing his red paper umbrella, he lifted his plastic cup to clink against mine. "New beginnings," he said. "I like the sound of that."

We spent a pleasant hour and a half, munching and chatting. By the time we were ready to go, I realized that Stefan's apology and the time here with Justin had erased—or at least muted—the bad memories of the time before.

When the valet brought his car around, Justin handed me the keys. "Would you like to try it out?"

I handed the keys back to him. "Thanks, but no. I'm not really into cars."

He shrugged and opened the passenger door for me. "No problem. Where to? Back to RIO?"

"Hmmm...how about Newton's condo? DS Scott has set up a command post there to work on the kidnapping, and I'd like to check in on his progress."

"Good idea." He put the car in gear, and we glided off.

Chapter 15
Command Center

I PUNCHED the code into the electronic lock on Newton's door and Justin and I entered. I'd been expecting a scene of bedlam, with people manning tip lines and sorting through evidence. Instead, Newton's living room was quiet.

Roland, Eugene's twin brother, sat on the couch, his shoeless feet on Newton's glass coffee table, staring into a computer with a frown on his face. The other cop who'd been with us the day of the kidnapping was seated at Newton's desk with a phone pressed to his ear.

Newton and Dane Scott stood together near the wall of windows, not speaking, just staring. Because the shades were drawn, I could tell they weren't enjoying Newton's multi-million dollar view of the ocean. I assumed they were lost in their own thoughts, and I could see despair in their drooping shoulders.

When the door clicked shut behind me, Newton turned and gave me a bleak smile. "No news," he said. "It's like they just vanished."

"They can't have just vanished. Somebody knows where they are," I said.

"Yes," Dane said. "But whoever it is, they aren't telling." His face was glum, and his eyes were sunken.

"What can I do?" I asked.

"You should both keep on doing what you're doing. Work. Whatever you normally do. This is on me." He stared at his feet.

Justin put a hand on Newton's shoulder. "Okay then. I'll hold down the fort while you're here. I'll be in the office if you need anything."

Newton nodded, and Justin turned to leave the condo. At the door, he looked back at me. "I'll call you," he said.

I felt my face flush. "Uh, sure," I said. I turned to Newton and Dane. "What can I do to help?"

"Not much," Dane said. We have the Coast Guard searching all vessels in the area, and we have eyes on their house. We've distributed a ton of those missing posters, but so far, no tips. I'm not sure…" He broke off at the sound of a ringing telephone. It was my line.

The cop who'd been sitting at Newton's desk looked up to make sure everybody was ready, and that the recording and tracing equipment was operating before signaling me to answer. "Yes, hello," I said.

An electronic voice responded. "If you want to see Gus and Theresa again, deposit the funds from his share of the treasure reward into my account by end of day. Otherwise, little Angel will be an orphan."

"Wait," I shouted. "We don't even have the funds yet."

The sound of the electronic chuckle that greeted my words sent chills through my body, but the sound of the click as the caller disconnected froze my heart. A few seconds later, my phone buzzed with an incoming text.

"When do you expect the money?"

Roland sprang into action trying to trace the text, but the cop who had been tracing the call shook his head. "Too short," he said. "Lost them on the third skip, and I'm sure there were at least six, if not more. Sorry."

I put my hand to my mouth in horror. "It was my fault. I should have kept quiet."

Dane put a hand on my shoulder. "The guy knew what he was doing. He'd have hung up anyway. It's nobody's fault."

Newton's eyes were hollow, and I noticed a tremor in his hand when he reached out to pat my arm. "Dane's right, Fin. It wasn't your fault he hung up. Seems like the guy's a pro. He knew exactly how long the trace would take."

Newton knew I always blame myself for anything that goes wrong, and I'd been working on learning to cut myself some slack. But my best friend and my third-father were at risk here, and I couldn't help but feel my rash words had added to their danger. I closed my eyes and inhaled deeply, trying—but not succeeding—to let the guilt go.

My phone rang again, and I gasped from the sudden hope that sprang up in my heart. I answered on speaker in case it was the kidnappers calling. "Hello," I said, my voice shaking.

"Hey, Fin. It's Benjamin Brooks here. Will you have some time to meet with me this afternoon? I have some questions I want to go over with you if you're free. And bring Angel if you want. I've totally fallen in love with her."

"Sure thing, Benjamin. I'm heading back to RIO right now. I'll see you in a few minutes."

"I'll drive you," Newton said. "Hang on a sec while I get Angel ready." He went down the hall while I shuddered, trying to recover my equilibrium.

"We'll find them," Dane said. "Don't worry."

I tried to smile at his reassuring words, but I couldn't make it stick. Newton returned with Angel, and she leaned into my arms with a happy smile. I kissed her soft cheek, slung her bag over my shoulder, and then we left the penthouse.

Chapter 16
Business Meeting with Benjamin

NEWTON DROPPED me off at RIO, but he didn't come in. He was anxious to get back to the command post at his condo in case any news came in about Gus and Theresa. I wanted to be there too, but I had to take care of business at RIO. I trudged down the hall to my office, carrying Angel and her voluminous diaper bag.

There was a stack of papers on my desk that hadn't been there when I'd left. My heart thudded. Maybe it was something from the kidnappers.

I hurried across the room, but even before I'd crossed the three steps that took, I saw it was a pile of forms of some kind. Disappointed, I sank into my desk chair and gave Angel a despairing hug.

"Knock. Knock," Benjamin said from the doorway. "Did you get the surprise I left you?"

"Sorry, no. What surprise?" I nuzzled Angel's neck so he wouldn't see the stress on my face.

"I signed the model release forms you requested. That's them on your desk." He jutted his chin toward the pile of papers. "I owe you an apology. I acted like a jerk when you asked me to sign the form. I realize now it's no big deal. Please go ahead and use the photos in any way you'd like."

"Thank you" I said. "I appreciate that." I noticed he wasn't wearing a shirt and tie today. He'd adopted the unofficial RIO uniform of cargo shorts and a RIO branded shirt. Instead of his highly polished loafers, he wore flip flops. He looked good enough that I almost missed what he said next.

"I've been an insufferable idiot since I started working here, and I apologize for that. I was stressed out. The pressure to live up to the standards set by the rest of the team here got to me."

That got my attention. "You have no need to put any kind of pressure on yourself. Maddy wouldn't have hired you if she didn't think you were up to it. I know what it's like to feel like you're not perfect, and believe me, it's not a good feeling."

He smiled. "But you are perfect—or practically. I've watched you in the RIO documentaries for years. I've seen you work here under tremendous pressure. I read about the murders you've solved and the people who tried to hurt you and how you bested them without batting an eyelash. You not only run the marketing team here, but you have the column at *Your World*, and unless I miss my guess, you're about to win an Underwater Conservancy award for your short film. You're a powerhouse in everything you touch. Is there anything you can't do?"

My mouth dropped open. "I make plenty of mistakes and there's a lot I can't do—like accounting and spreadsheets—stuff like that." I paused a moment. "Let's start over, with the assumption we're both very good at our jobs, okay?"

His lips twitched as he tried to hold back a smile. "I'd like that. Thank you. Now can I hold Angel while we talk? I love babies, and she is so darn cute…"

"She is pretty cute." I laughed. "I've got an idea. Let's have our meeting aboard the *Tranquility*. Much less stuffy than an office or conference room."

He reached over and picked up Angel and then slung her bag over his shoulder. "If I work here for a hundred years, I'll never get over the luxury of meetings on the deck of a boat while we enjoy sunshine and warm breezes. If I'm dreaming, don't wake me up. Now what else can I carry for you?"

"I've got it," I said, grabbing my tablet and electronic pencil. "Let's go."

We settled Angel on a blanket on the floor in the shade of the cabin with some toys to keep her occupied, and Benjamin and I sat in the captain's chairs nearby. We chatted amiably for a half hour while Benjamin asked his questions, and I provided the answers. We'd finished quickly, and now we were simply hanging out, getting to know each other, and enjoying the gentle rhythm of the boat.

"We should get back inside," Benjamin said at last. "But I'd like to pay you back for the time you spent helping me today. How about dinner tonight?"

"That's totally unnecessary, but sure—as long as it's nothing fancy and you don't mind eating early. I need to get the baby home soon, and if you don't mind, we can eat right after that." We gathered up Angel and her equipment and hopped off the boat.

We hadn't taken a single step along the pier when the roar of an approaching motorboat and a sudden splash of water stopped us in our tracks. Angel screwed up her pretty face in consternation at the unexpected shower, but Benjamin immediately crooned at her, jiggling her, and making her laugh. He really was good with her.

After I wiped the salt water off my face, I looked at the boat that had caused the splash. It was one of RIO's black Zodiacs we used for rentals. I was about to remind the pilot that this was a no wake zone when Stanley Simmons leaped out of the cockpit and landed lightly on the dock, still carrying his fishing tackle box.

"I'm so sorry, Fin. I'm really late getting back from lunch, and I was going too fast so I wouldn't be any later. It won't happen again. I promise."

I looked at my watch. It was after 4:30. Stanley was definitely late getting back from lunch. I knew that if Eugene caught him coming back this late there'd be harsh words and a cut in his paycheck this week. I decided to give him a break. "I won't tell Eugene this time, but in the future, please follow the rules when it comes to water safety. Someone could get hurt."

He nodded. "I promise I'll be more careful. Say, is that Angel? Can I give her a hug?" He reached out to take her from Benjamin.

"Just for a second. We're on our way out and in kind of a hurry," I said.

Benjamin reluctantly relinquished the baby.

Stanley cooed at her for a moment and then asked, "Where have Gus and Theresa been, anyway? Their boat's here but I haven't seen them around lately."

"They're away for a few days, but they'll be back soon." I sent a silent prayer that my words would come true.

"That treasure reward was supposed to be here by now, wasn't it? Are they away celebrating their big windfall?"

"No, I don't think they're celebrating yet," I said. "But we've got the legal team working on the reward. It should be here any day now."

Stanley handed Angel back to Benjamin. "That's good. I bet getting it will be a big relief to them. But right now, I've gotta get back to work. As you know, Eugene runs a tight ship." He grinned, then loped down the pier and across the lawn to RIO's back entrance.

Benjamin watched him until the door slammed shut behind him. "Who is that again?"

"Stanley Simmons. He works for Eugene in maintenance. He's been here for years."

"Simmons? Is he related to Gus Simmons?"

"I think so. He's a nephew or a cousin or something. Ready? We really should get going."

He hoisted Angel's diaper bag over his shoulder, and we walked across the lawn up the shell path toward the parking lot.

As we passed the tank shack, Oliver came out and locked the door behind him. "Hey, guys. Where are you off to?"

"We're going to return Angel to Newton's condo and then have an early dinner," I said.

"I'm done for the day. If you want, I'll take her to Newton's for you."

"Okay. But take my car. There's a full tank of gas and a baby seat in the back all set up. Easier than walking and you obviously can't take her on your bike. If you can, please bring the car back here tomorrow morning." I fished the keys out of a pocket in my cargo shorts and handed them to Oliver.

He grinned and took off across the lawn to the parking area. "Have fun and call me if you need anything."

Chapter 17
Dinner with Benjamin

BENJAMIN and I strolled slowly across the lawn to his car. Once seated inside, he asked, "So, where to? What kind of food do you like?"

"I'm a bit of a junk food junkie," I said. "So, unless you want burgers and fries, you'd better choose the place."

"Hmmm. How about The Wharf?" he said, mentioning one of the top restaurants on the island.

"Not sure we're dressed for it. Maybe another time. For today, how about Rackams? Good food, great drinks, super location. It's pretty touristy. Our casual clothes will fit right in."

"Sounds good." Benjamin put his car in gear and drove out of the parking lot. We left the car in a space on the street and walked inside the cool, dusky interior of the restaurant.

The front person seated us at a table on the deck, away from the noisy bar and shaded from the sun by a large multi-colored umbrella. Our table was close to the deck rail. We could look down and see the fish that always clustered nearby hoping for a handout.

We both ordered frozen drinks and sesame-crusted tuna. Our server brought a small bowl of pretzels to tide us over, but neither of us ate any. Benjamin was staring out at the ocean like he couldn't believe how beautiful the world was. I had to agree with him. We were lucky to live here.

The silence grew heavy, and I needed to break the ice. "Tell me about yourself, Benjamin. Where have you worked before and how did you end up in the Caymans?"

"I grew up in New Jersey. A small town no one's ever heard of. My family knows your grandparents. When I was looking for a job after I graduated from Yale, they put me in touch with Maddy. So here I am."

I swallowed hard at learning about yet another person acquainted with the family I never knew I had. "Yale, huh? What was that like?" I said instead of asking him about my grandparents. Those were the questions I really wanted the answers to.

Benjamin smiled and started talking about Yale, but I wasn't listening, still brooding over my unknown grandparents. To his credit, he noticed that something was wrong almost right away.

"Enough about me. Tell me what it was like growing up in this incredible place." Benjamin smiled, then sipped his drink, waiting for my response.

"Incredible, as you said. But lonely sometimes. I didn't go to regular schools, and there were no other kids on the *Omega*. I didn't even know Newton, my own father, until about a year ago." I paused, unsure of how open to be with this man.

"Neither set of grandparents came to my wedding or my college graduation. I didn't even know I had any grandparents at all until yesterday. Now I find out I have two sets I never knew. Justin told me he knows Newton's parents, and it seems you know Maddy's. I wonder why they never wanted to know me."

A shadow passed across his eyes. "I'm sorry. It must have been hard for you to learn about them this late in life. I wouldn't have blurted it out if I'd realized."

"You couldn't have known. And to be honest, I didn't feel I was missing anything until I heard about their existence."

"Still, it must have been hard to hear. I'm sorry I brought it up."

"It's not your fault. My parents are each brilliant in their own way, but they are clueless about kids. And relationships. And pretty much everything except their work."

We changed the subject and talked about everything except family while we enjoyed a terrific dinner. I discovered that when I gave him a chance, I liked Benjamin a great deal. Even so, as we were finishing dessert, I had to bite back a ferocious yawn.

Benjamin laughed. "C'mon. You're beat. I'll take you home."

"Can you drop me at Newton's condo? Oliver brought my car there. And Newton and I are working on something. I want to touch base with him on it."

"You mean the kidnapping? I should think you would want to catch up. You can fill me in about what's going on with that on the way over if you want. Maybe I can help."

I was surprised. "You knew?"

"You did a good job trying to cover up, but I'm not that oblivious to what goes on around me. Of course, I knew." He threw some money down on the table. "Let's go."

Chapter 18
Ransom Demand

THERE WAS no space in the visitors' parking area at Newton's condo, so Benjamin dropped me at the front entrance while he looked for a spot to leave his car.

The vibe was low when I walked into the penthouse. Everybody was in the same position they'd been in when I left this morning, as though they hadn't moved all day. Roland still sat on the couch, while DS Scott and Newton stood by the windows gazing into the distance. The cop running the call trace still sat at the desk, headphones at the ready. The mood was heavy and hopeless.

"No news yet on how to pay the ransom?" I asked.

Dane shrugged his shoulders. "He's called every hour, but always hangs up before we can get a trace. Insists he only wants the money if it comes from Gus's share of the reward."

Newton added, "We still haven't received the reward checks, but I've got the money ready to go from my own funds. He keeps saying he doesn't want my money. I've told him I'll make Gus pay me back when he gets his check. Of course, I won't really do that. The money doesn't matter to me. This is all about getting Gus and Theresa back safely. We're hoping he'll get tired of waiting for the reward and decide to give us the ransom instructions."

No sooner had he finished speaking when my phone began to ring.

"Why don't you answer this time," Dane suggested.

The cop with the headphones signaled me to wait through four rings, giving him the time he needed to connect.

At his nod, I answered. "Hello?"

That same electronic voice came over the line. "You have the funds? If you do, I'll give you the routing numbers. You'll have twenty-four hours."

"We don't have the reward yet, but we have the money from another source," I said.

"Not good enough. I've told you people the money must come directly from the reward funds." The call disconnected.

The cop trying to trace the call shook his head, meaning he hadn't been able to complete the trace this time either. Everyone in the room groaned.

"We'll keep trying," said Dane Scott. "Sooner or later, he'll agree to take the money no matter what its source. Or we'll find a way to spoof the account number, make it look like it came from the reward funds. We'll get Gus and Theresa back safely." He turned to Newton. "You're still willing to front the funds? You know there's a good chance you'll lose your money. Three million is a lot, even for you."

Newton nodded. "Gus and Theresa are too important to my family and me to do anything that might risk their lives. I'm ready to move forward. I can send a wire transfer within minutes, as soon as I get the routing numbers."

Dane reached out and put a hand on Newton's shoulder. "Good. We'll do our best to bring them home."

He'd no sooner spoken then the front door burst open. Maddy rushed in, followed by Benjamin, who was carrying her suitcase. She must have come back from her speaking tour and bumped into him in the lobby.

Maddy sped over to Dane and Newton. "Have you found them?" she demanded.

When Dane shook his head, she sobbed and turned to Newton for comfort.

He put his arms around her and patted her back. "They'll be returned safely, Maddy. Don't worry." His gaze met Dane's over her shoulder. Both men looked shattered.

After a few seconds, she broke away from Newton and turned to Dane, putting her hand on his arm. "What's the latest?"

He swallowed. "We received a ransom demand, but the kidnapper insists the money has to come out of the reward checks. He won't yield on the source of the funds. And as you know, RIO hasn't received the reward money yet, but your husband is prepared to put up the ransom out of his own funds."

"Ex-husband," she said automatically. Both men nodded and looked daggers at each other over her head.

Before the awkward silence stretched out too long, Benjamin said, "Where shall I put your suitcase, Maddy?"

She waved a hand in the air. "Doesn't matter. I'll bring it to my place later. Thank you for carrying it."

Benjamin parked the small rollaboard case near the door, next to a glass table that held a blue porcelain dish where Newton left his keys and his mail when he came home. "Anything I can do to help?" he said. "I already know what's been going on with Gus and Theresa."

Dane wheeled on me. "I asked you not to tell anyone. Who else have you told?"

I gulped. "I didn't tell him. I haven't told anyone."

Benjamin walked over and stood beside me. "That's true. She didn't tell me anything, but she didn't have to. I'm not an idiot, you know. I can put two and two together. You forget, I was on the *Sunshine Girl* when Fin realized they were missing. The look on her face when she found Theresa's phone, and all the mysterious goings-on since then gave away the whole sad situation."

Dane nodded. "You're right. Of course, you would have guessed. It's no excuse for my false accusations. I'm frustrated by this case. Fin, I apologize for being a jerk."

"Maybe I can find a way that the kidnapper will accept the funds Newton has offered without realizing the money didn't come from the reward. I'll start working on that as soon as I get back to the office," Benjamin said.

"Be careful," Dane said. "The kidnapper seems to have ears and eyes inside RIO. We don't want him to find out what we're doing and take it out on Gus and Theresa."

"Goes without saying. I'll be very discreet." Benjamin said.

By now, everyone present had a reason to be annoyed with at least one other person present. Obviously, the stress of the kidnapping and our worry about Gus and Theresa was getting to each of us.

We all stood there awkwardly until I noticed the tight lines of strain around Maddy's eyes. I remembered how much fund raising and being away from the ocean stressed her out, and I thought back to how Ray had always known what to do. Step one had always been a cup of hot tea and a lemon cookie, followed by a cuddle on the couch. I headed to the kitchen to get her the tea and cookies. With Ray gone, there was no one else who knew the ritual.

Newton's chef-worthy kitchen was equipped with an induction cooktop. It only took fifteen seconds to boil water for Maddy's tea. I poured the hot water into a Villeroy and Boch Marie Fleur teapot. Then I put the delicate china teapot on a small tray from the cupboard and loaded it up with a matching mug, a selection of teabags, and a small plate with two of her favorite lemon cookies.

When I entered the great room, everybody was still standing awkwardly exactly where they had been when I left. Apparently, there had been no conversation while I was gone. All their faces were starting to look extremely stressed, although Roland and the other cop were staring at the small tableau with unrestrained interest.

I smiled brightly. "Maddy, come sit on the couch and have your tea." I put the tray on the glass coffee table in front of the huge white leather sectional couch. I went to Maddy, took her arm, and settled her in a corner of the couch. "Which one?" I asked, holding up the selection of teabags. She pointed, and I plopped the bag into the hot water to steep before sitting beside her on the couch.

I put my arm around her shoulder. "We'll get them back safely," I said. "We have the best minds on the island working on finding them. There's nobody better than Dane's team. Or Newton. And Benjamin, Oliver, and Roland. And the guy on the phones. Everyone. Everybody we have working on this case is very good at what they do."

"Lucky is better than good," she said. "Remember we always say that?"

"Yes, we do. And that's why you and I are on the team. We bring the luck." I kissed her forehead.

She smiled at me and reached forward to pour herself some tea.

After the first sip, she leaned back against the couch and sighed. "Thank you," she said. "You always know what I need."

"That's because I love you," I said.

She reached out and clasped my hand.

"You okay now?" I asked. "I've got some things to take care of at RIO."

She and Newton locked eyes before she gave an almost imperceptible nod. "Can you spare a few more minutes? Your father and I have something we want to discuss with you."

Chapter 19
Adoption

"IT'S A LITTLE BIT SENSITIVE," said Newton. "Let's go to my study where we can have some privacy."

I could see Dane glance at Maddy. It was obvious that he didn't like Maddy and Newton having sensitive matters to discuss without him, but I didn't know if it was because he thought the topic might have some bearing on the case or because he was worried it was a thawing of the relationship between my parents. But he said nothing—just watched us walk down the hall toward Newton's study.

Newton shut the solid mahogany double doors behind us and waved us inside. "Would either of you like a drink?"

Maddy and I had taken seats on the massive claret-colored leather couch. We both shook our heads.

"What's up?" I asked. "Is this about Gus and Theresa? Have you found something out?"

"No, it's something different. It's about our family. Maddy, would you like to start?" he said.

She pushed her long white-blonde hair over her shoulder and looked at me. Her deep turquoise eyes were shadowy, and the little lines of stress I'd noticed earlier seemed even more pronounced.

"We want to adopt Oliver," she said. "Make him a legitimate part of our family. But only if you're okay with the idea."

I was confused. "But Oliver's an adult. He's almost finished with college."

Newton sat beside me and took my hand. "That's true, sweetie. But it's possible to legally adopt an adult, and we already feel like he's part of our family. We'd like to make it official. But only if you're okay with that. It will simplify his inheritance and make it possible for us to care for him in an emergency. There are a lot of legitimate reasons to adopt an adult."

"He's pretty much been on his own since Lily and Cara fled the island," Maddy said, referring to Oliver's twin sister and his mother, both of whom had gone to great lengths to hurt my family. "He shouldn't have to be alone like he is, with no family to rely on."

"He knows he's part of our family. He can always count on me for whatever he needs," I said.

"We appreciate that, and I'm sure he does too. But he was so happy when he thought he was Ray's son," Newton continued. "We can't bring Ray back, but we can make Oliver's use of the Russo name more legitimate if we adopt him because it's your mother's married name." He paused a moment. "And really, we're doing this because we both love him."

"I love him too," I said. "I already think of him as my brother. What does he think about the idea?" I asked.

"We haven't asked him yet, but we're hoping he'll be as thrilled about it as we are. We wanted to wait to tell him until we were sure we wanted to do it, and until we knew how you would feel about it." Maddy was biting her lip, a sure sign she wasn't telling me everything.

"There's something else, isn't there?" I waited for them to tell me the whole story.

"We're both US citizens, and Oliver is too. It will be easier if we do this in the states. We'd need to spend a few months in New York," she said. "All three of us. We'll need to be there while we make sure our residency requirements are met and while the procedure goes through the courts."

"But what about RIO? Who'll run RIO while you're gone?" I asked.

"You will, if you're up for it," Maddy said. "Benjamin can help you."

"And when he comes back, Gus will keep Fleming Environmental going. Until he comes home, Justin will handle any of the day-to-day stuff I can't do from New York. But it shouldn't be a problem."

I was hurt by their sudden burst of parental impulses toward Oliver. I thought about my childhood. Never seeing my biological father. No friends. Feeling alone. Completely unaware of the extended family I apparently did have—cousins, grandparents, aunts, and uncles. Who knew what other surprises lurked in my family tree? Why had neither of my parents thought to introduce me to their extended families? Why had I never asked?

But I balanced the missing parts of my life with what I did have. Ray Russo had been the best step-father—no, make that father—any child could ever hope for. Maddy, Ray and I had been happy together all those years while I was growing up. I always knew I was loved, even though Maddy spent more time running RIO than she did raising me, and Newton never even called me, never mind visited.

But I was lucky enough to spend half the year aboard the *Omega*, learning about the world's oceans and the amazing variety of sea life. I was educated by private tutors, putting me ahead of my peers to the point where I had a PhD in oceanography at the age of twenty-seven. I knew I'd been lucky, and although he was practically an adult, Oliver would be lucky to join our family too.

"But why now?" I asked, "With Gus and Theresa missing, it seems like we have enough to focus on."

Newton started the explanation. "We've been talking about doing this for a while—almost since Ray's death. And we had made the decision to go for it when Gus and Theresa were taken. We were going to put it off until they come back to us, but then we realized there are no guarantees in life. What if—God forbid—they never come back? Or what if something happens to one of us while we're waiting for the right time?"

Maddy continued the explanation. "One thing I learned from Ray's death is you never know. It's important to seize the time you have with the people you love, because you just never know." Her voice went low and cracked. I saw her struggling to hold back tears, and I knew her heart was still with Ray.

Newton reached out and put a hand on her back. "You'll always have us."

I took a step toward my parents and swept them both into a hug. "Well, I'll miss you guys while you're gone, of course, but it will only be for a short time. And when you get back, Oliver will be my brother for real. I think it's a great idea."

Chapter 20
Oliver Reacts

"Good. Then it's settled. He's on his way over. We can't wait to tell him," Newton said. "If he agrees, we'll be leaving for New York tomorrow. Does that work for you?"

I nodded. "Let me know what he says. I'll take him out to celebrate." I smiled at my parents. It was nice to see them happy together.

We left Newton's study just in time to see Oliver walk in through the front door.

"Hey, everybody," he said. "Any news?"

Dane responded. "No news, Oliver, but we still have hope. We'll be making the wire transfer as soon as the kidnapper gives us the go ahead."

Oliver didn't say anything, but he nodded grimly. "Fin, can I have a word with you please?"

"Sure, but I think Maddy and Newton wanted to talk to you right away."

"This will only take a sec," he said. "And we can speak again after they have their talk time, and you can tell me if you've had any ideas in the meantime."

He took my arm and steered me into Newton's study, shutting the doors behind us. He leaned against Newton's desk. "We have to find out who is stealing tanks from the dive shop. At least ten have gone missing every day for the last week. Some days fifteen."

"I still don't understand how that's possible," I said. "You log them out when someone uses them and log them in when they're returned. Maybe there's an error in your logging."

"That's what I thought, too. But I checked the serial numbers, and the missing tanks were all properly logged in. I did most of them myself. But they're gone. And it's not a serial number mix-up—the total number of tanks we have is off. I checked all the staff boats and the rentals. There aren't any unreturned tanks on them. Those tanks are gone." He turned his palms up in a gesture of puzzlement. "But I can't see how anyone could be stealing them. Or why."

"Hmm, let me think about this while you talk to Newton and Maddy. And don't worry about it anymore. I'll find the solution while you're…busy," I finished lamely when I realized Oliver didn't know he'd be out of town yet.

I was saved by Newton's discreet knock on the door. "Are you finished? Maddy and I would really like to talk to Oliver now,"

"Finished," I said. As I passed him, I whispered "good luck" in Newton's ear.

Back in the great room, it felt like the tension had ratcheted up several notches while I'd been away. "What's up now?" I asked Benjamin.

"Between Maddy cozying up to Newton and not hearing from the kidnappers, Dane is stressing out. It's affecting his whole team. What's up with you?"

"I'll tell you about it later." Then I remembered Oliver's concern. "Wait. Let me ask you something. Maybe you'll have a solution." I told him about the issue with the missing tanks.

"Hmmm," he said. "I think I may have an idea. I have a friend. He started a company, makes cutting edge RFID tags."

"What's an RFID tag?" I asked.

"It's a small radio transmitter, sometimes as small as a pinhead. They're used to manage inventory in a lot of industries. They work with a stationary receiver that records the movement of any tagged items around it. We can tag the tanks. Oliver won't have to manually log them in and out when he rents them, and it will eliminate any errors with serial numbers. And if tanks are leaving the dive shop and not coming back, we'll know that too."

I nodded. "Sounds expensive. And complicated. Can we afford it? Do we have the skills in house to run it?"

"We can afford it, and once it's set up, it runs itself. The only thing we'll need to do to keep it operational is add tags to any new tanks we buy and replace old tags when their power runs out. I bet my friend Chaunsey would set it up for free in exchange for a few days of vacation on Grand Cayman."

"Great. Offer to let him stay at my house. I won't be there for a while anyway—at least until we get Gus and Theresa back."

"Deal. I'll call him now. He's a little weird, but a genius at technical stuff. You'll like him." He pulled out his phone and stepped away to make his call.

I walked over to Dane. "You doing okay?"

"No," he said bleakly. "What's going on? Is Maddy getting back together with your father?"

"I don't think so," I said. "They have a new project they're working on together. I'm sure she'll tell you all about it as soon as she finalizes her plans. What do you want to do about your dive training? Wait until Newton gets back from his next trip or have private classes?"

He thought a minute. "Let's take a few days off until we get Gus and Theresa back and we nab the kidnapper. Then we can continue with those lessons, if you don't mind."

"Sure thing," I said. "In the meantime, don't worry. Everything will work out." I broke off when the doors to Newton's office opened and the three members of my family walked out. All of them were beaming, with big happy smiles on their faces.

"Hey, Sis," Oliver called out with a laugh. "You have no idea how often I've wanted to say that."

I rushed across the room to give my new brother a hug. No more "almost brother" or "almost sister." We were about to become a family for real, and the glow on Oliver's face said he was as happy as I was about making his status official.

Benjamin came over. "My friend Chaun arrives later tonight. He's bringing everything we need to set up. More than two thousand waterproof RFID tags, and a bunch of special long range readers. The readers can track any tag that gets within about twenty feet, even under sea water."

"What's this about?" Oliver asked.

Benjamin took him aside to explain his RFID tag idea, and Newton came over to let me know that since they were excited to get the adoption ball rolling, he, Maddy, and Oliver would be leaving at dawn tomorrow on Newton's private jet.

"You know we'd love to have you with us, but someone needs to stay here to run RIO—and to keep an eye on Fleming Environmental. Remember, you're still vice chairman of the company. While Justin is nominally in charge of day-to-day operations while I'm gone, you have veto power over anything you don't agree with. And you have complete authority to spend anything you need to, especially if it will help us get Gus and Theresa back safely."

I stared at him. "Just like that? I'm in charge of your multi-billion dollar operation?"

"Yep. It's good to be the boss," he said with a laugh. "You'll find out soon enough."

I already had all the jobs I wanted—or that I could handle. And I didn't have the heart to remind my father that whispers of nepotism had dogged my career my whole life. This latest plum job would only bring those whispers further out in the open. In this case, it probably wasn't good to be the boss—at least, not until I had enough seasoning to prove I'd earned it.

But I didn't say this to Newton, who obviously thought putting me in charge was a great idea. "Thanks, Newton," I said. "But it's been a long day. If you don't mind, I'm going to bed now."

Chapter 21
Chaun

I WAS STAYING in Newton's condo until we found the kidnappers. I only had to walk down the hall to the lavish guest suite to go to bed. As soon as I shut the double doors behind me, my cellphone buzzed with a text from Benjamin. *"Dive tomorrow with Chaun? 8 AM? I'll pick u up"*

"K" I sent back.

I was up at dawn to say goodbye to my family. Although they were leaving early in the morning, they weren't stressed out by the demands of travel, thanks to Newton's luxurious private jet. They'd have a full breakfast on the plane and be snugly settled in his condo before lunch. They had scheduled a meeting with the lawyers early in the afternoon. They weren't letting any grass grow under the adoption project, that's for sure.

Dane and his team were still hard at work, and I realized they'd been there all night, running down clues and guarding my family. Before leaving, I went over to thank Dane for his efforts.

He rubbed his face with his hands. "Today's the day. I'm sure of it."

"I hope so," I said, and surprised myself by kissing his cheek.

He looked as surprised as I was, but all he said was, "I'll call you if we hear anything new."

I took the elevator from the penthouse to the lobby and saw Benjamin's car parked out front. He was leaning against the car's hood, and a small man I assumed was his friend Chaunsey stood beside him, squinting in the golden Cayman sunshine.

Chaunsey barely reached Benjamin's shoulder, and he wore an unmarked blue baseball cap with the bill tilted to the back and the strap across his forehead. Long baggy red shorts of some heavy, shiny material grazed his kneecaps, and a long-sleeved black t-shirt hung on his torso, reaching nearly as far down as the hem of his shorts. The T-shirt had a logo for a company called ChaunID, which I assumed was the company Benjamin said Chaunsey had founded. He wore black high top sneakers and heavy, striped socks pulled up to his knees. He was sweating profusely in the already hot sun.

"So happy to meet you, Chaunsey. Thank you for coming on such short notice." I reached out to shake his hand, but he put both hands behind his back.

"No touching," he said. "No offense." His friendly smile said his refusal to shake hands wasn't personal—just his thing. "And call me Chaun."

"Sure," I said and then turned to Benjamin. "We can take the *Tranquility* for our dive. Afterwards, I'll treat you both to lunch in the RIO café and then we can get started on the RFID project. Sound good?"

Both men nodded. Benjamin held the passenger door open for me, and Chaun climbed in the backseat for the short ride to RIO. When we arrived, I said, "Chaun, would you like a tour before we dive?"

"Yes, please. But I only need to see your research labs and the IT department," he replied.

I started in the IT department, figuring Chaun would find it underwhelming.

I was right.

He looked at our small collection of servers and network routers and grunted. "Next."

We went in the back entrance to the research lab, and I showed him the heat, lighting, and filtration systems, then I walked him by the tanks holding a few of the more interesting research projects in process. He listened politely, but I could see he was bored.

"Rosie?" he said after a long sigh. "Where is Rosie?"

I was startled that he even knew of the little octopus. "How do you know about Rosie?" She had been the topic of my thesis, but unless they already had a deep interest in the topic, most people didn't make a habit of reading the papers of total strangers.

"I'm interested in artificial intelligence. Understanding how Rosie thinks provides insight into different ways of approaching a task. Great paper, by the way." He looked around as though he expected Rosie to jump out and introduce herself.

I bit back a smile. Benjamin had said he was a genius and a little bit different. That was clearly an understatement. "She's right over there," I said, looking over to the dim corner where Rosie's tank sat atop a small lab table.

Rosie's tank is small, and she is too. Even with her tentacles completely unfurled, she barely spans my palm. I was afraid Chaun would find Rosie as boring as he'd found our IT lab, but I took him to her.

He looked at her tank, with his hands politely behind his back, waiting for her to emerge from her shell. As usual, she somehow sensed my presence and peeked out within a few seconds of my arrival. When she was sure it was me, she oozed her way over to the front of the tank to say hello.

"Can I see her do her tricks?" Chaun asked.

"They're not tricks. They are learned behaviors, and they demonstrate great intelligence and the ability to engage in abstract thought."

"I know," he said. "I told you I'm into artificial intelligence right now and I want to see her so-called 'learned behaviors'."

"I guess we can spare a few minutes. Rosie loves to show off." I reached into a shelf under the table and pulled out the deck of special cards I use when I work with Rosie. Each card had a picture of a particular object on it. Matching objects, and some non-matching items, were piled in a corner of her tank. I selected the card with the picture of a red ball on it and pressed it to the glass. Rosie gazed at it, then she floated over to the pile and picked up the small red ball. She brought it back to my side of the tank and placed it on the gravel directly in front of me. I smiled at her. "Good girl," I said, dropping a small piece of clam in the tank for her.

Rosie picked up the clam sliver and passed it down her tentacle toward her beak. While she was moving the food, she changed color to a lovely coral pink—her way of saying thanks, and the reason for her name.

Next, I showed her a picture of a blue plastic jack—the kind used in old-fashioned kid's games. Rosie went back to her pile of treasures.

I could see she was pondering her choices. The pile included three identical jacks—one red, one blue, and one green—so this was a test of her ability to discern and differentiate not only by shape but also by color.

She delicately sent out a tentacle, the tip hovering over each jack in turn, until she finally wrapped the tip around the blue jack. She swam back to me and placed the jack next to the ball. Chaun gasped when he saw her returning with the right jack. I knew she would. I smiled at her and gave her another clam bit. As always, she flashed me her thanks.

"Can I try?" he asked.

"Not today. I think that's enough work for now, although you're welcome to come back for one of her regular training sessions. Maybe tomorrow?"

His face glowed as though I'd awarded him a prize beyond compare. "Oh wow. Thank you. I'd love that."

I led the way out of the lab and then down the crushed shell path toward RIO's marina. We stopped at the dive shop to get tanks and some rental gear for Chaun. "I'll need to see your certification card before I can rent you any dive gear," I told him.

He dug a frayed blue nylon wallet out of the back pocket of his long, baggy shorts and pulled out a brand new C-card. According to the date on it, he had passed his open water certification a mere one week ago.

"Congratulations on your certification. Do you have a specific dive site you'd like to see?" The Cayman Islands is a diver's paradise, and many of our dive sites are famous among divers the world over.

"Babylon, Stingray City, Aquarium and High Top," he said without hesitation.

I nodded. "We can do all those and more while you're here, but first I'd like to do a few easy dives to give you a chance to get used to the rental gear."

While we'd been talking, Todd, who was filling in for Oliver at the dive shop again, had been assembling a rental BCD, regulator, and weights for Chaun to try on. We were both surprised when Chaun pulled out his black AMEX card and said, "No rentals. I'll buy everything new."

Todd shrugged. "Fine by me. He put the rental stuff back in the storage closet and lifted two brand new BCDs off a display rack. One was a mid-range model, and the other a top-of-the-line version that carried an equally top of the line price tag.

Chaun didn't want to bother, but I insisted he try them on before making his decision. Still, I wasn't surprised when he pointed to the high-end version. We went through the same process with a regulator, dive computer, mask, fins, snorkel, octopus, and a mouthpiece for his new regulator. He also selected a large canvas gear bag, a two millimeter-thick shorty wet suit, and a shiny blue diveskin. Chaun barely listened to Todd's explanation of the pros and cons of each piece of dive gear. He quickly cut him off every time and pointed to the most expensive of the items under consideration. Clearly, money was no object for Chaun.

While he was selecting his gear, I texted June, Maddy's assistant, asking her to put together a VIP package for me to give him later. The package would include several t-shirts, a pair of cargo shorts with an elastic waist, at least one hat, a RIO-branded mug, a poster, a video, and a few other assorted items, plus a complete packet of RIO literature that explained our mission. I assumed the lightweight t-shirts and shorts in the packet would be more comfortable for Chaun than the heavy clothing he was wearing.

By the time I finished the text, Chaun was done selecting his gear. He held his card out to Todd, but I shook my head. "It's on the house. After you dropped everything to come and help us, it's the least we could do."

"Thanks." He slipped his credit card back in his wallet while Todd carefully folded Chaun's new divesuit and packed it and the rest of the equipment into the gear bag.

Before he packed the mask, Todd said, "Want me to treat this before you go?"

"What's that mean?" Chaun asked, turning to Benjamin.

"Scuba masks have a thin film on the lenses left over from the manufacturing process. Before you use a new mask, you need to remove the film, or it will fog up and you won't be able to see anything. In fact, you need to treat the mask every time you dive to prevent fogging, but the first time is the most critical. Got any toothpaste, Todd?" he asked.

Chaunsey looked mystified, but Benjamin squirted a large dollop of toothpaste from the tube Todd handed him into Chaun's new mask. He rubbed it briskly with his fingers, making sure he covered every spot. When he was satisfied, he took it outside and rinsed it in the communal rinse tank.

When Benjamin came inside and handed the mask back to him, Chaun took it outside again and rinsed it thoroughly with fresh water from the nearby hose. I could understand his aversion to the communal rinse tank. I knew Todd would have filled the rinse tank with clean water this morning and it was still early enough that no one would have used it yet today. But Chaun was obviously unhappy about physical contact with other people. That wariness apparently extended to anything that might have been left behind in the water when an unknown diver rinsed their gear. Understandable.

While Chaun was busy with the hose, I grabbed a bottle of defogging drops and put them in his equipment bag for later. "I think we're ready," I said. "This way to the *Tranquility*."

"Wait a second," Chaun said. "Let's put RFID tags on our tanks before we go. Then I can show you how they work. Sort of a proof of concept test." He grinned at me. "Where do you want them?"

"Can you stick them inside the boot?" I asked, referring to the black silicone bumpers on the bottom of the tanks.

Chaun and Benjamin pulled the tank boots off and then Chaun took two tiny sample-sized tubes out of his pocket. Mixed together, their contents made a special epoxy he'd brought with him to stick the one inch by two inch RFID tags to the tanks. The epoxy cured quickly, and after a minute, they put the boots back on the tanks. Now we were good to go.

Chapter 22
Diving with Chaun

BENJAMIN HOISTED the bag containing his own gear as well as the new one Chaun had bought, and the three of us headed down the pier. I carried a tank in each hand, and Todd, ever eager to help, followed us with two more. While Benjamin stowed the gear bags under the benches along the *Tranquility*'s gunwales, Todd brought out two more tanks and I showed Chaun around the *Tranquility*.

He followed me around with a big smile on his face. "I always wanted a chance to take a trip on this boat. I wish it was still called the *Maddy*, though. Then this would be really cool."

I smiled at him. "Well, as you know, Maddy's my mother, and my stepdad named the boat after her. When he passed away, both Maddy and I felt it was time for a change. I like the name *Tranquility*. It expresses the feeling I get when I'm on board."

Chaun politely said nothing, but the look on his face said it all. The *Maddy* was famous. The *Tranquility* was just another boat. Even though they were the same vessel, I could see that the name change was a disappointment to him.

Before we cast off, I explained my dive plan. "For this first dive, I want to stay close to home. I'll take you out to one of the sites where we do training dives for our classes. Once I see you can handle more advanced sites, we can go anywhere you want, okay?"

I climbed up to the flying bridge and he sat on the bench opposite Benjamin. The site I had in mind for our first dive was only a short distance from our dock. At RIO, we called it training spot one.

At this site, the top of the reef was down about forty feet, and it was very flat and open, with a sandy surface. It was ideal for practicing skills. But only a few feet away, it dropped down to a gently sloping wall that went to about one hundred feet of depth before plateauing again. After the second plateau, the drop off went down for miles along a sheer vertical wall. I didn't plan for Chaun to go beyond the first plateau. The mini wall was plenty advanced enough for such a new diver, and there was a lot more to see in the shallow areas anyway.

I started the engines, and we made the short trip to the dive site. I pulled up to the mooring ball, and Benjamin hooked it with a long pole. He tied the boat to the line, but I discreetly checked the knots when I climbed down from the bridge. I didn't know Benjamin's capabilities that well yet, and I didn't want to surface from the dive to find my boat drifting out to sea.

Satisfied that we were secure, I said, "Okay. Pool's open."

Benjamin had already slipped into his diveskin, but Chaun was sitting idly on the bench. "Feeling okay, Chaun?" I asked. "Are you seasick?"

He shook his head. "I'm fine, but is there a changing room?"

I tried not to show how startled I was by his question, but it was hard not to laugh. "No. Sorry. You can go below if you want. Or change in the water. Or right here on deck, which is what most people do." Of course, most people were already wearing their bathing suits. I had no idea what Chaun wore under his baggy shorts.

He sighed deeply, showing his disappointment in the accommodations once again, but he said nothing. He pulled his diveskin out of his bag and went below. I turned my back, facing the stern to give him whatever privacy I could. I shimmied out of my shorts and t-shirt, revealing the one piece tank-style bathing suit I wore under my clothes most days. Then I stepped into my diveskin and pulled it up over my shoulders.

I continued staring out over the *Tranquility*'s stern until Benjamin said, "The coast is clear."

Chaun emerged from the cabin and stood near the ladder to the flying bridge while I got busy setting up my regulator and BCD on a nearby tank. Benjamin chose a tank on the same side of the boat. Chaun walked over and sat on the bench, apparently expecting one of us to do his setup for him.

"You okay over there?" I asked. "Do you need help setting up?"

"I'm fine," he said, "But I thought as captain you'd do it for me."

"That's not how it usually works unless you're on a tourist boat," I said.

"I'm a tourist. This is a boat. Ergo…" he said.

I smiled a fake smile. He was here to help us, after all. "Happy to be of service," I said. It took me less than a minute to assemble his regulator to his BCD and tank. I turned on his computer and checked the tank pressure. All looked fine.

Benjamin had assembled his own rig and was sitting on the bench waiting for Chaun to be ready.

"Okay," I said. "Here's the dive plan. I'll go in first in case either of you has a problem in the water. Benjamin, please help Chaun. Once he's in, then you go. I suggest we all use a giant stride entry. It's the simplest. After we descend, we'll stay beneath the boat at about forty feet. Chaun, I'm going to ask you to perform a few basic skills. Once that's over, we can head for the first wall if you want. We'll level off at sixty feet for a total of forty-five minutes dive time, unless either of you uses up more than half the air in your tank before then. At either of those turnaround points, we'll come back to the plateau for ten minutes or so, then proceed up the mooring line. We pause at fifteen feet for a three minute safety stop. Throughout the dive, I will lead, and you will follow. Got it?"

Benjamin nodded quickly. Chaun stuck out his lip, but after a tense second or two, he nodded. "Fine."

"Okay, first let's make sure you're weighted properly. How much weight do you usually carry?" I asked him.

"Uh, thirty-five pounds? I think that's about right." He looked puzzled by the question.

"I think that's way too much. Try this." I handed him two three pound weights and waited for him to insert them in the weight pockets of his BCD.

He stared at the weights in his hands like he didn't know what to do with them.

"Sorry. You must have been trained with a weight belt instead of a weight-integrated BCD. I think you'll find this way is much more comfortable." I inserted a weight in each of the front weight pockets of his brand new BCD. "Now let's see how that works out. Jump in and I'll check it."

He looked at me and it seemed that he had no idea how to don his gear or enter the water. I had serious misgivings about the quality of his dive training.

Benjamin looked concerned, but he didn't say anything about Chaun's training or lack thereof. "You put it on like this," he said. He sat on the bench in front of his rig and slid his arms through the openings in his BCD. He fastened the Velcro cummerbund, then stood up and tightened the shoulder straps.

Chaun had been watching carefully, and when Benjamin finished his demonstration, Chaun donned his gear using exactly the same motions. I slipped into my gear, grabbed a selection of weights in case we needed to make some adjustments, and then both Benjamin and I helped Chaun over to the dive platform.

I did a giant stride entry off the platform, popped back to the surface, and gave Benjamin the okay sign letting him know I was in control of my dive. I removed the regulator from my mouth and said, "Your turn, Chaun."

He forgot to put his regulator in his mouth before he did his entry. He was spluttering when he bobbed to the surface. I swam over to him and put the regulator in his mouth. I used the controller on his BCD to add a few puffs of air to his vest to keep him afloat. "Breathe," I said.

After a few breaths through the regulator, he calmed down enough for me to check his weighting. "Now I'm going to let the air out of your BCD. When I do that, I want you to inhale and hold your breath," I told him. "You want the water to be right above your nose. Got it?"

He nodded.

"Please get in the habit of using the proper hand signals to let me know what's going on, okay?" For divers, 'Okay' is signaled by making a circle with thumb and forefinger, or by placing the tips of your fingers on your head with the elbow held out to the side. I showed him the two versions of the okay sign, and he nodded again.

"Hand signals," I said.

He made the "top of head" okay sign. I pulled the purge valve on his BCD to release the air that was helping to keep him afloat high in the water. He sank an inch or two, inhaled, and came to rest in the water exactly where a properly weighted diver should be. The water reached halfway up his mask.

"Excellent. That's perfect. We'll be ready to dive as soon as Benjamin does his entry. Remember, we're going to stay under the boat until I say otherwise. I'm going to want you to show me how you clear your ears and clear your mask, how to operate your BCD, and all the hand signals. I'll write on my slate what I want you to do next. Benjamin, if you wouldn't mind demonstrating the skills as a refresher for Chaun, that would be great."

Benjamin stepped off the dive platform, bobbed to the surface, and gave the okay sign. Then I lifted my arm and turned a thumbs down.

While diving, the thumbs down means descend, and the thumbs up means ascend. Novice divers sometimes have a lot of trouble realizing that in the water, those two familiar signals have an entirely different meaning than they do on land.

We descended feet first, stopping every few feet to clear our ears. I made my motions exaggerated enough that Chaun would see what I was doing. He cleared his ears every few feet at the same time I did, seemingly without difficulty. I began to relax a little.

When we were a few feet from the bottom, I put Chaun through the basic skills of diving, and he performed reasonably well, although each time I asked him to perform a skill, he watched Benjamin's demonstration with an eagle eye before he made a move.

Maybe he was intimidated by diving with me. Many people had grown up watching the RIO annual documentaries and had seen me diving in all sorts of conditions. I'd been diving since I could walk, and I had a reputation as a superb diver. It made some people self-conscious to dive with me. Maybe Chaun was one of those people.

When I was satisfied that he could hold his own, I signaled for them to follow me. We dropped off the edge of the reef at forty feet onto the mini-wall. I checked for current and used the directional hand signal to let them know which way we would be going. I swam slowly into the current, pausing often to point out interesting reef dwellers or to look out into the blue to see if we could catch sight of any larger denizens.

We saw a pair of Queen Angelfish swimming regally around a large elkhorn coral, and a tiny blue blenny peeking out of a crevice in a bright yellow brain coral. Two turtles swam by out over the ledge, and then I pointed out a nearly invisible trumpet fish hovering upside down and hiding among the coral, waiting for unwary prey to come by.

As one, we turned in awe toward the open ocean where two large mantas swam past, their thirty-foot wingspans blocking the view beyond them. The majestic creatures took no notice of us until, arms outstretched, Chaun swam directly toward them as fast as he could, leaving a flurry of bubbles in his wake.

The mantas paused, then began descending. There was no sense of hurry in their movement, but they departed at a rate no human could hope to keep up with. Unfortunately, Chaun continued chasing after them, descending quickly over the sloping second wall and heading toward the steeper vertical drop off that went straight down for miles. As he swam, he seemed oblivious to how deep he was going, and he was already well past the sixty foot depth his basic certification qualified him for.

Alarmed, I took off after Chaun. I could swim much faster than he could, so I quickly caught up to him. I grabbed his arm and pulled him up short. He tried to shake me off, but I held his computer in front of him so he could see his current depth and air supply.

We were at one hundred sixty-five feet, just a few feet shy of the depth at which regular air can become toxic.

Chaun smiled dreamily at me. Great.

He was narc'ed as well as in danger from oxygen toxicity and decompression sickness—the dreaded bends. Worse, Chaun had exerted so much effort chasing the stunning mantas that he'd nearly sucked his tank dry.

And even worse than that, his computer had entered decompression mode, meaning that he'd already spent enough time at depth that he would need to make one or more decompression stops on the way to the surface in the hope of avoiding the bends.

His tank pressure was in the red zone—meaning very little air remained—and he had a long swim and required decompression stops ahead of him. His heavy breathing was ragged from exertion.

I still had plenty of air, and my breathing was slow and steady. For Chaun, this was a bona fide diving emergency, and he was still tugging at my arm trying to get free to chase the mantas even deeper.

I was a much stronger swimmer than Chaun. With a two-handed grasp on one of his arms, I was able to drag him up a few feet at a time despite his struggles to follow the mantas. I looked around for Benjamin. I could have used his help saving his friend's life, but he was about sixty feet above me gazing down at the mantas as they retreated into the blue.

Once the giant rays had disappeared into the distant haze, Benjamin looked down and saw me struggling with Chaun. He quickly descended and grabbed Chaun's other arm. Between the two of us, we were able to keep him ascending. I took a chance on releasing Chaun's arm to look at his dive computer. It showed he was scheduled to make a decompression stop at one hundred twenty-five feet. I held the computer up where Benjamin could read the screen. He made the okay sign.

We stopped at the required depth and hung out. Chaun was exhausted by his struggles. He hung listlessly in my grasp. Still, I didn't dare let him go in case he decided to take off again. You never could know what a narc'ed diver might think made sense.

Our first stop was almost over when Chaun emptied the last of the air in his tank. He began writhing and twisting, pulling on my regulator instead of using the simple out of air signal—a finger drawn across one's throat.

I calmly pulled my "spare air" out of my BCD pocket and flipped it to the on position before pushing the mouthpiece into his mouth. The spare air is a small hand-held scuba tank with an attached regulator mouthpiece, designed to be used in emergencies. Typically, a spare air tank can only provide a few breaths of air. Chaun sucked in a huge lungful of air, and I knew he would drain this small tank within a few minutes.

I caught Benjamin's eye over Chaun's head and made a sign toward the spare air to see if he also carried one. I relaxed a little when he made the okay sign. I hoped we might be out of the nitrogen narcosis zone by the time Chaun had drained both our spares, and maybe he'd be in a more reasonable frame of mind to buddy breathe.

As we hovered near the wall, I looked down and to my left and saw a flash of golden light at what I judged to be about 180 feet down. Usually, if you see a flash underwater, it's silvery, like a flashlight reflecting off fish scales. I couldn't imagine what could be causing this flash of gold, but I couldn't investigate right now.

Chaun's computer gave the okay to move up to the next decompression stop, so we swam up to the recommended level and hung there. By the time we reached the new depth, I could see that the spare air I'd given Chaun was approaching empty.

These tiny canisters are designed to hold only a few breaths of air for an emergency, and Chaun was breathing so heavily he was emptying the tank quickly. If he tried to inhale and got no air, he'd go into panic mode again. I was concerned he would drown all three of us if we tried to buddy breathe, but we would soon have no other alternative if we were going to get him back to the surface safely.

We'd no sooner leveled off when, as I'd feared, the spare air I'd given Chaun reached empty, and he began to panic. I signaled to Benjamin to deploy his own small canister. He gave me the okay sign and flipped its mouthpiece to the open position.

I reached over and pulled my small tank out of Chaun's mouth and Benjamin immediately replaced it with his canister. We did it quickly enough that Chaun didn't have time to panic any further.

Because of the required time for decompression stops, I was worried about getting Chaun to the surface with our current air supplies. And trying to buddy breathe with him would be a recipe for disaster. He clearly wasn't capable of safely performing that complex maneuver.

Then I had an idea. I pulled out my underwater slate and balanced it against Chaun's tank. I wrote, "Stay w/Chaun. Follow deco rules. Buddy breathe only if must. I'll bring fresh tanks."

While we hovered there, I caught Benjamin's eye and showed him the note on my slate. He nodded. I knew Benjamin was an advanced diver, but this was not a normal underwater occurrence. I let go of Chaun's arm, hoping Benjamin had understood my improvised message and that he'd be able to handle Chaun while I was getting fresh tanks from the *Tranquility*. I couldn't ask Benjamin to undertake the dangerous ordeal I was about to begin.

I slithered out of my BCD and handed it to Benjamin. He'd be able to use the air in my tank to satisfy Chaun's air hunger if it took me more than a few minutes to get back with more full tanks. As soon as Benjamin had clipped my BCD to his own, I swam rapidly toward the surface.

The speed of my ascent from this depth and the immediate return to the same depth would be dangerous for me, but I could see no other way for all three of us to get back to the surface safely. Even so, the success of the plan hinged on Benjamin being able to control Chaun. I wasn't sure he could handle Chaun's panic attacks if one occurred while they were alone at depth, but I knew it would be faster for me to retrieve the required tanks than for Benjamin, who didn't know the equipment aboard the *Tranquility* the way I did. And I didn't want to ask him to undertake the dangerous "bounce" dive profile I was about to undertake.

I shot to the surface, swimming as fast as I could, even though it meant I was ascending faster than the safe pace. While I ascended, I let out a thin stream of air from my mouth to prevent my lungs from being over-pressurized as the compressed air I'd been breathing expanded with the change in ambient pressure from the sea. I kept my eyes looking up at the surface, staring at the *Tranquility*'s shadow and praying that Chaun would remain docile and that Benjamin could manage him if he panicked.

I reached the *Tranquility*, but before I climbed the ladder I risked looking back to Benjamin and Chaun. It looked like Chaun had used all the air in the spare air tank I'd given him, and he was thrashing around, making it hard for Benjamin to give him my BCD and tank. I saw Benjamin hand his own regulator to Chaun, who grabbed it.

Rather than waste more time, I hurried up the final rung of the ladder. I went below to the emergency locker, where I had stowed four scuba tanks of Nitrox, an oxygen enriched breathing gas. Nitrox can only be used at relatively shallow depths—above ninety feet with the

36% blend we used at RIO—but the reduced nitrogen load would help reduce Chaun's and Benjamin's necessary decompression time. And my own.

I carried three of the tanks, two old regulators— the only two I had on board—and a spare BCD to the stern of the boat. Then I put a sturdy web strap around two of the tanks and hooked them together using the attached D-rings. I connected one of the spare regulators to a tank, and then I dropped all the tanks over the side, clipping them to the boat. I set up the third tank with the spare BCD and regulator and put the rig on. All this took less than a minute or two.

Just in case we had more problems, I grabbed the *Tranquility*'s first aid kit and pulled out another spare air and the small canister of pure oxygen all RIO boats carried and stuffed them in my BCD pocket. Then I stepped off the dive platform, detached the two tanks from the boat and reattached them to my BCD so they followed me as I swam. They were bobbing around, getting in the way of my kicks, but I ignored the hassle and kept descending as quickly as I could to rescue Chaun and Benjamin.

After what seemed like eons, I saw Benjamin below me, struggling to keep Chaun from grabbing the regulator out of his mouth. It was easy to see that Benjamin was in trouble, and I redoubled my efforts to reach them quickly before the situation went completely south.

As soon as I reached the two men, I grabbed the lift handle on the back of Chaun's BCD and towed him up above ninety feet where we could safely use Nitrox. I wasn't too worried about cutting this stop short because I knew his dive computer would automatically recalculate the depths and times for the remaining safety stops. We'd simply make up any lost time on the next one.

Chaun continued to struggle, but I was behind him where he couldn't reach me. I was safe, but because Chaun was breathing from Benjamin's tank at this point, the octopus regulator was ripped out of Benjamin's mouth as I pulled Chaun up.

I looked behind me to where Benjamin hovered, a thin stream of bubbles leaving his mouth for safety. I handed him the small spare air tank from my BCD pocket and pointed to one of the Nitrox tanks hanging from the clip on my BCD. Benjamin gave me the okay sign and took the small tank.

After taking a breath from the emergency air tank, he left it in his mouth while he unfastened the cummerbund of his BCD and slipped it off his shoulders. He unfastened the strap holding his tank to the back of the BCD and shut it off. He purged the residual air from the hoses by hitting the purge valve on his regulator and then removed the regulator assembly from the tank.

Now he had no hands available to attach his regulator to the Nitrox tank, and I had my hands full with Chaun. He looked at me quizzically. I pointed to the used tank and pantomimed dropping it. He did, and it began sinking.

Benjamin quickly connected his regulator to the full Nitrox tank and set it up in his BCD. Then he slid the BCD over his head onto his shoulders, settled the cummerbund and shoulder straps comfortably and removed the spare air from his mouth. He purged the new regulator of water, stuck the new regulator in his mouth, and he was good to go, having done a complete equipment changeover at eighty-five feet of depth. Even I was impressed, although I'd done the maneuver myself hundreds of times while Ray was training me. I gave Benjamin the okay sign and a big smile.

We now had sufficient breathing gas to complete Chaun's decompression, but since his computer hadn't been set for Nitrox, there was no way to make it take the reduced nitrogen load into account. That meant we still had to do the full recommended decompression profile as though we were using regular air. Using Nitrox was a good safety measure for all of us at this point anyway, which was okay by me. Nothing about this dive had in any way conformed to safe diving practices. Every bit of margin we could get would help.

When this decompression stop was over, we ascended to the next level to wait out our penalty time. We were now above sixty feet, and the effects of Chaun's nitrogen narcosis were subsiding. The madness slowly faded from his eyes, and he remained docile as we completed the rest of the decompression sequences and climbed back onto the *Tranquility*.

Chapter 23
A Cage

CHAUN STOOD near *Tranquility*'s stern, shivering, and refusing to look up. Benjamin took a seat on the bench and removed his gear without comment. I did the same thing on the opposite side of the boat, trying hard to control my anger at Chaun.

"Sit down," I said to him tersely when I'd finished removing my gear.

He scurried across the deck and sat on the bench as far away from me as he could get. He made no effort to remove his gear, just stared at his feet and said nothing.

"That certification card you showed me. That was a fake, wasn't it?" I kept my voice steady.

"Might have been," he said. "The guy I got it from said it was good, but…"

"Did you take classes? Do checkout dives?"

He bit his lip and shook his head.

"Diving like that—when you had no idea what you were doing— you endangered all our lives. You could have died. We all could have died. You know that, right?"

I pulled an oxygen canister out of the boat's first aid kit and handed it to Chaun. "Put this on, and don't remove it until the doctor says you can. Got it?"

He nodded. "Sorry. I didn't realize…"

"Don't apologize. Report to the RIO classroom at seven a.m. tomorrow. I'll take care of the problem then. But today, I want our doctor to check you out—you too, Benjamin—and then I want you to start on the RFID project we brought you down here for. And I don't want you anywhere near boats or diving until I say so." I thought a minute. "Don't even go in the pool at my house until I clear you. Got that?"

He nodded again, looking downcast.

"Good. Stay there. Do not move."

His misery was apparent, but I wasn't about to relent and let him off the hook. Instead, I went below and picked up the radio to call RIO. "Please have Doc and her crew meet the *Tranquility* at the dock. ETA three minutes. I have three possible decompression sickness patients, one who just recovered from nitrogen narcosis. Giving him pure oxygen right now."

Since Todd was still manning the dive shop, he was the one who took the message. "Jeez, Fin. What the f… I mean, heck, happened?"

"I'll fill you in later. Thanks, Todd."

"Benjamin, do you want to come up on the bridge with me?" I turned to climb the ladder, and he followed me up.

"You were pretty impressive down there," I said. "I didn't realize you were such a skilled diver. And you were so cool under pressure. A lot of divers would have panicked, and that could have been a disaster."

His cheeks turned pink. "I was with one of the most famous and accomplished divers in the world. I had to step up. I just kept thinking 'What would Fin Fleming do?' Then I did that."

I laughed. "I have to confess I had no idea what to do. It never occurred to me he lied about his diving experience, or that he would be that reckless. Luckily, I had put those Nitrox tanks in the storage area below the other day. Even though we finished the dive on Nitrox, Doc is probably going to stick us in the recompression chamber to be on the safe side. Sorry about that."

He shrugged "First time for everything."

"Believe me, one time in a recompression chamber is too many. It's boring and uncomfortable. But at least we'll have each other for company."

He smiled and turned away, but not before I noticed the pleased expression on his face.

Since we hadn't been far out from the RIO marina, we were there within a few minutes. As I docked the *Tranquility*, I saw Doc and her team lined up at the end of the pier with three gurneys and several oxygen tanks. Benjamin tied the lines to the cleats on the dock, and as soon as I shut down the engines, the medical team rushed toward us. The rubber wheels of the gurneys made a racket clacking against the wooden dock.

I rolled my eyes. Doc loved a little bit of drama every now and then.

Chapter 24
Recompression

"CHAUN IS THE WORST OFF. He went into decompression mode at about 165 feet. He also sucked a couple of tanks dry on the way back. He was intermittently without air, but for only a few seconds each time. We brought him up from about one hundred feet on Nitrox, and he's been on O2 since we surfaced." I glanced at my watch. "About five minutes' worth."

She nodded, and leaned over Chaun, who'd been strapped to a gurney. "Don't worry, Chaun. We'll take care of you. There's nobody better than the medical team here at RIO when it comes to diving-related injuries. Please let me have your dive computer. I need to check your profile."

She spoke to her team. "Please prep him for recompression."

Next, she turned to Benjamin. "What's your story?"

"Nothing special. I joined Fin in trying to get Chaun safely to the surface. I stayed with him on the ascent. But I'm fine."

She rolled her eyes and held out her hand. Computer please." Then she turned to her second team. "Prep him for recompression too."

The second team jumped into action, lifting Benjamin onto the gurney, and putting an oxygen cannula in his nose before hurrying him off to RIO's infirmary.

"Why don't you lie down, Fin. No need for us to argue about it. No matter what you say, I know you did something crazy and heroic. Maddy would kill me if I let anything happen to you. Let's save each other the aggravation."

I opened my mouth to protest, but realized she was right. Instead of arguing that I didn't need treatment, I hopped up on the gurney, handed her my dive computer, and inserted the oxygen cannula in my nostrils myself.

"Wow. You really must have done something wild this time. I've never known you to give in this easily. You'd better tell me so I can be sure I've got you covered in the recompression protocol."

I told her all the details of what had happened and what I had done. She walked alongside the gurney as we rolled across the lawn and down the long sunlit halls to RIO's infirmary, nodding her head as she took in the details. Benjamin and Chaun were already in the infirmary, dressed in RIO scrubs and waiting outside the recompression chamber for my arrival before the medical team loaded us all into the tank.

Doc handed me some scrubs when the gurney stopped rolling. "Change quickly, please. I want Chaun under pressure as soon as possible."

"Ok, but will you send someone to get a couple of copies of the Basic Open water course book to take in there with me? Chaun lied about his certification status—even showed me a fake C-card—and I want to rectify his lack of certification as quickly as possible."

She nodded to one of her team, who trotted down to the dive shop to pick up the books I'd requested. "And bring a mask too," I hollered at his back. Then I went into one of the nearby cubicles, pulled the curtain, and dressed in the loose fitting scrubs.

When I emerged, Doc handed me a hooded sweatshirt. "You'll probably need this." It was often cold and dank in a recompression chamber, and I wasn't looking forward to it. I shrugged into the sweatshirt and then I walked through the hatch into the chamber. Benjamin and Chaun followed me in. I immediately climbed into the top bunk—the one near the heat vent. I'd been here before.

Chaun and Benjamin took the bunks on the opposite side. The medical staff hooked us up to IV fluids and doppler monitors and put pulse oximeters on our fingers to measure the oxygen levels in our blood. Before they finished with the IVs, one of the EMTs rushed in with the textbooks and mask I'd requested, as well as sweatshirts for Benjamin and Chaun. When nobody was looking, he slipped me a half dozen of the famous chocolate chip cookies from RIO's café. I smiled my thanks, and he winked at me. He also dropped a selection of old magazines on the empty bunk.

When the EMTs had finished hooking us up, I gave Doc the okay sign, and she shut the door. For a few minutes, all we could hear was the hiss of pure oxygen entering the chamber, increasing the pressure to the equivalent of one hundred sixty-five feet of sea water.

Chaun was looking around the cramped space with open curiosity. "How long until we get out?" he asked.

"Could be here overnight," I said. "Depending on the protocol used. But it's up to Doc. Maybe she'll take pity on us and let us out in time for dinner."

"You're kidding! What exactly will this treatment do? And why do I need it?" He sounded petulant.

"It's just physics. You'd know what it was about if you hadn't tried to cheat by faking your certification," I said. I was annoyed that I was stuck in here, especially with Gus and Theresa still missing. I needed to be out doing something.

"I apologize for that. I didn't realize it would be a problem. Will you please explain it to me now?"

I relented. "For you, the treatment is probably going to address a combination of things. First you need to understand diving physiology. The air in the tanks is under pressure. There are more molecules of oxygen and nitrogen in a given volume than there would be at sea level. As you dive, your body takes in more nitrogen molecules than it would have on the surface, and the extra nitrogen molecules have several adverse effects on your body."

"Like what?"

"First, at depths below sixty-feet, you may experience a phenomenon known as nitrogen narcosis, which is also called rapture of the deep. When suffering from nitrogen narcosis, you may experience intense feelings of euphoria, or confusion. You don't understand the consequences of your actions. You may even hallucinate."

He looked contrite. "I do remember being pretty out of control while we were diving."

"Yep, you were," said Benjamin. "You nearly killed us all."

I was as angry at Chaun as Benjamin obviously was. I shot Benjamin a "stay cool" look before I continued my lecture. "That's why we're going to make sure you have the training to avoid narcosis as much as possible, and to recognize it if it does happen so you can be extra careful. The good news is, the feelings dissipate naturally as you ascend, assuming you don't get confused enough that you forget which way is up. I believe you were suffering from rapture of the deep today, which is probably why you took off like that and why you drained your tank without seeming to care…"

I scowled at him. "…and why you had no problem grabbing Benjamin's and my air supplies away from us."

He looked down at the floor. "I'm sorry. I really didn't know what I was doing."

"I know that. And the good thing is that over time, you can build up a tolerance to excess nitrogen. You may not suffer from nitrogen narcosis as frequently, or at least, you might recognize the symptoms if they occur."

"But Chaun, you were in even more danger than you realized. First of all, the concentration of oxygen in regular air becomes toxic below one hundred seventy feet. You were right about at that point when I caught up to you. You could have suffered convulsions, seizures, and even died." I paused a moment. "And when I dove down to rescue you, I might have died from oxygen toxicity as well. Nobody is immune to that."

He bit his lip and opened his mouth to speak. I shushed him with a gesture,

"But that's not the worst of it. Back on the surface, you could have succumbed to decompression sickness because you violated the safe dive profile. And again, you endangered Benjamin and me, because we had to stay with you to make sure you followed the required decompression protocol. We couldn't be sure you understood the gravity of the situation, because of the narcosis and because you lied about your training."

"Decompression sickness isn't pleasant. It too is caused by excess nitrogen in your body tissue. As you ascend to sea level, the nitrogen bubbles get larger because there's not as much pressure on them. The large bubbles can cause all kinds of problems. Joint pain. Brain trauma, like a stroke. Even permanent paralysis. Not even counting lung barotrauma and pneumothorax. And because we had to save you, you exposed your dive buddies to the same risks. And since you didn't monitor your air consumption, I had to do a rapid ascent and rapid descent to bring you more air so you could complete your decompression stops. Bounce diving like that is extremely dangerous for the diver, and it makes the likelihood of decompression sickness even greater for me. You were completely irresponsible today."

Chaun's face reddened and he looked at the floor. "I didn't know…"

I cut him off again. "I know you didn't know. You couldn't know because you didn't have the proper training to dive. And that's why I am going to take on the responsibility for your training, starting right here, right now." I tossed one of the basic Open Water instruction manuals to him. "Read the first two chapters and do the exercises. Let me know when you've finished. If you have a question, ask. Otherwise, shut up and read because I am so angry right now I could…I don't know what I could. Just read."

I lay down on my cot and rolled over. The silence in the chamber was deafening.

After a few minutes, I heard a tiny whisper. "I'm sorry."

Chapter 25
Recompression Chamber

Chaun sat back on his bunk, opened the textbook, and started reading. I pulled out my phone to text Dane Scott. I needed to let him know that I was stuck in the recompression chamber and wouldn't be by for at least several hours—maybe not even until tomorrow morning. I also asked him to text me if there was any news.

He replied to the text immediately. *"Still won't accept Newton's money. Holding out for receipt of treasure $$. How does he know? Insider?"*

The thought that the kidnapper was a RIO insider was chilling—like an ice cube on my back. The story about our recovery of the treasure—and the sizable check we were due—had been widely reported. It wasn't like the news of the reward had been a big secret.

But the recently negotiated payoff date and amount had not been publicly shared. Dane was probably right. I'd said we hadn't received the reward yet, but that was yesterday, and the reward was well overdue from the date the government-backed syndicate that had claimed ownership of the treasure had promised we'd receive it. So, if anyone knew we still hadn't received the funds yet, it very well might be an insider.

I thought of everyone at RIO like family. Who among the team could be behind such a betrayal? And who would hate Gus and Theresa enough to use them this way to get money?

The only people I'd ever met who were that evil were not around. My ex-husband, Alec Stone, had left the island after the treasure expedition returned from Belize, and apparently, he was now living in New York with a good job. Oliver's twin sister, Lily Russo and his mother, Cara Flores, were both greedy enough to try to pull this off, but neither of them had been seen around recently—possibly due to the outstanding arrest warrant for drug trafficking that was hanging over their heads.

Other than those three, I didn't know of anyone who would be heartless enough to kidnap a new baby's parents for money. Or anyone with a reason for keeping track of when we were due to receive the reward.

There was no answer to the question Dane had asked and nothing I could do about it from inside the chamber. I was trapped and feeling frustrated by my inability to take any action. So, I was surprised but happy when Chaun announced "I'm finished. Can we go over it now?"

I glanced at my dive watch. It didn't seem like it had been long enough for Chaun to have completed the work I'd assigned him, even though Benjamin had said he was a genius. "Hand me your book. I'll check your answers to the exercises, then we can go over anything you don't understand."

I was only slightly disgruntled to see that he'd answered every question correctly. "Good job. Any questions?"

He shook his head. "It's just physics." He winked at me. "Should I keep reading?"

"Do what you like. I'm going to sleep. It's been a long day." I rolled over in my bunk and turned out the overhead reading light.

The next thing I knew it was morning. I slid off the bunk and passed out the cookies the EMT had given me last night. "Breakfast," I said.

Chaun took a bite of his cookie. "I finished two more chapters. Should I keep reading?"

"Let's break it up a little." I tossed the mask on my bunk to him. "Show me how to clear a mask."

"There's no water," he said.

"I know. I want you to show me the technique. We'll practice in the water once we get out of here."

He put the mask over his head, and like many novices, he put the strap low on the back of his neck, which makes it hard to get a good seal between the mask and the face. Then he pulled the straps tight— so tight that the mask's skirt buckled against his skin. Those two circumstances would leave him with a constantly leaky mask in the water, but he demonstrated the motions of the mask clearing skill well, exactly as he had when I'd tested him on the dive.

I crossed the chamber. "Wear it like this," I said, adjusting the fit of the mask. "It'll be much more comfortable and won't leak nearly as much."

I'd no sooner handed the mask back to Chaun when I heard the hiss of escaping air and felt the pressure in the tank begin to abate. Doc's voice came over the loudspeaker. "You're all free to go as soon as the airlock opens, but no diving for twenty-four hours. Fin, this means you too."

I grinned at the camera where I knew she'd be watching me.

"I mean it, Fin," she said. "No diving."

The door opened and we walked out of the recompression chamber. Doc stood outside and asked us each to sign some paperwork. When it was my turn, I whispered in her ear. "Can I take him in the pool? Shallow end only? Mostly snorkel work. I'm afraid he'll take it into his head to dive beyond his skill level again, and I want to get him up to speed as fast as I can."

She bit her lip. "Shallow end only. Nitrox or snorkel only. And you and Benjamin stay on the sidelines. Got it?"

"Got it," I said.

"Before you go, I want to show you something. It's pretty exciting, and I hope you and Maddy will help me test it out." She smiled like the Cheshire Cat.

"What is it?"

"You'll see. Hurry. Todd is waiting to move the boxes over to the *Omega*." She took off down the hall to the loading dock. It was all I could do to keep up with her.

"Wait for me here," I said to Chaun and Benjamin. "I won't be long."

When we entered the shipping and receiving area, Todd was waiting next to three large wooden crates. Doc grabbed a crowbar off the wall, ready to pry the crates open herself.

Todd took the crowbar from her. "Let me. You never know when you'll need those magic medical hands. We can't take a chance on injuring you." He used the crowbar to pry the top off the largest of the three crates.

The contents of the crate included a folded length of a heavy, bright yellow material, and several bars that looked like stainless steel. At intervals the yellow material was broken up by clear pockets that looked like windows or portholes.

I nodded sagely. "Nice. What is it?"

Doc rolled her eyes. "Portable diving bell. A totally new design. Lightweight, portable, easy, and safe enough for recreational divers. A friend from school recently received the patent on the design. You set it up almost like an umbrella. You can feed breathing gas either from a surface supplied hose or from tanks, and it keeps the air pocket the same size, regardless of depth because the pressure is balanced as the air is replenished."

"You can eat, sleep, decompress, whatever you want in this baby. I was hoping you and Maddy would join me on a test run. Fancy a few days underwater?"

I was impressed. "Count me in. I'm sure Maddy will want to be in on it too. When do you want to try it out?"

"Let's give it a few days until things settle down around here," she said. "When we're all less stressed out about you know what." I realized she knew about Gus and Theresa being missing but didn't want to say anything in front of a crew member. Not much gets by Doc.

"Good idea," I said. I can't wait to try it out."

"Try them out, you mean. I have three. One for each of us. Private rooms." She laughed. Then she turned to Todd. "Please load these onto the *Omega*. You can put them in the cargo area. No need to keep them on deck. We won't need them for at least a week."

Todd nodded and tilted the first crate onto a hand dolly to take it out to a Zodiac for transport to the *Omega*.

I walked back to the infirmary, where Chaun and Benjamin were waiting.

"Ok, Chaun. Let's go to the pool. Change back into your swimsuit in the locker room. You can keep the scrubs." He picked up his bathing suit and dive gear as we left the infirmary. We stopped by the café to pick up some coffee, and then I led him down the hall to the gigantic Olympic size saltwater pool where RIO did its diver training classes.

The three of us were changed and on the pool coping within a few minutes. "Hop in, Chaun. Clear that mask again, this time underwater."

He put on his mask and pulled the straps tight. I cleared my throat.

He removed the mask, loosened the straps, and redonned the mask, this time barely tightening the straps enough to keep it in place. Underwater, the pressure would create a tight seal between the mask and his face, as long as the straps weren't tight enough to cause the soft silicone to buckle and leak.

He learned fast. I'd give him that.

"Good. Now do two laps. Surface swim only. Any stroke you like. No mask, no fins."

"That's quite a distance," he said. "Without fins."

"Sure is." I sat on the edge of the pool with my feet dangling in the water, sipping my coffee while I watched him.

He gulped, placed his mask on the edge of the pool and started swimming.

Benjamin took a gulp from his coffee and swallowed. "He didn't know he was putting us in danger, you know."

"I do know. And I'm making it my mission to make sure that from now on, he does know, so he won't do it again."

"He's doing us a favor..."

I cut off Benjamin's words. "And I'm doing him a favor. The only difference is his favor might save me some money, but my favor could save his life."

After a moment of quiet, Benjamin said, "Do you need me for this? I have some work to do. I'll go with you when you're done here. How long do you think you'll be?"

"Depends on his stamina," I said. "I'll let you know."

He nodded and left the pool house, presumably to go to his office to enjoy his coffee in peace.

When Chaun finished his laps, I had him get out of the water and sit beside me on the side of the pool with his regulator in his hands. "Name each part of the regulator assembly and its purpose," I said.

He complied, and I put him through his paces for another half hour or so.

"Hungry?" I asked at last.

"Starved," he said.

"Go change. I'll buy lunch as I promised." I texted Benjamin to let him know to meet us in the café. I had reserved the private room where we held the dive class celebration parties, because I didn't want to discuss Chaun's RFID project in the public areas.

It wasn't quite noon, but we were all starving. We made quick work of lunch. We grabbed a couple of lemonades on the way out of the café, and then we strolled across the lawn to the dive shop where Chaun had stashed his RFID equipment when he arrived yesterday morning.

The first thing he did was download and install an app onto the shop's computer. He promised the app would be able to tell us the whereabouts of every tank that had a tag, as long as it was within range of the scanners. I was skeptical, but Benjamin nodded.

"Good. That's exactly what we need. Now what's next?" he asked

Chaun opened a black rolling suitcase, and out tumbled thousands of small black pellets, like the ones he'd shown me yesterday. "These are the tags we'll use," he said. "They are waterproof, won't degrade even under intense pressure in seawater, and can be read from about twenty feet away."

"Only twenty feet?" I said. "That's not very far."

He gave me a sly look. "It's a function of physics."

"Touché," I said, and we both laughed.

He continued. "Most tags can only be read from two to three feet away, and very few can function at all in seawater. You're lucky Benjamin knew enough to call me. These are state-of-the-art."

He opened a sealed compartment in the larger suitcase and removed several large tubes of the special epoxy. "And this is the glue that will hold them in place. Should we put them all in the boot?"

I nodded. "Let's get started."

We set up a little assembly line. Todd, still manning the dive shop, brought the tanks over two at a time. Benjamin removed the boot from each tank, then passed it to Chaun, who used the epoxy to stick the tag to the tank's bottom. Then he passed the tank to me, and I replaced the boot and carried the tank to the other side of the dive shop. That way we knew which ones had been tagged.

Working together, we'd still only finished about thirty-five tanks by the time five o'clock rolled around. "This is more time-consuming than I thought it would be," I said. "This will take days."

"No worries," said Chaun. "I'm here until it's finished. But before we quit for the day, let me set up the readers." He pulled another black rolling case out from behind the counter. This one was smaller than the first one, and when he unzipped it, it contained several small black boxes. He affixed one to the inside wall near the dive shop door. He walked down to the dock and fastened one to the gate that opened to the dock. Working quickly, he attached one to the dock at every slip.

Then he walked back to the dive shop, selected a tagged tank, and carried it outside the shop and down to the dock. He lugged the tank out along the pier for a short distance, turned around, and reversed the process.

When Chaun returned to the dive shop, he went to the computer on the counter and opened an app. "Ta Da!" he said, swiveling the screen around to an angle where Benjamin and I could see it.

The app showed the tank leaving the shop, entering the marina, and returning to the shop a few minutes later. It had registered at each checkpoint along the dock. We knew exactly where it had been and when it had been there.

"It's perfect, Chaun. I can't thank you enough for setting this up."

He blushed. "And I can't thank you enough for this free vacation in paradise, the use of your house while I'm here, saving my life, and teaching me to dive." He grinned. "Plus, lunch. So, if you buy me dinner too, I'll call it even."

I laughed. "Pushy, but it's a deal. The whole RFID project will be a godsend to RIO. I'll agree to call it even. Let me know when you're ready for dinner."

"Ready," he said with a smile.

Chapter 26
A threat

"SURE. We can leave right now and finish this up in the morning. I need to make a stop on the way, if you can postpone dinner for a few minutes."

Since my car was still in the parking lot at Newton's condo, Benjamin agreed to drive us. We were outside RIO's entrance, walking across the parking lot to his car, when someone called my name.

"Fin. Got a minute?" It was Stanley Simmons, Gus's cousin who was a member of RIO's maintenance crew.

Mindful of my responsibilities filling in for Maddy as RIO's leader, I smiled. "Sure, Stanley. But only a minute. What's up?"

"Just wondering how Angel's doing. I haven't seen her around for a while. Everything okay?"

I smiled at him. It was sweet of him to worry about his cousin like this. "Angel's fine. She's staying at my father's condo while Gus and Theresa are away. He's got a whole nursery setup there for her, with every toy you could imagine, and a full-time nanny to watch over her. She's so spoiled she may never want to leave."

"Good. That's good. I just…I worry about her. All the time."

"No need to worry. She's in good hands. But right now, I've got to run."

I slid into the front seat of Benjamin's car, and we headed directly over to Newton's condo. I wanted to check in with Dane and also give Angel a little bit of love and attention. The nanny was competent, but I wanted Angel to have time with someone she knew well.

Benjamin pulled up in front of Newton's building, and I got out of the car to run up the steps. "I won't be long. Five minutes, tops," I yelled over my shoulder as I pulled open the heavy glass front door.

Seconds later, the elevator doors opened, and I entered the penthouse. I needn't have worried about Angel feeling neglected. She was sitting on Roland's lap while Dane held a stuffed giraffe in front of her. He was making the giraffe wiggle and dance, and Angel was laughing in delight. Her nanny sat in the sunshine on the balcony, reading a book.

"I guess there's no news," I said from the entryway.

The cops instantly assumed a more somber demeanor. Blushing, Dane put the giraffe on the couch behind his back. "No. There are no new leads. Nothing from the posters we put up. We had another call from the kidnapper, but he still says he'll only accept the ransom from the treasure reward. Isn't there anything you can do to hurry that up? The longer this goes on, the more danger for Gus and Theresa."

"I don't know what I can do. I'll talk to Benjamin again—see if he can identify everyone who would know whether the reward has been paid yet. And I'll talk to Justin too. Maybe he can find a way to make it seem like we have the reward, but we take the ransom from the money Newton offered. Or I can put out a fake press release saying we've received the funds. I don't know what the holdup on the reward payment is, but I'm sure it's dangerous for Gus and Theresa if we wait much longer."

"Just be careful. As we've discussed, the kidnapper most likely has someone on the inside at RIO or Fleming Environmental. They might know if we try to fake it, and that would make things even worse for Theresa and Gus."

"Got it," I said. "I'll make sure we think it through and that we have everything perfectly in place before we do anything. No leaks. No obvious fakery."

I picked up Angel, gave her a kiss, and crooned into her tiny perfect ear. She was so sweet. My heart broke with worry about her parents, and what would happen to them if we didn't find them soon.

"I've got to run. Text me if anything changes, please." Reluctantly, I handed Angel back to Roland and left to rejoin Benjamin and Chaun.

I opened the door to Benjamin's car. "We have reservations at The Wharf. Is that good for you guys?"

They both agreed that it was the perfect place, and we drove off to one of Grand Cayman's most popular waterfront restaurants. At the restaurant, we left the car with the valet and approached the reception stand.

"Fin! It's been a while. How are you doing? How's your mother?" said the host, who'd known me since I was a child.

"Maddy's fine, thanks. These are my friends, Benjamin and Chaunsey. We'd like a table near the tarpon please."

"You got it," he said. He grabbed three menus and led us to a table on the restaurant's wharf, next to the railing.

As soon as we sat down, several large tarpons swam up to the edge of the dock and surfaced, opening and closing their mouths in silent supplication. The fish who came here were used to getting handouts from the restaurant's patrons, and they weren't shy about letting you know what they wanted.

I didn't believe in feeding wildlife, but at this point, these particular tarpons were more like pets than wildlife, since they'd spent their entire lives under the wharf here, enjoying the easy pickings of tourist handouts.

Our waiter arrived and we ordered margarita's all around. Chaunsey asked for a cup of conch chowder, but Benjamin and I decided we'd hold off until our main meal.

When they brought his chowder, Chaun dug in eagerly. "It's delicious," he said. "What's in it anyway?"

"Potatoes, tomatoes, onions, spices, broth, clam juice, conch meat…"

Chaun broke in. "Conch meat? I thought conch was just a word, like 'New York style' or something. What's a conch?"

Benjamin and I looked at each other. "We'll show you a picture later," I said. "Just enjoy the chowder for now." While most people found the conch's shells gorgeous, the squeamish had been known to find the large slug-like mollusk itself off putting.

When Chaun had finished his chowder, the two men took turns

tossing pieces of their dinner rolls to the hungry tarpon hovering near the water's surface below us. The waiter came back to remove Chaun's dish, and we ordered our dinner. I sat back, feeling the tequila and the setting sun start to drain the tension away.

We each had another cocktail while we finished our dinners, and Chaun ordered dessert. While he was spooning coconut cream pie into his mouth, my watch buzzed that I had an incoming text. I glanced down.

The text was from Justin Nash at Fleming Environmental. *"Need to C U. Can we meet @ RIO 2nite?"*

Good. I wanted to talk to him about setting up a transfer from Newton's accounts—but making it look like it came from Gus.

"Excuse me," I said and left the table to reply with a text of my own. *"After 9. Work 4 U?"*

He sent back a thumbs up, so I returned to the table.

Chaun had finished his pie and was sipping a cappuccino. "This is a great place, Fin. Thank you for a fabulous dinner. I don't deserve it after nearly killing you two the other day."

His reminder of our ill-fated dive made me realize how bone-weary I was. He must be feeling the same—maybe even worse. "You deserve a nice dinner. But you must be beat. Let's get home."

I paid the bill, and we left the restaurant. Benjamin drove us to my home on Rum Point, and we all went inside.

Almost immediately, I bit back a yawn. "All set for the night, Chaun? Because I'm beat."

He nodded. "Thank you. This place is fantastic, and much nicer than a hotel."

Benjamin opened the front door for me. "C'mon. I'll get you back to your father's place, Fin. Chaun, I'll pick you up in the morning."

We were halfway back to Georgetown before I remembered my day wasn't over yet. "Can you drop me at RIO instead of Newton's condo? There are still a few things I need to take care of today."

"Anything I can do to help? You've had quite a day, and you said you were beat."

"Thanks, but this is Fleming Environmental business. I have a meeting with Justin."

"Why don't you call him and ask him to meet you at Newton's

condo? If it's about Fleming Environmental, you'll be right there if you need to reference any documents or files. And when your meeting is over, you'll be able to go right down the hall to bed."

The idea of going straight to bed sounded wonderful. "Good idea. I'll call Justin and suggest the switch."

But Justin didn't answer when I called, and he didn't respond to my text. "I can't reach him. I guess I'll have to stick to the original plan."

"I'll wait for you and drive you to Newton's when the meeting's over," he said.

"No need. Justin can drop me off in his super fancy, ultra-expensive new car." I laughed. "He's very proud of that thing, even though all it does is get you from Point A to Point B, same as my Prius. But it makes him happy. Who am I to judge?"

Benjamin said nothing while he concentrated on his driving, and it wasn't long before we pulled into RIO's parking area. I hopped out of the car. "Thanks for the ride. And for everything you did yesterday. You were actually pretty amazing."

"Back 'atcha," he said with a smile. "See you tomorrow."

I heard the sound of a boat approaching the marina, so I trotted off in that direction. I hit the dock at the same time Justin moored one of RIO's black rental Zodiac's in the spot next to Gus and Theresa's boat. He wrapped the excess line in a neat circle next to the cleat.

He seemed surprised to see me. "You're early," he said. "I expected to have time to clean up the boat before you arrived." He was wearing a Lycra diveskin, still wet.

I glanced into the rental boat, where I saw a dive gear bag open on the floor, a mask and regulator spilling from the opening. There was one tank aboard, its dust cap dangling from the valve, the universal signal that the tank had been used. "Were you diving alone, at night? That's not smart."

He flushed. "I needed to clear my head. But you're right. It wasn't smart. I promise I won't do it again." He gave me his impish grin. "Next time I'll wait for you."

I laughed. "Good idea. Let's have our meeting on the deck of the *Tranquility*. It's a nice night."

"Be right there." He unzipped his diveskin and pulled his arms out of the sleeves, tying them around his waist so they wouldn't dangle. Then he zipped himself into a fleece jacket with the Fleming Environmental logo on the chest. Before I turned away to walk down the pier to my boat, I noticed that the blue of the jacket matched the color of his eyes.

I waited while he returned his empty tank to the drop off area outside the tank shed. We settled at the galley table onboard the *Tranquility*. I offered him some lemonade or coffee, but he declined, so we got right into the topic he wanted to discuss.

He folded his hands on the table in front of him and stared at them for a moment before speaking. "I'm concerned about how much money Newton is plowing into RIO. The monthly donations alone are hefty but adding in the extras like paying for the surveillance camera system and offering to pay the ransom out of his own pocket—those things add up. His expenditures are outrunning his revenue."

"But surely Newton understands that. And he must have reserves. Assets that are his alone, not part of Fleming Environmental," I said.

"That's what I wanted to talk to you about. Do you have any ideas where he might have assets like that stashed? Off-shore bank accounts? Trust funds? Personal investment accounts? Anywhere?"

I was floored. I'd always been told my father was a multi-billionaire. If that was true, he'd have a hard time spending down all his assets no matter what he did. "Why come to me about this?" I asked. "Have you discussed your concerns with Newton?"

"No, I didn't want to embarrass him, and I thought you might know where he has the bulk of his wealth stashed. If you did, we could figure this out together. Put both our minds at ease about it."

"My mind was at ease before," I said. "Now it's not. What gave you the idea that Dad's personal finances were in jeopardy?"

Now he blushed. "Sorry. I can see this conversation was a bad idea. Forget I brought it up. I'll discuss it with Newton when he gets back. I should go now." He got up and left the boat, hurrying quickly down the pier and across the lawn.

I watched him go. It wasn't until after I saw his car leave the RIO parking lot that I realized I was now stranded here without a ride home. I'd driven in with Benjamin this morning, and I didn't have a car with me. Dane had told me not to sleep on the boat until he'd caught the kidnapper, but it looked like I didn't have a choice since my car was still at Newton's place. I turned out the boat's lights and lay down on the daybed.

I had just pulled a lightweight blanket over me when I heard the sound of a boat approaching the marina. I peered out the window and saw another one of RIO's black rental Zodiacs approaching the dock.

The boat hovered near the usually empty slip next to the one where Gus's boat was moored, but the boat Justin had been using was still occupying that spot. After a moment, the captain backed up and moved the boat to an empty slip on the other side of the dock.

I watched as a man jumped out of the boat and wrapped the lines around the cleats on the pier. I noticed that whoever it was wrapped the excess line in a neat round pile around the cleat, and I remembered that we thought the kidnapper might have this habit.

I dug out my cellphone to text Dane, forgetting that the phone's screen would light up as soon as I touched it. The bright light was like a beacon in the dark of the marina. The man from the Zodiac quickly ran off down the pier. He disappeared into the shrubbery surrounding RIO's grounds before I could even finish the text to Dane.

I didn't have anything at hand I could use for self-defense, so I went below *Tranquility*'s deck and locked myself in the engine compartment to await the arrival of the police. It seemed like forever until I heard the sirens approaching. Even then, I waited until I heard Dane's voice calling my name before I came out of my cramped and smelly hiding place.

As soon as I appeared on deck, Benjamin hurried over, leaping past the police contingent to crush me in his arms. "Are you all right?"

I stepped back from his embrace. Benjamin was the first man to hold me like this since Liam had left, and I wasn't sure how I felt about being held. Or about Benjamin. "I'm fine. What are you doing here? I thought you went home?"

He blushed. "I was worried about you, so I waited in the parking lot outside Newton's condo. I was going to stay there until you were home safe. When I saw Dane and his team rush out with sirens ablaze, I was afraid something might have happened to you. Anyway, here I am. I'm glad you're okay."

"Thanks. It was nice of you to worry about me, but not at all necessary."

Dane came over then, carrying a large flashlight. "Are there more lights out here? It would help us to follow his trail if we could see better. It's too dark we'll never be able to pick up a clue until morning."

It was only when he mentioned the darkness that I realized the lights that usually lit the pier, the boat slips, the dive shop, and the walkways that crisscrossed the lawn, were not on. They were on a timer, so they turned on automatically at sunset.

"That's odd," I said. "They usually go on at dusk. But Todd is filling in for Oliver, and he's not as familiar with the dive shop operation. Maybe he accidentally turned off the master switch when he left. He might not have realized what he was doing."

"Maybe," said Dane. He didn't sound convinced. "Do you know how to turn the lights back on?"

"Of course." I clicked on the flashlight app on my phone and used the beam to light the path to the dive shop. The main switch was in a box on the back side of the small building, the side where no customers or outsiders generally went.

I opened the panel box and reached up to turn the switch back on, but Dane stopped my hand a millimeter before I touched it. "We'll want to check for prints first. Now that I know where the control is, we can take it from here."

Benjamin was standing behind us. "This doesn't seem like a secure place to keep the main control. It's right out in the open, where anyone could access it."

"That's true. We had most of these lights installed last year after an incident when someone tampered with the scuba tanks. But we didn't want to disrupt the dive shop operations. That's why we put the controls outside. I can see now that was a mistake."

"I'll take care of getting it moved," he said. "And we won't disrupt anything." He pulled out his own phone and dictated a reminder into it.

Dane interrupted before I could thank him. "You two should go home now. We've got this from here."

"I'll drive you to Newton's condo," Benjamin said. "Your car's still there, right?"

I nodded, and we walked across the lawn. I was so tired I fell asleep on the ride. Benjamin woke me up when we arrived. "Do you want me to walk you up or can you make it on your own?"

"I'm fine. Thanks for asking." I bit back a yawn and reluctantly slid out of the car.

Chapter 27
Stewie Returns

I COULD BARELY STAY AWAKE LONG ENOUGH to brush my teeth, and I slept like a hibernating bear until the rising sun kissed my eyelids. I'd been tired enough that I'd forgotten to close the room darkening blinds. I knew if I got out of bed I'd be up for good, so I tried burrowing my face into one of the pillows.

It didn't work. I reluctantly decided to start my day. While I waited for the shower to heat up, I looked in the mirror. I'd aged at least ten years since yesterday. My skin was grey and pasty, and my eyes were ringed with darkness.

I dragged myself to the kitchen, filled a mug with fresh hot coffee, and tiptoed through the silent condo so as not to wake Angelica, her nanny, or anyone of Dane's team who had managed to grab a quick forty winks. I hurried across the parking lot to my car.

By the time I arrived at my desk at RIO, I was feeling almost human. I started reading an astonishingly boring research paper, but it was tough going.

Another cup of coffee would do it, I thought, but I wanted to finish reading this research report from one of our top oceanic geology scientists before I did. I knew if I stopped now, I'd never be able to force myself to finish reading the dry material.

I was rubbing my bleary eyes when a cup of coffee materialized on the center of my desk. "Bless you," I said, assuming it was Maddy's assistant June who'd brought it. I looked up to say thank you.

The man in front of me was almost unrecognizable from the man he'd been the last time I saw him. In his late fifties, he was as fit and trim as a much younger man. His eyes were clear and bright, and his grip on his own coffee mug was rock steady. His clothes were clean and pressed. His hair was still damp from a shower, and he was clean shaven.

He looked so different from the broken man he'd been when I last saw him that if it hadn't been for the brightly colored Hawaiian shirt partially tucked into his baggy cargo shorts, I might never have realized who he was.

"Stewie. Welcome home." I smiled at the man who had been like another father to me until he succumbed to the lure of alcohol. My late stepfather Ray Russo had two close friends his whole life. One was Gus Simmons, the kidnap victim, and the other was this man, Stewie Belcher.

Unlike Ray and Gus, Stewie had never really grown up. He continued to drink and party, while his two friends went on to educate themselves and to achieve admirable career and life success.

Stewie had remained a divemaster, refusing promotions or additional responsibilities, living off tips, and lapping up the free beer tourists bought him while listening to stories of his dive adventures. He'd never married or had a family. His wakeup call had been his inadvertent contribution to Ray's death.

He'd never gotten over his part in the tragedy, even though we'd forgiven him for what happened. He'd thought he was doing what Ray wanted, and he couldn't have known what was to come.

Still, the guilt ate at him, and we all knew it. We also knew that until Stewie could forgive himself, he'd never kick his drinking. This was his second stint in rehab since that awful day. From the look of him now, it seemed like this time he'd stuck to the program.

Stewie sat in the visitor's chair in front of my desk and took a sip of the fragrant coffee. "Where's Gus? I went by his place when I got back on island last night, but there was nobody around. He and Theresa off on some exotic jaunt for your dad's business?"

I knew Dane wouldn't want me to tell anyone outside the small circle of people that already knew about the kidnapping. I paused a moment to decide what to say before speaking. "I'm not sure where he is right now."

"I thought you and Theresa were pretty tight. She didn't tell you where they were off to? And what about Angelica? Did they take Angel with them wherever they were going?"

"Angel's staying at my father's place. She has her own nursery and a full time nanny."

"Hmph. Must be nice," he said. "I slept in my car last night. Had to shower in the locker room here. I need to talk to Maddy about getting my old job back. She's not out at sea—I saw the *Omega* on her mooring. Do you know what time she's coming in today by any chance?"

"She's out of town for a few weeks," I said. "I can ask her to call you when she gets back."

He looked crestfallen, and he took another sip of coffee. "I don't have a few weeks. That reward check hasn't come through yet, and I spent everything I had on rehab." Another sip. "You know Maddy fronted me most of the money for this go around too, don't you? I put everything she gave me toward the bills. I'm tapped out."

"I can lend you…"

He put up a hand, palm facing out. "Don't say it. I've known you since you were a toddler. I can't take money from my best friend's kid, even if she is rich. I still have some pride. I'll find a way."

He turned to go.

I was afraid I might regret it, but I knew it's what Maddy would have done if she'd been here, because it's what Ray would have wanted. And I remembered Stewie as he'd been back when I was a child. Funny. Loving. Always ready to lend a hand or offer a quick word to make someone feel better. He'd spent a lot of time with me and Ray. I'd loved him like another father. Funny how I'd gone from having no father at all to having several father figures—each one different, but all of them loved. I knew what I had to do.

"Stewie, Oliver is away too. Can you run the dive shop while he's gone? Todd's been filling in, but they need him back on the *Omega*. Having you run the dive operation would be a big help to me, and we can talk to Maddy about something more permanent when she gets back. How's that sound?"

His face glowed as though he'd won the lottery. "Thank you," he said. "Your confidence in me means a lot. When do you want me to start?"

"Right now. Why don't you go to HR and get the paperwork done? Meanwhile, I'll arrange for you to get an advance on your salary to tide you over."

He walked back into my office and shook my hand. I pretended not to see the tears in his eyes. "You won't be sorry. I promise."

"Good. Come back here when you've got everything set with HR and I'll take you down to the dive shop. Oliver's made a few changes, and Todd can show you the new methods. Then you're on your own." I smiled at him.

As soon as he'd left my office, I called HR and told them about the offer I'd made to Stewie. "And I want to give him a substantial pay increase." I named a figure that caused our HR director to suck in her breath.

"I hope you know what you're doing," she said.

"That makes two of us," I replied.

When I'd hung up, I walked around the corner and down the hall to Benjamin's office. He must have just arrived, because he was dropping his keys in the top drawer of his desk when I walked in.

"Wow. After all you've been through the last few days, I didn't expect you in this early," he said when he saw me.

"I didn't expect to be here this early either, but I'm glad I was here because I was able to take advantage of a great opportunity." I told him I'd hired Stewie and asked him to cut a check for an advance on Stewie's salary.

Benjamin looked skeptical. "I've heard Stewie's kind of a loose cannon. His reputation's not very good. Are you sure you want to do this?"

"Very sure," I said. "Speaking of loose cannons, where is Chaunsey this morning?"

He laughed. "He can be a handful, but he means well, and he'd give you his last nickel if you needed it. I know he can be off-putting, but he's a good guy. He's already hard at work at the dive shop, and the sun is barely even up. I'm on my way to check on him now."

"Good. I'll join you in a few minutes, as soon as Stewie finishes up in HR."

Chapter 28
Missing Tanks

I'D NO SOONER GOTTEN RESETTLED at my desk when Stewie returned. "I'm ready," he said. "It was quick because they had all my info from when I worked here before. Except an address. I lost my rental while I was away. I gave them your address. I hope that's okay?"

"I'm sorry but you can't stay at my house, Stewie. I already have someone else staying there. But if you need a place, I can get you a hotel room for a couple of nights." I handed him the envelope with the check Benjamin had cut for the advance on Stewie's salary. "And this should be enough to cover a deposit on a new place, and for you to buy some food and necessities until your regular paycheck is due."

He took the envelope as if he were accepting the Holy Grail from the hands of King Arthur himself. "I don't deserve this kindness. Thank you."

"Not to be too blunt about my expectations of you, but the best way to pay me back would be by not screwing things up this time." I sighed. "You know we all care about you, Stewie. We want you to be healthy and happy."

He nodded. "I understand. I won't let you down."

"C'mon then. Let's get you started." We walked down the hall to the rear exit next to Maddy's office. As soon as we were outside, I could hear Chaun's high pitched voice. He sounded panicked.

"I left them right here. They're gone. Every one of them. Those were my test units. I need those tanks, and they've gone missing." He stabbed his forefinger at Todd's chest, as though he thought Todd had secretly taken the tanks on purpose to ruin his day.

Stewie and I sped up our approach. "What's going on?" I said. "What tanks have gone missing?" I could see how distraught he was.

"The tanks. The ones we put the RFID tags on yesterday. We left them right here." He pointed at the concrete slab where we kept the supply of tanks ready to rent to day-tripping divers or for the RIO staff to use. "Remember? There were thirty-five of them here last night, and they're all gone. Every one of them is missing."

RIO had thousands of tanks in a continual rotation. Most of them were either on the *Omega*, locked up inside the dive shop, or stored in the nearby supply shed for quick access if we had a run on rentals. We did keep a handful of tanks on an open concrete slab near the entrance to the dive shop overnight for the use of the staff or walk in rentals. We called it the ready area, and we left a sign-out sheet with the tanks, which could be taken by anyone. We'd always relied on the honor system, and until recently, we'd never been burned.

Transient divers were expected to pay when they returned the tanks, and the staff was supposed to return any tanks they took within a few days. We'd occasionally had someone use a tank overnight and return it without paying, but for the most part the system had worked fine for the more than thirty years that RIO had been in operation.

But this morning, the concrete slab was bare, giving off waves of reflected heat in the hot sun. "Were there any tanks at all here when you got in this morning, Todd?"

"Not full ones. Just that empty over there." He pointed to Justin's used tank. "I thought it was odd that there were no tanks in the ready area. We never run out of tanks overnight. And I left most of them chained up, like I always do."

"Nobody's blaming you for anything, Todd. I'm simply trying to figure out what happened. Where do you keep the key to the chain's padlock?" I asked.

Todd pointed to the door jamb. "Up there. We like to leave it accessible in case any of the research staff needs a tank at night or in the early morning. We always leave a bunch of loose tanks out too." He wrung his hands. "I'm sorry."

I patted his arm. "It's not your fault. We'll figure out what's going on. These aren't the first tanks that have gone missing."

Chaun perked up when he heard that other tanks had gone missing before the ones he'd tagged. "You people have a real problem here. I didn't realize how badly you need my help. Let's get moving." He was wearing an acid-yellow RIO branded tank top, but he made a rolling up his sleeves motion that made me smile.

Stewie held out his hand to shake. "I'm Stewie Belcher. How can I help? What do you need?"

Chaun gazed at Stewie's outstretched hand with a look of horror. I spoke up before things got really tense. "Chaun doesn't shake hands, Stewie. It's nothing personal." Then I had an idea how to bring Stewie up to date and soothe Chaunsey's angst at the same time.

"Stewie, let me introduce you to Chaunsey. He's helping us stop the missing tank problem by putting his company's RFID tags on all the tanks, so they log themselves in and out automatically."

Stewie surprised me by nodding. "Great idea. That'll cut down on a lot of paperwork. And it'll help us find the tanks that are due for inspection fast." He looked at Chaun with admiration. "Your company sounds really awesome." He paused a moment. "By the way, is Chaunsey your first or last name?"

"Yes," said Chaun. "But call me Chaun."

Stewie laughed, and Chaun grinned back at him. I was astonished at Stewie's knowledge of RFID technology and that he'd come up with another use for it. And that he'd laughed at Chaunsey's joke about his name.

Chaun went into the dive shop to retrieve his case full of tags, and Stewie started carrying tanks outside to set them up for the application of the tags.

"Todd, can you stay here today and show Stewie the new procedures Oliver implemented? And maybe help with the tagging operation whenever things are slow? Once we get all the tanks tagged, you can go back to your real job on the *Omega*."

"Great," said Todd." I can use the extra hours." Todd and Oliver both tried to live on their dive shop earnings, and both of them were perpetually broke. He continued, "I don't mind helping out here, but I prefer being on the ship."

"No problem. We'll get you back aboard the *Omega* as soon as we can." I looked at Stewie and Chaun, who were busy pulling the boots off the first batch of tanks. "Looks like you guys don't need Benjamin or me, but you know where to find us if you do."

Benjamin and I walked along the crushed shell path to RIO's back door. It was situated between his and Maddy's offices, and right down the hall from mine. When we were inside, I said, "Hopefully this will be a normal day now, and I can get some actual work done."

Benjamin nodded. "There's always something going on here, that's for sure."

We parted outside his office, and I continued down the hall and around the corner to mine. I sat down at my desk for what felt like the first time in days and flipped on my computer to see what had been going on at RIO while I'd been otherwise occupied.

The computer had barely finished booting when my phone rang. I glanced at caller ID and read *Your World*, the outdoor focused magazine where I had a monthly column. I adored Carl Duchette, the editor in chief. I happily picked up the phone to chat. "Hey, Carl. What's up?"

An unfamiliar voice said, "Hold for Mr. Stone, please."

Before I knew it, I was bewildered and on hold.

"Hi, Fin." I recognized the voice of a man I despised. Alec Stone, my horrible ex-husband. Why would he be calling me from the *Your World* offices?

"What do you want, Alec?"

"I was calling to give you the news. I'm the new editor in chief here at the magazine, and I have some ideas on how to improve your column. Got time to chat?"

"Not until you tell me what's going on. Where's Carl?"

He snickered. "Carl retired right after the board of directors suggested he should. They asked me to take over and lead the magazine in a new direction. They've always been impressed with my photographic work, ever since that first spread I did…"

"You mean the one that featured all my photos and your byline? That work?"

"Are you going to rehash that again? It was an innocent mistake, and now I'm in a position to offer you an even bigger showcase for your work than Carl did. Here's my idea…"

"Not interested."

"You will be. I'll double your rate and give you more pages. You'll still have free rein to choose the locations and the topics…"

"I hear a but coming," I said.

Well, here's the thing. I think it would get more leverage for the magazine if we did the column jointly, you know? We can put both our work in each month…kind of a 'his-and-hers' viewpoint, you know. You can write the text, and we share the byline. What do you think?"

"The answer is still no. No way. No how. No, never." I hung up.

I shut my eyes and took a deep breath. This couldn't be happening. It had to be one of Alec's nasty tricks. I loved my gig at *Your World*, and each month when my work appeared under my byline, I felt that I'd regained some of the credibility I'd lost when Alec had taken my work as his own.

The phone rang again, and caller ID showed it was from Carl Duchette's direct line. I answered quickly. "Carl, you'll never guess what Alec is saying…"

He interrupted me. "I bet I can. He said that I retired and he's the new editor in chief at *Your World*." Here he paused. "I'm sorry to say, Fin, he was telling the truth."

"That's not possible," I said. "You know what kind of a snake he is. You'd never let him get your job."

"I'm afraid I had no choice. Apparently, he's been cozying up to the members of the board, and he convinced them that my talents were out of date. They asked me to step aside and let him take over the reins."

"But don't they remember what he did? Why would they want a thief on their staff?"

"Because they don't know he's a thief. I'm ashamed to admit I never told them. Remember, you asked me not to make a big deal out of what he'd done because you didn't want to hurt Alec's career. I knew better, but I let it slide because I was embarrassed that I hadn't seen through him right from the start. Now we're both paying the price, and all I can do is say I'm sorry once again."

"It's okay. It's not your fault. It's the way Alec works. He's a sneak and a weasel as well as a thief. But I'll miss doing that column. I loved the gig."

"You'll be resigning then?"

"Yup. As soon as we hang up."

"I'll keep my ears open in case I hear of anything with one of *Your World*'s competitors. I still have a lot of contacts and friends in the industry, and I will do whatever I can to make this right for you." He sighed. "I hope you'll forgive me, but I have to go. They've given me until noon to clean out my office and it's getting late. Goodbye, Fin."

I said goodbye and then opened up a new document on my computer to begin drafting my letter of resignation from *Your World*.

Before I finished the message, Stewie and Chaun dashed into my office, followed by Benjamin. Stewie was panting. "They're gone. Our whole morning's worth of work. All the newly tagged tanks have gone missing."

"How can that be? Weren't you guys right there working?" I asked.

Chaun stepped forward. "We went to the café to get something to drink. It was my idea. Then I spent some time in the gift shop checking out the posters—that one of you and the stingray is pretty awesome —and…"

For a moment I stopped listening, remembering the day Liam had taken that photo of Susie Q the stingray and me. With an effort, I brought my attention back to the men standing in front of my desk.

Chaun was still talking. "…So, I might have kept Stewie away from the dive shop a little longer than we'd planned. And when we got back, all the tanks were gone."

"Maybe they're not missing. Did Todd bring them inside the shop or rent them out while you were gone?"

"No, we sent Todd back to the *Omega* after he showed me the new systems. It didn't make sense to have him hanging around while I was right there. They needed him on the *Omega*…" Stewie's voice trailed off.

"You left the shop unlocked and unattended? Is there anything else missing?" I asked.

"No, it's only the tanks, at least as far as I can tell," Stewie said.

"Chaun, what does your app say about the tanks' locations? Can you tell where they are?"

He looked sheepish. "I was so surprised they were gone I forgot to check the app," he said, grinding the toe of his flipflop into the floor. "I can check now."

"Let's all go and check," I said. "We need to get to the bottom of this."

The five of us headed out the back door and crossed the lawn to the dive shop. Chaun walked up to the computer and opened the app he'd installed. A puzzled look followed by a frown crossed his face. "They were moved down the pier to the slip next to yours, Fin. But they aren't on the dock, and there's no signal from them now. They must be out of range. Could they be underwater?"

"Chaun, what would it look like if someone loaded them on a boat and then pulled the boat away from the dock?"

His face cleared. "It would look exactly like this." He spun the screen around to an angle where we could see it. "That must be what happened. They've been stolen."

"Yes, I figured that much out already," I said. "Can you track them?"

"Not unless they're near a reader. I told you this technology only has a range of a few feet…"

"Yes, you did tell me that." I turned to Benjamin. "Where do we stand on the surveillance system I asked you to get quotes on?"

Benjamin blushed. "I've been waiting for Justin to approve the cost and I need to follow up."

"No need to wait any longer. Consider it approved. If you need to add a bonus for fast install, that's pre-approved too. I want the installation started today. Make it worth the contractor's while to put us at the top of their customer list." One thing I'd learned from watching Newton operate is that money talks, and a lot of money talks so loud and fast the results can feel like the roadrunner just whipped past you in pursuit of Wile E. Coyote.

Benjamin opened his mouth and closed it again. "Will do."

"Great. Now, Chaun, show me where we lost track of the missing tanks."

Chaun grabbed a handheld reader and we followed him down the pier to the empty slip next to my boat. There was no signal from any tanks as we walked by the other boats.

"What if the tanks were underwater?" I asked. "You told me we could read them within about a twenty foot maximum range."

"Yup. How deep is the water here?" he replied.

"About twenty feet deep. If they were dropped a short distance away from the dock and they were on the bottom, they'd be out of range, right?"

"Correct," he said.

"Is that reader waterproof?" I asked him.

When he nodded, I took the reader from him, walked onto the *Tranquility*, and donned a tank and my fins. I clipped the reader to a D-ring on my BCD where I could see it easily. "They're probably not here, but it's worth a shot," I said. I put on my mask and stepped into the water.

I started a grid search. I swam past the end of the dock about twenty feet and moved out about fifty yards. Then I swam in a straight line for about one hundred yards before turning at a right angle and heading to shore. When the water was too shallow to swim in, I turned right again and swam along the dock until I was a few feet shy of its end. Then I repeated the swim, except I shaved about five feet off each leg of the square. I was making a series of boxes, each slightly smaller than the previous one.

I heard bubbles and looked over to my left. Stewie was in the water, beginning a search pattern on the other side of the dock. Good. That would make the search go faster.

When I had covered the entire area on the left of the dock, I climbed back aboard the *Tranquility*. Nobody said anything as I switched over my tank and headed for the far end of the marina. "Send Stewie down to this end when he finishes his grid," I said.

I stepped off the dock and began making a grid search off the end of the pier. This time I made each side of the grid about five feet larger than the previous iteration, because I was in a more open area. I covered a large swath of the sea floor without seeing any of the missing tanks, but as always, being in the water calmed me down and soothed my soul. When my tank was nearing empty, I kicked back to the *Tranquility* and climbed aboard. A few minutes later, Stewie came up the ladder, looking morose.

"Nothing," he said. "You?"

I shook my head. "That means that whoever took them brought them someplace farther away. We'll find them. Meanwhile, we should keep all the tanks inside the shop. If any of the staff want to dive, they can sign out tanks like anyone else. And if they plan to do a night dive, they'll have to pick up their tanks before you close for the day. I'll send a notice out when I get back to my office. I should have done that as soon as the first tanks went missing, but I didn't want to change a long-standing employee benefit for what seemed like an isolated incident. I didn't realize the extent of the problem at first and then I was distracted by…never mind what I was distracted by. I should have acted sooner. This is on me, and I will do whatever needs to be done to stop the thefts."

Stewie nodded. "Consider the changes done. No more loose tanks. And I'll do some discreet inquiries around town. See if there've been any new dive operations opened up. Or if anyone has a new grudge against RIO."

Just then, one of RIO's black rental Zodiac's zoomed up to the marina and into the empty slip next to *Tranquility*. The boat was moving so fast, it bashed into the dock and bounced backwards before the pilot managed to regain control. Benjamin, Stewie, and I all frowned at this blatant disregard for safety—and for RIO property.

The boat's captain backed up, slowed the engines, and headed into the slip at a better clip. Obviously, he did know how to dock the boat correctly—but he had chosen not to. He wore a hat with a broad floppy brim that kept his features shadowed. I couldn't tell who it was.

"Who rented that boat?" I asked Stewie. "Put him on the blacklist." The blacklist contained names of people we would no longer rent boats or tanks to because of disdain for the rules and bystander safety. The list included speedsters, people who returned our property late or badly damaged, and divers who went into decompression mode multiple times.

Stewie said, "I don't know who that is. There aren't any open rentals on the books. Todd and I checked first thing."

When the boat was safely tied up to a cleat, the captain raised his head and I saw his face clearly for the first time. It was Justin Nash,

Newton's assistant. What was he doing using one of our boats in the middle of the workday, especially without signing it out?

He hopped nimbly up onto the pier. "Sorry about that crash, Fin. I was so worried about my grandmother I wasn't paying attention to what I was doing. I'll pay for any damages." Justin was already loping down the dock toward shore.

I scurried to catch up to him. "What's wrong with your grandmother?"

"Possible heart attack. I have to get to her before it's too late."

He darted away before I could tell him that working for Newton didn't give him free rein to take RIO equipment without following the sign-out procedures we had in place. The man was worried about his beloved grandmother. I could make our position clear when he returned.

I walked back to the group standing near the *Tranquility*. "We'll do an expanded search for the missing tanks later. Stewie, maybe you can put together a search plan. Will you let me know when you've finished?

"Sure. But I want to finish tagging the remaining tanks we have in the dive shop first. That way we have a better shot at tracking them if they go missing. Is that okay?"

I was already trotting back toward RIO and my office, but still in motion, I shouted back over my shoulder. "Fine." Normally, I would have stayed to help put together the search plan, but I wanted to get that letter of resignation to *Your World* before Alec started to think he'd won.

I sat at my desk, finished the letter, and did a final check of spelling and grammar. When I was satisfied, I clicked send on the email with the resignation letter attached.

The hourglass was still spinning when my phone rang. "What now?" I thought as I answered.

It was June. "DS Scott is here to see you. He's in the conference room…"

I didn't let her finish. I dropped the phone. This must be about Gus and Theresa. Maybe he'd found them. Joy gave wings to my feet, and I skidded down the hall and around the door to the conference room.

Eugene, RIO's head of maintenance, and Benjamin were already seated around the large cherry wood table.

"Come in. Sit down," Dane said solemnly.

I put a hand to my throat. "Are they okay?"

He shook his head. "Sorry. This isn't about Gus and Theresa. It's about Stanley Simmons. I know he's worked here a long time, so this will be hard to hear. There's been an accident. Stanley's in Cayman Hospital in a coma. They don't know if he'll make it."

I gasped. "Not Stanley. I just saw him the other day."

Eugene bit back a sob. Stanley had worked for him in maintenance for years. They bickered a lot, but deep down everyone knew they were the best of friends.

"What happened?" I asked.

"It looks like he was speeding along Conch Point Road. He may have fallen asleep or something because there weren't any skid marks or signs of braking. Anyway, he hit a tree. His car caught on fire. He's lucky a bystander pulled him out, but it's still touch and go."

"What was he doing out there?" I asked.

"We don't know. Do you have next-of-kin information for him? There wasn't any information in his wallet." Dane was staring at his hands.

"He has a wife and six kids, but I think she left him recently." I looked at Eugene, who nodded. "But HR probably still has her contact info." I pushed the button on the speaker phone in the center of the table and dialed the HR director. When she answered, I told her about Stanley's accident and asked her to find his next of kin info. "And text it to Benjamin Brooks' phone," I said. I didn't want her or anyone else to text my phone while the kidnapper was still using it as a primary communication tool.

In a few minutes, Benjamin's phone buzzed. He slid it across the table to Dane.

Dane stood up. "I'll go tell her."

"Benjamin, why don't you go with Dane to represent RIO? Find out if Stanley's wife needs anything." I stood up too, ready to head back to my office.

"Are you sure you wouldn't rather go? I can hold down the fort here," said Benjamin.

"No, the employees know me better than they know you, and they'll feel more comfortable hearing about Stanley's accident from me. Neither of us knows Mrs. Simmons, so it won't matter which of us sees her. And I'll go see her later when I get things cleaned up here.

Benjamin nodded. "Makes sense."

I bit back my tears for Stanley. "You have free rein," I said. "Whatever she needs."

Benjamin and Dane left the conference room, and I took a deep breath to begin the process of letting the employees at RIO know what had happened. I called HR again, asking for information on the grief counseling team we'd used after Ray's death. "Let them know we may have employees reaching out over the next few days," I said. "And make sure the contact info is up to date on our employee portal."

I composed an email that went out to all hands, letting them know what had happened to Stanley. I offered to meet with them in person or by teleconference, and I also told them about the grief counseling we'd made available.

Then I turned to Eugene, who was still sitting on the other side of the conference table, seemingly in shock.

"What will you need to keep maintenance running? Let's figure it out together. We can make two plans. Short-term over the next few days until we know what's going on with Stanley. Then we can take our time to look at mid- and long-term options."

The big man was quiet for a minute. "I can handle things without him for a few days. It's pretty slow around here right now. No parties or guests until Maddy gets back. We can go from there once he wakes up and we know how long his rehabilitation will take."

I had to admire Eugene's optimistic faith. From what Dane had said, it didn't sound as though Stanley was expected to make it. He was well liked. Everybody would be praying and sending positive thoughts into the universe on his behalf. Maybe that would be enough to pull him through this crisis. I hoped it would be.

I gave Eugene the rest of the day off and told him to take as much time as he needed before he came back. His voice was rough when he thanked me. He trudged out of the conference room, head down and shoulders hunched.

I returned to my office and drafted another all-hands memo about the changes in tank and boat access. We'd always let our employees use the rental boats and tanks whenever they wanted, with no reservations required, whether they wanted the equipment for business or personal use. But the loss of this many tanks, and the reckless use of the boats wasn't good for business. We needed to tighten up our equipment usage procedures. I had hoped to put this off until Maddy's return, but the problems were escalating too quickly for me sit by any longer. I copied all the employees at Fleming Environmental Investments too, since it seemed at least some of them—at least Justin—felt they were covered by RIO's free tank and rental boat policy.

Within minutes after I hit the send button, I received the first in a barrage of angry emails questioning why I'd felt the need to change such a long standing policy. I was debating whether to send out a clarifying message explaining the missing tanks when one of our senior researchers appeared in my door.

"Dr. French," I said. "What can I do for you?"

He pushed his glasses up on his nose and wiped his sweaty hands on his cargo shorts. "Fin, I know your mother left you in charge while she's out of town, but I'm sure she didn't mean for you to change long standing policies…"

I drew in a breath. "Why are you so sure she didn't want any changes? Maybe that's exactly why she put me in charge."

He did a double take, before turning and walking away, muttering under his breath. All I heard was the word "whippersnapper," and then my computer dinged with another incoming message.

Again.

Again.

The employees were up in arms over the change. I'd known this would happen. It was one of the reasons I'd let the thefts go on this long.

I toggled off the alert so I could think, but then I heard more muttering from the hallway outside my office as employees gathered to question my decision en masse.

I thought about explaining about the missing and misused equipment in another email, but that would sound like I was accusing the employees. I didn't think any employee was stealing tanks but providing open access for employees was also providing open access for whoever really was taking the tanks.

The high pressure steel tanks we used were expensive, and our budget was tight. I didn't want to spend our money on unnecessary tank replacements when there were so many worthy research projects that had to go unfunded.

On the other hand, I didn't want an employee revolution. My head was spinning as I looked for a solution that would keep everybody happy.

Shattering enough that we were dealing with the horror of the kidnapping. Even beyond that, today had been filled with terrible events.

And why did the worst days always include three bad things? I didn't know why, but it seemed to be true. Justin's grandmother. Stanley's accident. More delays in receiving the salvage reward payment.

I shut down my computer and did what I always do when I need to think.

I brushed passed the small cluster of employees lurking down the hall from my office, giving them a bright smile and a cheery greeting as I went by. I felt rather than saw them turn to watch me as I walked away.

I pushed open the door next to Maddy's office and strode across the lawn to the dive shop. Stewie and Chaun were on the lawn, working on tagging tanks. I waved but didn't stop to talk. I went into the shop and picked up one of Chaun's tag readers and continued across the marina. Down the pier. Onto the *Tranquility*. My dive gear and at least two filled tanks were on board. I was good to go. I started the engines and pulled out.

Chapter 29
Tank Recovery

I'D DECIDED to see if I could find and retrieve the tank Benjamin had jettisoned the day we were trying to save Chaun from himself. I didn't have too far to go. If I found that tank, it would be one less tank that RIO needed to replace, and it would help me feel like I'd done at least one thing positive about the tank situation.

I moored on the ball where we typically tied up for our dive classes, even though I knew I'd have to swim quite a way because Chaun and Benjamin had been far past the wall, out in the blue, when we'd had to go through the tank swapping maneuver.

Once the boat was secure, I donned my dive gear and made a giant stride entry off the *Tranquility*'s dive platform. As soon as I hit the water, the stress and anxiety of the day washed away, and I found myself relaxing. My breathing and heartrate slowed. The creases in my brow smoothed out. If they hadn't been clamped tightly around my regulator mouthpiece, my lips would have curved into a relaxed smile.

I dropped down to about thirty feet of depth to make the swim to the area where we'd been struggling to get Chaun safely back to the surface. I'd been so intent on saving him that I hadn't taken a careful reading on our location. I knew I might have to search around a little bit. I didn't mind. I needed the underwater time to soothe my ragged soul.

I swam slowly along the edge of the reef, peering down the edge of the wall to see if I could catch a glimpse of the tank anywhere below. I was hoping it had snagged on a coral outcrop or landed on a ledge. I reached the turnaround point of my air supply without seeing anything. I swam slowly back to the *Tranquility*, rising gradually in the water column as I went.

I climbed up the ladder, doffed my gear, and grabbed some water to wait out my surface interval. While I waited, I tried to figure out why someone would be stealing our tanks. We'd kept them in the open for the convenience of our researchers since we'd first opened the current RIO building over thirty years ago, and with the exception of an occasional rental tank that didn't get returned, we'd never had a problem with any of them going missing. Why would that suddenly change?

I hadn't come up with any new ideas by the time my surface interval was over. I switched over my gear and stepped into the water. Because I wanted to cover more distant areas of the reef on this trip, I kicked along the surface for a short way before I began my descent. When I thought I was almost to the area where I'd had to turn around on the last dive, I exhaled completely and sank below the surface.

Once over the reef's drop-off, I swam slowly along the wall, peering below, and looking for any sign of the missing tank. I was almost at the turnaround point for my air when the tag reader gave a chirp. I looked down and saw the missing tank.

As I'd hoped, it had snagged on a rocky outcropping and was sitting at about one hundred fifty feet, maybe a little deeper. After a quick debate, I decided to retrieve it on this dive. I knew my own limits, and I knew I'd have no trouble getting back to my boat, even if I emptied my tank completely.

But retrieving the tank was not as simple as I'd hoped. The valve had tangled in some coral, and I had to work hard to free it without damaging the coral any further. At last, it was free, and I slipped a nylon strap with a D-ring over it and attached it to my BCD for the trip back to the surface.

Because I didn't want to damage the coral, I'd been hovering out in the blue, over the abyss while I'd been working to put the strap on the tank. As I swam back, I glanced below and saw a pile of tanks on a ledge far below. Without meaning to, I'd discovered what might be the location of RIO's missing tanks.

Unfortunately, I didn't have enough air or bottom time remaining to start the recovery process now. I swam to the reef edge directly above the ledge. I pulled a bright yellow plastic ribbon out of my BCD pocket and tied it to the coral to enable me to find the location more easily. Then I headed back to the *Tranquility* and home.

After securing my boat, I stopped by the dive shop to leave the recovered tank. It was late in the day now, so I was surprised to see Stewie and Chaun, still affixing RFID tags to the last few scuba tanks.

"Good job," I told them when I realized how hard they must have worked to get through all those tanks this quickly.

"By the way, I think I found the missing tanks," I said. "Stewie, want to help me with the recovery mission tomorrow?"

"Absolutely," he said. "Where are they? How did you find them?"

"Pure luck," I said. "I went out to try to find a tank we jettisoned the first day Chaun dove with us. Luckily, the tank was one of the first units tagged with an RFID device. The reader chimed as soon as I got within twenty feet of it. While I was working on the recovery, I just happened to see a big pile of tanks on a ledge, way down deep. It's not a common sight. I assume they must be our missing tanks."

"That's terrific. You always were a lucky lady."

I laughed. "Chaun deserves some thanks here. His RFID tags and readers functioned perfectly."

"So does that mean I can go with you on the recovery mission tomorrow?" Chaun asked.

"No. You most definitely can't go. It's a technical dive, well beyond your skill and training."

He pouted.

"But I promise to finish your dive training when this is over," I said. "And you can always say you played an instrumental role in the tank recovery.

His face brightened.

Stewie chimed in. "I assume we're leaving early. I'll get Todd to cover for me. Chaun and I are almost done here."

I looked at my dive watch. "Chaun, I'll tell you all about it over a late breakfast tomorrow when Stewie and I get back. Right now, I have to be someplace and I'm late."

Chapter 30
Silence; Not Golden

I STEPPED through the unlocked door of Newton's condo to see Dane, Roland, and the third cop sitting glumly at the table, picking at the remains of sub sandwiches.

My heart plummeted. "Bad news?" I asked, barely able to choke the words out.

"More like no news," the third cop said. He rose to throw his trash into the nearby waste basket.

"Quiet, Morey," said Dane.

Well, at least now I knew the third cop's name.

Dane continued. "Sit down, Fin. Are you hungry? We've got a couple of extra subs around if you are."

"No thanks. Not hungry. What's going on?" My hands were shaking with fear for Gus and Theresa.

"We haven't heard from the kidnapper for a couple of hours. He went from calling every sixty minutes to not calling for hours. We don't know what it means, but it can't be good." Dane's voice was flat.

I bit my lip in consternation. "That's not necessarily bad, is it? Maybe he figured calling wasn't helping anything. Maybe he had something else to do today."

"Yeah," said Roland. "There's a lot of maybes, but none of them sound like good news for the Simmons family." He crashed his chair back from the table and left the room. I could see by the set of his shoulders he was working hard to keep control of his emotions.

I was in shock myself. Eyes blinded by tears, I stumbled over to the couch and sank down in the corner, clasping a throw pillow to my chest for comfort. My heart felt broken. Theresa, my best—my only— friend. Gus—a man who was like another father. He'd always been there for me, ever since I was a little girl.

And Angel. My heart broke for little Angelica too. It was unthinkable that she might have to grow up without her parents. I prayed that the kidnapper hadn't gotten tired of waiting for the reward money and killed Gus and Theresa. Maybe he was simply tied up, unable to make his hourly phone call.

Just then the nanny brought Angel into the room. "I think she'd like a change of scene. Anybody want to play peek-a-boo?"

With a heavy heart, I rose and took the baby from her arms. I put her in the corner of the couch, with a rolled up blanket between her and the edge to keep her safely upright. I sat beside her and covered my eyes. "Peek-a-boo."

She laughed, that sound of pure joy that only babies can make, and I smiled at her. We played the game for fifteen minutes or so, and she laughed with delight each time I uncovered my eyes.

Soon Dane came over and sat on the floor near her, taking over the eye covering part of the game while I feigned surprise each time he "reappeared." Angel continued to find our antics entrancing, but even her glee couldn't lift the heavy sorrow from our hearts.

Chapter 31
Recovery Mission

I WAS BACK at RIO shortly before sunrise the next morning, loading up *Tranquility* with tanks of Trimix—a blend of air, oxygen and helium that would allow us to dive safely below 170 feet without fear of succumbing to oxygen toxicity.

We'd use Nitrox during our descent until we reached ninety feet, then switch tanks to use the Trimix. That would help minimize our nitrogen uptake and reduce the risk of nitrogen narcosis. The only problem was that since helium molecules are so small, the helium in the Trimix would extend our decompression time because we'd absorb a lot of helium during the dives. It would be a long and arduous day.

I'd finished loading the last tanks on my boat when Stewie arrived with Todd and Chaun.

"Good morning, Fin," Stewie said. "I'm sorry you had to do all that yourself. You should have waited for me. Actually, I had planned to load up all the tanks before you got here. Chaun came by early to see us off, and he offered to buy breakfast while Todd and I went over the dive shop schedule. I apologize for losing track of the time. It won't happen again."

It was unlike the Stewie of the last few years to apologize for anything or to take responsibility for a gaffe. For a moment, I was rendered speechless. When I'd recovered from the shock, I said. "Okay. Why don't you get the cage and load it on one of the Zodiacs? Then we can still get an early start."

"Aye, aye, Captain," he said, doffing his hat. He trotted off to the maintenance shed to get the lift cage we would use to bring the tanks to the surface.

"Is it okay if I stay in the dive shop with Todd while you're gone? I want to watch how the tank rental process is working now that the new RFID tags are in place." Chaun looked as though he thought I might say no.

"Sure," I said, "if it's okay with Todd. But remember, he has work to do, so try not to bother him. And you have to stay out of the water."

"Thank you," he said. "I can only stay a little while anyway. I have business to attend to myself."

Stewie was trotting back across the lawn, pulling a wheeled cart with the metal lift crate on it. The eight-foot wide by four-foot high sides of the crate were collapsed, allowing it to lay flat. He rolled the cart over to the part of the marina where we kept the rental Zodiacs. With ease, he lifted the pile of metal and loaded it on the largest of the rental boats.

This was indeed a new Stewie. The Stewie of the last few years would have whined and asked for help. Lots of help.

When he had the folded crate secured, I said "Looks like we're ready. See you guys later. It'll probably be late afternoon before we're done."

There's no rule that says you need to file a dive plan like there is for airline pilots, but this was an extremely dangerous and technical dive. I wanted to make sure Todd knew when we were expected back in case anything went wrong.

I walked down the pier to the *Tranquility* and started the engines. After guiding my boat out of the slip, I waited for Stewie to come up behind me in the Zodiac. Then we headed out to the recovery site.

As soon as we arrived, Stewie idled his boat a few feet away while I anchored the *Tranquility* over the area where I'd spotted the tanks. Once I gave him the signal that my boat was secure, he putted over and tied up to the *Tranquility*'s bow, letting out a long line to ensure the two boats were in no danger of colliding while we were underwater. When he was sure his boat was secure, he unfolded the crate, secured the corners with quick release U-bolts, and attached the assembled crate to a line. He dropped the cage-like crate over the side and let it sink. Then he jumped in the water and swam the few strokes to the *Tranquility*.

Because we'd be doing technical dives using multiple mixed gases, our BCDs were equipped with back-mounted tank boards that allowed us to carry two tanks. One tank would contain Nitrox for use in the shallow parts of the dive and the other tank would contain Trimix, for use at depth. We connected a separate regulator to each tank. That way, all we'd have to do to switch from one gas to the other was put the other regulator in our mouths and breathe. I put colored socks over each of the regulator's second stages—the part that goes in the diver's mouth—so we could easily tell which was which in an emergency.

We clipped extra tanks of both gases to the side mounts of our technical BCDs, which were less bulky but also had less lift than our regular buoyancy control devices. We stuffed our voluminous BCD pockets with inflatable lift bags and small canisters of CO_2, and we each included a small spare air tank for emergencies.

Because the equipment was heavy and cumbersome, it would be easier for us to don it in the water than it would be to put it on in the boat and try to walk even the few steps to the dive platform. We dropped our BCDs and tanks over the side of the boat and clipped them to D-rings, so they'd stay put. When we were ready, we put on our masks and fins, stuck our snorkels in our mouths, and did giant stride entries off the platform.

Both Stewie and I were in our BCDs within a minute of hitting the water. We gave each other the okay sign and then, before beginning our descents, we swam on the surface to where the assembled crate floated below us at about seventy-five feet. On the way down, we breathed from the Nitrox tanks until we were just above ninety feet, then we switched regulators and began breathing from the Trimix tanks.

As soon as we reached it, we each grabbed a side of the crate and pulled it along with us as we descended down the wall toward where I had seen the tanks. The line for the crate unspooled smoothly behind us. At 150 feet I saw the florescent marker I'd tied to the reef. I knew we were close. We passed the ribbon wafting gently in the current and descended to 185 feet. The first few tanks came into view, lying in a jumbled heap on a rocky outcrop.

I continued down, swinging around to face the wall as I neared the ledge holding the tanks. I was stunned to realize that the ledge was actually the lip of a large underwater cavern. Most of the cavern had been hidden in the coral growth. All I'd seen before were the few tanks that had been visible on the ledge, but there were at least 300 tanks sitting in a messy pile further back from the ledge.

I was horrified to see how many of our tanks had gone missing when I saw the huge pile that had been abandoned. I estimated the value of these tanks at a few pennies under $100,000, a huge sum to the perennially cash-strapped RIO. We brought in plenty of money through donations, and Newton and Maddy both put in a lot of their own funds, but quality research is expensive. Every penny counted.

The theft of this many tanks made no sense to me. Why would anyone take our tanks and leave them here, deep in the ocean?

Stewie did a double take when he saw the mound of tanks and looked at me quizzically. I shrugged. At this point, I had no explanation.

I tugged the crate as close to the ledge as I could get it without endangering the delicate coral. Stewie and I each grabbed two tanks and placed them carefully in the crate, which would hold about eighty tanks. We didn't want to try to bring that many to the surface with only the two of us, especially since we were now in decompression dive mode. We wanted to minimize the time we'd have to spend hovering while our bodies off-gassed the excess nitrogen and helium we'd absorbed during our dive. We stopped loading the crate when it was about three-quarters full. We needed to head to the surface before the recommended decompression times became too lengthy.

Before we could ascend, we had to prepare the crate to surface along with us. Stewie and I each pulled lift bags from our BCD pockets and attached one to each of the four corners of the crate. Then we hovered at opposite corners, and holding the lift bags open, we released a few blasts of CO2 from the canisters we'd brought with us into each bag.

As we ascended, the CO2 would expand, increasing the buoyancy of the crate, making it nearly effortless to bring to the surface, despite the fact the crate and the tanks it held weighed more than one thousand pounds. In fact, as we got closer to the surface, our biggest problem might be keeping the crate from getting away from us and ascending rapidly due to the CO2 expansion as the ocean pressure decreased.

Stewie and I were in decompression mode because we'd been at depth for a long time loading up the crate. We hadn't expected to be under as long as we were since we'd thought we'd only be retrieving about ten to fifteen tanks. I was glad that I'd insisted we carry all the extra breathing gases to ensure we wouldn't have to worry about skimping on deco time.

Luckily the decompression stops recommended by our technical dive computers weren't too long, making our ascent time shorter than it might have if we'd stayed below even a few minutes longer. Even so, our total dive time would run to more than three hours.

At about ninety feet, we switched from breathing trimix to Nitrox. The extra oxygen in the Nitrox gas would provide a further margin of safety against decompression sickness. While we waited out our deco stop time, we carefully tilted the lift bags on each corner of the crate to release a small quantity of the CO2 to help control its buoyancy when we reached the shallower depths where the gas would expand more quickly as the pressure of the ocean above us lessened. I wondered and worried about the motive for the tank thefts the whole way up.

At ninety feet we switched over to breathing from the spare Nitrox tanks we'd dropped on a line before we began the dive. Neither Stewie nor I were low on air yet, but we thought it would be prudent to conserve the air in our tanks. You never know what can happen underwater, and the crate was heavy and unwieldy. If it somehow got away from us or tilted too far to one side, we might have to spend additional time maneuvering it back into position, and that would use up precious air.

It seemed like forever before we finally surfaced near the bow of the *Tranquility*. Stewie tied the crate to the boat's stern, then he removed his gear and attached it to the boat. He took off his fins and climbed the ladder while I stayed in the water, steadying the crate.

Within a few seconds, he passed down a BCD with a single Nitrox tank and regulator so I could stay in the water without all the cumbersome gear I was wearing. I swam to the ladder and turned my back to it before I slipped out of the technical BCD with its heavy tanks.

Stewie grabbed my gear by the lift handle on the back of the BCD and carried it over to the tank rack along the side benches. He returned quickly and began removing the tanks from the crate and stowing them aboard the *Tranquility* while I kept the crate steady. When the crate was empty, I unlatched the clips that held it together and collapsed it, making it flat once again, I attached it to a cleat on the *Tranquility*'s hull and climbed the ladder.

Stewie handed me a towel and, after drying my face, I wrapped it around my shoulders. We'd been in the water a long time, and even at a steady eighty-five degrees like the water in the Caymans, the ocean eventually leaches out your body heat.

I walked into the galley and put on a pot of coffee to warm us up. While the coffee brewed, I radioed Vincent, the *Omega*'s captain.

"Vincent, we have a problem." I explained what I had found below and my plan for retrieving the rest of the tanks. "Can you bring the *Omega* here? We'll need a couple of technical dive teams who are comfortable with decompression diving. See if you can get a few of the crew to volunteer to dive. I think Stewie and I will have to sit out the next few hours, and I'd like to finish this up today if we can."

The *Omega* was in port for routine maintenance in preparation for this summer's documentary research voyage, but Vincent agreed he'd be there as soon as he could get the ship moving.

Stewie and I sat in the galley and drank our coffee in companiable silence while we waited for the *Omega* to arrive. Although RIO's research vessel wasn't anchored far away, it was a large vessel, and it took time to get her underway. We had just taken the last sips of our second cups of coffee when we heard the thrum of her engines as she approached.

I'd given Vincent coordinates that were closer to the location of the submerged tanks than the spot where I'd anchored the *Tranquility*. He anchored near there to minimize the swim time for his dive teams.

When he'd finished with the anchoring process, Stewie and I swam to the Zodiac and used it to reach the *Omega*, towing the crate along with us.

Vincent had assembled two teams of four divers and supplied another crate. It was possible that between the teams, we'd have all the missing tanks on the surface by the end of the day.

I stood in front of the group and gave the briefing, describing the terrain, the current, the depth where the tanks were located, and the landmarks, including the florescent marker that would let them know they were in the right area. "Anything you'd like to add, Stewie?" I said when I'd finished.

"Nope. Your briefing was very thorough," he said with a smile. "Ray would have been proud."

There was a moment of silence as everyone remembered Ray Russo, my late stepfather, who had been one of the greatest and most accomplished divers in the world. Everyone at RIO had looked up to him and admired his skill. Stewie's compliment was quite a tribute in front of this audience, and it made me blush.

I waited until everyone raised their eyes to me again, and then I said, "Thank you, Stewie. That means a lot." I paused. "Okay, team. Let's go." The divers scrambled to their feet and shot to the *Omega*'s stern to gear up.

They used setups similar to the ones Stewie and I had used, with multiple tanks, mixed gases, and redundant systems. Without being asked, Stewie attached regulators to several tanks of Nitrox and then sent them down below on a tether. These safety tanks might never be used, but if any of the divers ran low on breathing gas during a decompression dive, the tanks could save their lives. He also lowered the two crates, each on its own line unspooling from a thousand yard reel.

The first team of divers stepped off the dive platform and began their descent. I watched from the edge of the platform as they neared the crate. The divers stationed themselves so there was a diver on each corner of the crate and started their trip to deep water.

As soon as the first team was out of the way, the second team entered the water, swam to their crate, and followed the others down, being careful not to get close enough to the line to get tangled. It wasn't long before both teams were out of sight, even in the clear waters that surrounded Grand Cayman.

Stewie and I went to the galley to see if we could find something to eat. It had been a long day, and diving uses a lot of calories. The *Omega*'s cook had some hot soup and grilled cheese sandwiches ready for us, and we sat at a table in the corner and chatted while we ate.

Chapter 32
Returned Tanks

I<small>T WAS</small> a couple of hours later when we finally sighted the first team making their ascents. They were still down about twenty feet, making a last safety stop before surfacing. When they'd completed the stop, they towed the crate full of tanks to the *Omega*'s port side. Vincent lowered one of the davits usually used to deploy the lifeboats, and each of the divers attached a hook to one of the crate's corners. Then they swam to the dive platform to get out of the way.

Slowly and carefully, the crate full of tanks rose until it was level with the deck. *Omega*'s crew made short work of pulling the tanks out of the crate and stacking them in the nearby dive shed. By the time they'd finished unloading the first crate, the crew with the second crate was ready to surface. The process began again.

Each crew had brought up more than 125 tanks. Coupled with the sixty-five Stewie and I had brought up, I realized my original estimate of the quantity of tanks in the pile had been darn close. Someone had jettisoned more than 300 of RIO's tanks.

I couldn't imagine what the purpose of dumping all those tanks had been, but I knew I'd have to get to the bottom of it. Whatever the reason, the vandalism couldn't be allowed to continue. The perpetrator had to be identified and stopped.

Vincent's crew had stowed all the recovered tanks, and they were ready to head back to port. I asked him to have the tanks delivered to the dive shop on RIO's grounds. Unless I was mistaken, every tank had been completely emptied of air, leaving open the possibility that water had found a way into it.

We'd need to put every tank through a complete inspection process to make sure there was no water or debris inside, and carefully dry out any tanks that had been compromised. This could entail a process called tumbling, where a quantity of small abrasive stones would be put inside the tank. After that, the tank would be placed in a machine that shook it in a prescribed pattern for a few hours while the stones buffed off any rust or foreign substances. Then we'd need to visually inspect the inside of the tank again to be sure it was pristine before we could put the tank back into service. It would take weeks to get through all these tanks, a total waste of time and resources.

I was angry. I couldn't imagine a motive for this senseless act.

Stewie walked over and put a hand on my arm. "Don't worry. You'll figure this out. In the meantime, I'll take care of getting the tanks back into shape as quickly as possible, even if I have to work late every night."

"Thanks, Stewie," I said, marveling again at how this latest stint in rehab had transformed him. He was a completely different man.

"Need anything else? If not, I'll bring the Zodiac back and then get started on those tanks. Chaun and I can put the RFID tags on the ones that don't have them yet while I'm doing the inspections. Kill two birds with one stone."

"Good idea," I said. "I'll be right behind you."

Chapter 33
A Surprise at the End of the Day

I'D TAKEN my time bringing the *Tranquility* back to the marina, and by the time I arrived, Stewie, Todd, and Chaun were already hard at work on the recovered tanks. I waved as I walked by, but I didn't stop. My job involved a lot of diving, but it also included a great deal of paperwork, especially with Maddy out of town. I envisioned a deep stack of documents requiring my review and signature to keep RIO's business running.

Ugh. I hate paperwork.

With a sigh, I sat down at my desk and glared at the expected stack of papers. If anything, the pile was even higher than I'd imagined it would be. I picked up the phone.

"June, are any of these papers routine stuff—something I can just rubber stamp? Or do they all need analysis?" Maddy's assistant knew everything about how RIO ran, and I knew she'd give me the straight scoop.

"I already sorted them for you," she said. "The stack is broken into several bunches. The ones with the yellow clips are routine. I usually sign off on those myself with Maddy's initials. I didn't know if you wanted to do things that way…"

"Yes," I said. "I want you to do that. What else?"

She laughed. "The ones with the blue clips would have gone to

Liam for analysis and approval. I didn't know if you were ready to let Benjamin sign off on those on his own yet…"

I thought about my hatred for spreadsheets and how easy Benjamin made them look. "Fully ready," I said. "Benjamin will have to sink or swim."

"Oh, I'm pretty sure he'll be just fine. I didn't want to overstep though because he's still so new."

"Never be afraid you're overstepping with me. I trust you, and I need your help," I said.

Her voice held a hint of the pleasure my words had given her when she said, "Given all that, the only things left for you to review are the papers on the bottom of the pile. I'll be right over to get the projects you're delegating."

True to her word, June was in my office almost instantly. "I'll drop Benjamin's assignments in his office, and I'll take mine. Do you need anything else?"

"No, I'm all set. Thanks for the help." I smiled at the mere handful of papers awaiting my approval.

Now I understood how Maddy managed to run RIO, network for her near-constant fundraising, and still stay on top of her own research. When she returned from New York, I planned to talk to her about getting an assistant of my own. I needed someone like June to keep me organized.

I picked up the first sheet, which was an approval form to transfer Todd's salary expense for the hours he'd worked in the dive shop from Vincent's department to mine. No problem. I initialed the form and set it aside just as my phone rang. I answered. "Fin Fleming here."

A female voice said, "Dr. Fleming, this is Genevra Blackthorne with Quokka Media. I understand you're no longer working for *Your World*. Is that correct?"

I'd never heard of Quokka Media, and I was surprised that the news about my leaving *Your World* was out already. Both of those facts seemed like good reasons not to provide any information to this person I didn't know. "Why do you ask?" I said.

"The CEO of Quokka is familiar with your work, and he's authorized me to offer you a job as managing editor of our newest title, *Ecosphere*. You'd have complete control over your own content calendar, a staff of assistant editors, and an unlimited travel budget. You can showcase those parts of the world that most interest you. And it comes with a substantial pay raise over what you were earning at *Your World*. How does that sound to you?"

"It sounds too good to be true. Which is why I don't believe it's a real offer. But either way, I'm not interested. I have enough on my plate here at RIO."

"We understand that. We would do everything in our power to minimize the demands on your time while still making good use of your incredible talent. We're all excited about the possibility of you joining us."

"Control your excitement. I won't be joining."

"Our CEO will be very disappointed," she said. "What can we offer you to make you reconsider?"

I thought a moment. "This whole thing sounds like something Alec Stone would cook up to try to catch me violating my non-compete. Is that weasel behind this?"

She stifled a giggle. "No, I assure you this has nothing to do with Alec Stone. And actually, Quokka has already bought out your non-compete. There's no concern there."

"How dare you? I haven't agreed to your offer."

"Oh, don't worry," she said. "No strings attached. We simply didn't like seeing a person with your talent shackled by an unfair contract. You're free to sell your photography and to work wherever you want, although we certainly hope you'll decide to join us."

"Don't count on it," I said as I hung up.

The phone rang again almost immediately. This time it was Benjamin.

"The salvage reward just hit the bank account. Can I come to your office to discuss how it should be distributed?"

"Sure thing," I said. "Maybe now we have a chance of getting Theresa and Gus back."

But I was speaking to an empty line, because when I looked up, Benjamin was standing in the door to my office. "This is too important to delay even a minute," he said.

"Agreed. What have you got?"

I whistled when Benjamin told me we'd gotten the full amount of the reward. We'd originally thought we were negotiating our salvage fee with the government of Belize, but it turned out that it was actually a syndicate composed of several governments who each had a vested interest in the treasure.

And since the treasure's owners had been dragging their feet on paying the reward, we'd been afraid they would try to renegotiate our share of the salvage value. Which would have left Gus in a very tight spot.

"The agreement was simple," I told Benjamin. "The principals in the expedition each got an equal share. Maddy, Newton, Oliver, Gus, Stewie, Liam, and me. Gus and Stewie would get their shares directly. Everyone else agreed to sign their share over to Stefan Gibb and his brothers, Noah, and Austin, as restitution for Dylan Gibb's death during the trek. I think there's a trust or foundation already set up for each of them."

"Got it," he said. "I'll get the wire transfers out today. Do you know where I can reach Stefan Gibb and his brothers to get their account info?"

"Not sure about the two younger brothers, but you can reach Stefan at Nelson's. He recently bought the place. He should know how to reach the other two."

My phone rang. Benjamin left.

"Hello," I said warily. I was afraid it would be Genevra, the woman from Quokka again.

"Hi, Fin. It's me, Carl Duchette. I heard you turned down an offer from Quokka. I think you should reconsider."

I sighed. "Doesn't the nature periodical industry have anything to do besides worry about my career? And why don't you take the job? You'd be much better at it than me."

He laughed. "I already have a new job. Today's my first day as managing editor-in-chief for Quokka. I'm excited, and *Ecosphere* will be our flagship title. Please say you'll join."

"If Genevra had said you were involved right up front, maybe my answer would have been different."

"Sorry. It just became official a half hour ago, and then I was in a meeting with the board of directors."

"Are you the mysterious CEO Genevra mentioned?"

"Um, no. I'll be working with him. He's terrific. You'll like it here. Please say you'll join us?"

"This mysterious CEO isn't my father, is he?"

"Newton? Oh gosh, no. Definitely not Newton. But like your father, he has only your best interests at heart." Carl sounded flustered.

"What's this CEO's name again?" I asked.

"Oops. My other line is ringing. Let's talk soon. Meanwhile, I'll ask Genevra to call you again with more details." He hung up.

I leaned back in my chair. This was turning out to be a good day. It was true. Both good and bad things seemed to come in threes. We'd recovered the missing tanks, received the long delayed reward, and I'd been offered a flattering new career opportunity.

I had no intention of taking the job with Quokka, but it was nice to be wanted. Meanwhile, I decided to go see Dane and Angel, and see if we'd heard from the kidnapper. If he really was a RIO insider, it wouldn't be long before he heard that we'd received the salvage fee we'd been waiting for.

Chapter 34
A Quick Return

As soon as I walked into Newton's condo, I could tell the mood was black. Dane was staring out the window, every line of his body showing he felt defeated. Roland was on the couch, head in hands. Morey, the third cop, stared at his computer screen, his hands hanging loosely by his side. "No news yet?" I asked.

Dane turned. "Nothing. I'm afraid…" He stopped, before saying the dreaded words out loud.

"Well, I have some good news. We got the salvage reward money today. We can pay off the kidnapper as soon as we hear from him. Benjamin is ready to make the payment. It won't take more than a minute once we have the account number."

Dane nodded slowly, showing his weariness.

"When was the last time you guys ate? Or slept?" I asked.

They responded with blank stares, and I realized they couldn't remember. I knew that since he was out of town, the contents of Newton's kitchen offered slim pickings. I decided to call out for food to keep the troops going.

They were too drained for me to expect them to agree on a restaurant or a menu. I called the concierge at the Ritz.

"Can you have the kitchen rustle up four or five of everything on the menu, including soup and dessert? Urns of coffee and tea with cream, sugar, lemon. An assortment of sodas and bottled water. Deliver it all to Newton's condo ASAP?"

She didn't even pause. "Of course, Dr. Fleming. It'll be there in under an hour. Maybe a little longer of you want souffles…"

The team here needed food, and they needed it now. "Skip the souffles, and anything else that will take a long time. Speed is the keyword here."

"You got it," she said. "Shall I charge the order directly to Mr. Fleming?"

I agreed that Newton would foot the bill. Then I sat next to Eugene. He was barely keeping his eyes open.

"Why don't you lie down here on the couch? I'll wake you if anything happens," I said.

It was a sign of his bone-deep fatigue that he did it without protest. Within a few minutes, he was snoring softly.

I walked over to Dane. "How can I help?"

Before he could answer, the front door of the condo banged open. Newton, Maddy, and Oliver stood silhouetted in the light from the hallway.

"We're back," Oliver said. "At least for a few days." He dropped his suitcase next to the door and hurried over to give me a hug.

Newton and Maddy entered close behind him and stood next to me waiting their turn for a hug.

I was happy to see my family, especially with all the current troubles at RIO, but surprised at their change in plan. "Why are you back this soon? I thought you'd all have to stay in New York for weeks, if not months."

"We had permission from the judge to come back for a few days. Special circumstances." Newton brushed his hair back from his forehead, and I noticed the brand new platinum ring on the fourth finger of his left hand.

A quick glance at Maddy's hand showed a matching ring. I looked up to catch Oliver's eye, giving him a questioning look.

He shrugged.

Dane must have seen the rings, too, because I heard him suck in a breath, although he said nothing. He stood up straighter and looked away.

The doorbell rang. "Who's that?" Newton said.

"I ordered some food for the team. They haven't eaten for a while, and they were hungry. But don't worry, I must have had a premonition you were coming home tonight because I ordered plenty for everybody." I walked over and let the crew from the Ritz wheel in their carts of food and drink.

Maddy smiled. "Thank you. I'll eat in a few minutes. I want to say hello to Angel first." She took off down the hall to see the baby.

"Dane, you and your men help yourselves. There's plenty to go around." I linked arms with Oliver. "We need to catch up," I told him.

We walked down the hall to Newton's study. "What's going on?" I said when I'd shut the mahogany double doors behind us. "Are those wedding rings?"

He nodded. "Yes, they are. The lawyers told them the adoption process would go more smoothly if they were married. So, they got married. Then the judge let them come here for their "honeymoon." We're only here for a few days. We have to be back in New York soon." He bit his lip. "I'm sorry, Fin. It must have been a shock."

"Probably more shocking to Dane than to me," I said. "Maddy and Newton have always been close, but I didn't think there was anything more than friendship and respect between them."

"I think you're right about that. I expect they will divorce again as soon as the adoption becomes final. It's just that they're both so busy they wanted to take the shortcut when it was offered." He bit his lip. "I hope you're okay with it. I know children of divorce often hope their parents will get back together, but I don't think this is the way the fantasy usually looks."

"You've got that right," I said.

When Oliver and I returned to the great room, Dane was sitting on the piano bench eating a turkey club sandwich. You'd have thought he didn't have a care in the world. Newton walked in right behind us, carrying Angel, and Maddy trailed behind him.

Newton stuck out his tongue at Angel. and she laughed like it was the funniest thing in the world. Because it was Newton, it kind of was.

"Dane, what's the latest on the kidnapping?" he said while bouncing Angel in his arms.

"No news. We haven't heard from the kidnapper in more than a day. We finally have the salvage reward money ready to go, but there hasn't been any more communication letting us know how to pay the ransom." Dane folded his arms across his chest, daring Newton to criticize him or his team.

"Fin, what have you seen? Noticed anything unusual?" he asked, turning to me.

No, just my parents getting remarried after more than twenty-five years apart, I thought.

I shook my head and watched Maddy join Dane on the piano bench. She put her hand on his arm, spoke a few words in his ear, and then they stood and left the room. Newton watched them go, but he said nothing.

"My turn," Oliver said, pulling Angel from Newton's arms. He blew kisses into the crook of her neck, and she laughed again.

I couldn't stand it anymore. My family was all caught up in romance, and my best-friend and her husband were missing. I knew there was nothing they could do about that. Bad enough they'd decided to rush the adoption.

Okay, I understood their fears of not being able to care for Oliver in an emergency. That made sense, but still, it seemed callous to be running off to get married in the middle of a life-or-death crisis. And here was my father, kissing a baby like nothing was wrong, when Gus and Theresa were still missing. Kissing a baby when he hadn't even bothered to see his own daughter for twenty-five years.

As soon as that thought entered my brain, I realized I was jealous of the way Newton doted on Angel. She was so sweet, and her parents were missing—she deserved as much loving as we could give her. I was ashamed of my jealousy, but that didn't make it go away. I needed to be alone to think this through.

"Goodnight," I said before walking down the hall to my room.

Chapter 35
A Cage

I WROTE in my journal for a while about my mixed feelings for Newton. I'd come to love him, and we were friends, but I rarely felt like he was my father. I also knew I couldn't go back and rewrite the past, and Newton hadn't neglected me because he didn't care. It was more because he was clueless.

Well, clueless or not, I loved my father, and I knew he loved me. There was no reason for me to feel jealous because he'd matured enough to love and nurture a baby who wasn't me. He'd always done the best he could. I resolved to be content with our growing friendship.

Now that I'd worked out my feelings on paper, I could finally go to sleep. I slept soundly for several hours, until I woke up unexpectedly and remembered the glint of metallic gold I'd seen on my solo dive when I discovered the location of the stolen tanks. I'd meant to investigate it when Stewie and I were retrieving the tanks, but I'd been so overwhelmed by the sheer number of tanks we had to recover that I forgot to check it out.

Even if I'd remembered the quick glimpse of whatever it was, I wouldn't have been able to investigate during the recovery dive. We'd barely made it back with enough breathing gas as it was, because of the hard work of loading the tanks and the long decompression requirements.

It wasn't that I thought the gold I glimpsed was treasure of some kind—there was something about the unusual color that said it might be worth investigating. It could be an artifact from a long ago wreck or it could be a piece of trash someone had dumped illegally. But whatever it was, something about it kept calling to me. I resolved to get up early and do a quick dive to check it out.

But I still couldn't sleep. A quick glance at my nightstand told me it was 3:30 a.m., and I knew I'd never get back to sleep. I decided to get up and make that dive that had been worrying me. Then it would be over and done with, and I'd still be on time for work. Sounded like a good plan.

I crept out of my room and down the hall. Morey was asleep in the big leather Eames chair, and Roland was sacked out on the couch. There was no sign that Dane or anyone else was in the condo, but someone had cleared away all the leftover food from the delivery last night. My money was on Oliver.

I drove the short distance to RIO and stopped by the dive shop to pick up tanks. We stored all the Trimix and Nitrox tanks in a small, locked room in the back so untrained divers wouldn't be tempted to dive beyond their experience. Luckily, I knew where we kept the key.

I pulled out four tanks each of Trimix and Nitrox, even though I was diving alone and only planning a single dive. The Nitrox and Trimix tanks were easy to tell apart from each other and from tanks filled with regular air because each of the mixed gas tanks had a brightly colored stencil that identified the gas inside.

Since the breathing gas was blended by hand, I tested the mix in each tank with a small portable gas analyzer. The chances of finding a problem with the blends was slim, but even a few percentage points of variation could prove fatal. I would be breaking enough safety rules on this dive without breaking that one too.

I grabbed a powerful underwater flashlight off the shelf to supplement the ones I kept on the *Tranquility*. I picked up a pony bottle—a small tank slightly bigger than the spare air canisters Benjamin and I had used when we rescued Chaun. It would give me a few extra minutes of air if I ran into trouble on the upcoming dive. Then I left a note for Stewie asking him to charge the items to my account. I included information about where I'd be diving and when I expected to return—just in case.

I carried the tanks down the pier to my boat. When everything was put away, I cast off and headed out to sea. The sun still wasn't up by the time I anchored over a spot I thought would be very close to the golden gleam I'd seen.

I dropped two of the Nitrox tanks over the edge on long lines as safety gas, set up my technical dive rig with a tank of Nitrox and a tank of Trimix with separate regulators, clipped an additional tank of each to the d-rings and carried the heavy assembly to the dive platform. With a short line, I attached it to a cleat on the hull and dropped it into the water.

I put on my mask and fins, put my pony bottle on a free D-ring, and holding tight to my new flashlight, I stepped into the inky ocean. My gear was only a few swim strokes away, so I was there quickly to don my BCD. I put the regulator connected to the Nitrox in my mouth and sank beneath the waves.

The water was dark enough that the only visibility came from the beam of my flashlight. I moved the beam back in forth in front of me and also below me. Every few feet, I checked my depth to make sure I didn't inadvertently go below the safe range for Nitrox before I switched over.

At eighty-five feet, I made the switch between gases by swapping the regulator I was breathing from and continued my descent. At one hundred eighty-five feet, the beam of my flashlight picked up the florescent marker I'd left, pointing the way to the cavern where the stolen tanks had been.

I swam further along the wall, past the cavern, and dropped another twelve feet, because the metallic glint I'd seen had been lower than the tanks. I played my flashlight along the wall, up and down, as I swam slowly ahead.

The wall curved out a little bit because of a large chunk of rock a few feet ahead. I followed the curve. As soon as I'd rounded the rock, I caught the gleam of gold color ahead at about two hundred feet. I quickly swam to it.

As I approached, I saw that the gold metal was more likely brass. The object was about four feet square, made of separate bars shaped into a crosshatch pattern. At first, I thought it must have been part of a wreck, but there'd been no news of a modern wreck in this area and the grid was too new to have been underwater more than a few days. On closer inspection, I realized it was affixed directly to the wall.

Curious about its purpose, I examined the edges of the grid. Someone had driven eye bolts into the rock at regular intervals to attach the grid plate to the rock. I wondered briefly if someone had been using a passage from the surface to transport illegal substances or polluting chemicals.

The top of the grid was locked onto to one of the eye bolts with a large padlock. I examined the lock and shook it, but there was no hope of opening it or shaking it free. I swam down the side and realized that the edges of the grid had been attached to the eyebolts with heavy plastic zip ties. Whatever was on the other side of this brass plate wasn't meant to stay there permanently.

As soon as I realized that this makeshift cage was temporary, I knew. Cold dread filled my soul. Was it possible?

I don't like carrying the traditional dive knife, but it's important to have a cutting implement with you in case of underwater entanglements. I fumbled in the pocket of my BCD for my scuba scissors and removed the protective sheath from the tips.

The zip ties were made from tough, heavy plastic, and I needed both my hands to use the scissors on them. I attached my flashlight to my BCD, allowing me to use both hands to attack the ties more effectively. It was still slow going. Cutting through the ties was more like sawing or gnawing at the plastic than cutting in a single snip

It took a minute for the first tie to snap apart.

Another minute for the next.

And the next.

I kept going around the grid until I had removed enough of the durable ties to open the cage door. Swallowing my fear, I swam inside, aiming the beam of my flashlight straight ahead.

The passageway was narrow, but wide enough for two divers to swim abreast without getting caught on any crags or rocks. I was betting that the passage led to a wider cavern.

There were a few lumps of a waxy looking substance I couldn't identify strewn at intervals along the way. I picked one up and stuck it in my BCD pocket to examine later. Luckily, other than those lumps, the bottom and sides of the passage were free of silt and debris, as though they'd been swept clean. Otherwise, it would have been too dangerous for me to proceed without a safety line. As it was, my heart was pounding with fear of what I might find as I continued my swim.

After a few feet of staying level at the same depth, the passage curved upward. I continued swimming, shining my light along the sides of the passage to make sure there were no branching tunnels that might prove confusing on my exit. Confusion at this depth meant death.

When the passage had risen about twenty feet, it began to widen as I'd suspected it might. And then my head broke through the surface, and I was in a pitch dark underwater cavern with a pocket of air. I pointed my light around the area.

"Fin, is that you? I knew you'd come," a familiar voice shouted. "Help me get Gus out of here!"

I splayed the light in the direction of her shout and saw Theresa sitting on a narrow ledge, panting with excitement. Gus was lying beside her, his head on her leg. Even in the dim light I could tell he was unconscious.

Oh my God. I'd found them. It was pure dumb luck that I'd seen that metallic glint. Even luckier that I'd been unable to sleep last night so I'd decided to investigate. Thank God for my luck.

I had no idea how they'd gotten down here, but I knew only an evil person would have done this to them. To anyone, really. And I knew it would take every ounce of skill I had along with a lot of resources to get them safely to the surface.

I looked around to see what resources I had at my disposal.

A large yellow tent supported by steel bars was floating atop the water nearby. I recognized it as one of the experimental portable diving bells Doc had recently received. I could see the wrinkles in the tent fabric that told me the air inside was losing the battle against the sea.

While I watched, a clump of something fell from the roof of the cavern into the water. I didn't get a good look at it before it floated away, but I assumed it was the same substance as whatever I'd just put in my pocket. I looked at the roof of the cave. It was lined with the substance, but there were holes in several locations that said whatever it was, it was losing the war against the relentless ocean.

I could hear Theresa's raspy breathing. She was panting with fear and excitement.

I spit out my regulator mouthpiece and pushed my mask down below my chin. "Stay calm, Theresa. We don't want to use up what air there is left in here."

"I know. I've been very careful, but he hasn't brought fresh air for a long time now." She coughed as though her lungs had suddenly realized there wasn't much oxygen left in the small gas pocket that kept the cavern free of sea water. "Aren't you going to get us out of here?" Her voice cracked.

"Yes. Yes, I am definitely going to get you out of here. But you have to know it's not as easy as simply swimming out. You're down pretty deep, and you've been here for a couple of days. You've absorbed a lot of nitrogen. We'll need to do decompression stops to get you to the surface. And we've got Gus to consider. He's unconscious and he isn't supposed to be diving anyway because of his heart. We'll want to get Doc involved, and we'll need to take extra care to get him out of here safely. Let me think for a minute," I said.

Theresa bit her lip, but she kept quiet, letting me think.

I ran through about a hundred possible rescue scenarios before I realized there was only one that would work, even though it was extremely risky for me. Theresa wasn't going to like it either, but I knew she'd agree for her husband's sake.

"I'm going to leave you here while I go to get more help. Like I said, I need Doc to help me with this. She'll know the best way to get Gus to the surface without risking his life. And I need more tanks for you. There's not enough gas left in my tanks to get all three of us out of here safely."

Theresa started to cry. "Please don't leave me here. I'm scared. What if you never come back?"

"Don't cry. It uses too much oxygen. And I will come back. I swear I will save you both. I won't lose you or Gus. You have my word on that."

She stopped crying and gave a little nod. "What should I do while you're gone?"

"Keep doing what you've been doing. Sit quietly and take care of Gus. I'll leave you my tanks as an emergency air supply, but I don't think you'll need them. You can have my light too." I kicked over to her and held out the heavy underwater flashlight. "If it starts to get hot, hold it underwater until it cools down."

She took the flashlight and placed it carefully on the other side of the ledge, away from Gus. "What will you do without a light or air tanks?" she asked. "I know you're a superstar under water but even you have to breathe."

I cut short my laugh because I didn't want to waste the oxygen. "I have a spare light in my pocket and a pony bottle to breathe from. It'll get me to the surface if I'm careful," I said. I didn't mention the risk of decompression sickness or pneumothorax from ascending too quickly. She didn't need any more worries. And I had an emergency beacon in my BCD, and another one on the *Tranquility* in case I ran into problems.

I slipped out of my BCD and together, Theresa and I managed to get it up on the ledge beside her. "I'll be back," I said, imitating Arnold Schwarzenegger.

I heard her laugh just before I ducked under the water to swim back down the passage.

Chapter 36
Rescue

When I emerged from the passage, the vast darkness around me was broken only by the feeble beam of my backup flashlight. Its tiny ray of light was no match for the ocean depths.

But the ocean is my happy place, and I wasn't frightened of the dark. I flipped up the regulator mouthpiece on the pony bottle and stuck it in my mouth for a sip of air. I didn't take in much. I wanted to save it in case I needed it later, plus oxygen is toxic at this depth. I wanted to minimize my use of regular air until I was out of the danger zone. I gave a mighty kick and rose through the darkness.

I should have been making decompression stops, but I didn't. First, because I wanted to get the rescue effort organized as quickly as possible.

And second, because I didn't have enough air in my pony bottle to stop anyway.

When I passed the florescent marker I'd placed, I veered off in the direction where I knew I'd left the *Tranquility*. I rose straight up the wall, keeping to a consistent pace trying to move quickly but without outpacing my smallest bubbles. Going faster than the smallest bubbles was a direct path to decompression sickness.

Soon enough I reached the edge of the wall, and I swam atop the reef toward the *Tranquility*'s anchor line. The Nitrox tanks were floating near the line, and I stopped for two minutes of steadily breathing Nitrox in hopes it would be enough to stave off the effects of all the nitrogen I'd absorbed. When I was so tense I couldn't wait any longer, I swam the rest of the way to the surface and climbed the ladder to *Tranquility*'s deck. The sun was just breaking over the horizon.

I dropped the pony bottle to the deck and ran into the cabin, grabbing the radio to call RIO.

Stewie, who was manning the dive shop, answered the call. "Good morning, Fin. You're up early."

"I've found Gus and Theresa. Gus is unconscious. I need Doc to figure out how to get them safely to the surface. The diving bell. The habitat. The ROV. Whatever it takes. She'll know best."

"Where are they? Why do you need that stuff?" he asked.

"They're being held underwater in a cave. Close to 200 feet down. They've been there…"

Someone pulled the radio from my hand and ripped the cord out of the console. I watched it plunk into the water a few feet away from the hull. I whipped around to see Oliver's friend Todd standing behind me. Only then did I notice the black RIO Zodiac tied to *Tranquility*'s bow.

"You?" I said.

He smiled, the same sweet accommodating smile as always. "Yep. Me," he agreed.

"But why? Gus and Theresa never did anything to you, did they?"

"No," he said. "They didn't. And as far as I can tell, they never did anything much for you or RIO either, but Gus gets hurt and he lucks into a great job with your father's company. He stays safe at home during the treasure expedition, but you cut him in for an equal share of the reward money. I don't get it."

"He was partners with Ray…"

"Do you know how sick I am of hearing about the great Ray Russo? He was a guy like anyone else, not a saint. And he wasn't even that good a diver. I mean, he died while diving, right? But anyone who was friends with him gets treated like gold, while the rest of us get nothing."

"I think you're being unfair," I said. "We've always treated you well. We rely on you. We pay you…"

"Nowhere near what you're paying Gus." He glared at me. "I acted as body double for Oliver on the expedition. I fill in at the dive shop whenever you need me. I work like a dog. It's always 'call Todd' if you need something. But when it comes to getting a big payoff, you're all like 'Todd who?' Well, I'm sick of it. So, this is how I'll get my payoff."

"Not without my signature you won't," I said.

He scowled at me. "I didn't want to play it this way, but I guess I have to. Gear up."

"What for?"

"You'll be joining Gus and Theresa in their new home. But don't worry. You won't be together long enough to get sick of each other's company."

"So, you'll be setting them free?"

"Nope. They'll stay down there until they run out of air. And you'll be right there with them. Thinking of how it's all your fault." He grabbed my arm. "Gear up."

I jerked my arm out of his grasp and pushed. He stumbled back a few steps, before the backs of his knees bumped into the bench that lined the hull, forcing him into a sit. I bolted to the ladder of the flying bridge.

I'd only climbed the first two rungs when he grabbed the strap of my bathing suit and pulled me off the ladder. The strap was sturdy and stretchy, so it didn't rip, but it dug painfully into my shoulder. I tumbled to the floor.

Todd rushed at me, a wicked looking dive knife in his hand.

I let him get close, almost close enough to cut me with the knife, then I kicked him as hard as I could between his legs. He doubled over and dropped the knife.

I stood up, but when I reached for the knife, Todd charged, and we both tumbled over the side of the boat into the water. I had less than a half second to gasp in a breath of air before I was under water.

Todd was above me, holding onto my shoulders and pushing me down deeper.

Clearly, he didn't know me.

The ocean was my friend.

Instead of struggling to reach the surface as he'd expected. I wrapped my hands around his wrists and pulled him down with me. I swam down as hard as I could, dragging him along.

Down and down.

We kept going.

We passed the drop-off where the reef became a wall.

Fifty, sixty feet under, and still I pulled him down.

Todd began to struggle, trying to escape my grasp, but he couldn't get free of my grip.

Seventy feet, and we were still locked in a struggle.

Eighty.

Ninety.

I estimated we were at one hundred feet when I let him go.

I knew I could get to the surface.

He could have too, but he started to panic.

Rather than make a smooth swim to the surface, he was flailing around out over the blue.

I began my own ascent.

Todd kept flailing.

I debated going to his rescue. He was only down this far because I'd dragged him with me, but I'd only dragged him to throw him off guard because he was trying to kill me. And he'd kidnapped Gus and Theresa and held them captive under deplorable conditions. There was a good chance that he'd panic and drown us both if I tried to save him.

And then I remembered all the times he'd willingly helped out at RIO, going above the minimum requirements of his role. His friendship with Oliver. His cheerful smile no matter what I asked him to do.

I started swimming toward him. I'd do my best to bring him to the surface. After that, it would be up to the law to punish him.

And then it was out of my hands. From the deep blue, the huge silky shark we'd seen the first time I dove with Benjamin approached and circled slowly around Todd.

Classic silky attack behavior.

Todd saw the shark and began to panic even more. Instead of holding still, he was waving his arms in a shooing motion, pushing his hands right into the shark's face.

Many sharks are attracted by random motion, because it mimics the death throes of a fish struggling for its life. The best thing Todd could have done would be to hold still, or swim gently and evenly toward the surface.

Instead, he kicked out with his right foot, missing the shark by a few inches. Then he made a fist and punched the shark in his snout. The silky butted Todd's belly.

It might have been a warning shot or an exploratory poke.

Still Todd didn't head for the surface. He kept flailing, inflaming the shark.

The shark opened its massive jaws and lunged hard, ramming into Todd's shoulder.

There was nothing I could do to stop what was about to happen.

The silky made another circle, his mouth open.

Another circle. Mouth now gaping wide.

I looked away.

The water below me turned a misty brown as I reached the lip of the reef. I was too far down for the true color to show because the water absorbed colors at depth.

But I knew the cloud was red.

Blood red.

I glided across and up, barely moving my toes for propulsion, heading toward the *Tranquility*'s anchor line. I stayed close to the line as I rose, keeping an eye out for the shark, but he was still busy with Todd.

I climbed the ladder and threw myself onto *Tranquility*'s deck, but I didn't have time to rest. I still needed to muster the rescue team for Gus and Theresa.

I climbed up to the flying bridge and thumbed on the backup radio.

"What happened?" Stewie said when he answered.

"Long story. Just get Doc and the *Omega* out to where we recovered the tanks the other day. Make sure she knows she needs a way to get Gus and Theresa to the surface without risking decompression sickness. Maybe those new portable diving bells she was so excited about the other day would work."

"She'll need something. They've been held underwater at around two hundred feet all this time. And please call Maddy and Newton if you would. And DS Scott needs to know. Over." I dropped the mic and put my head in my hands, sobbing.

Chapter 37
An Amazing Invention

I WAS STILL in shock when I heard the thrum of *Omega*'s engines as the ship approached. Vincent anchored her in the same spot he'd used the last time. As soon as the ship was secure, one of the lifeboats dropped down and made its way toward the *Tranquility*. I could see Doc standing in the bow, peering across the water at me, one hand shading her eyes and the other steering the boat.

Less than a minute later, Maddy's boat, the *Sea Princess* pulled up next to me and dropped anchor. Behind her came Stewie, with Benjamin, Dane Scott, and Chaun in one of RIO's black Zodiac rental boats.

I wiped the tears from my face and eyes and climbed down from the flying bridge to join my parents on Maddy's boat. She threw a line to me, and I wrapped it on one of the cleats embedded in the hull. I dropped a fender over the side to keep the boats from banging into each other, then I pulled hard on the line, and the two boats came together. I stepped up on the gunwale and dropped onto the deck of *Sea Princess*. I gave Oliver and my parents each a hug.

Oliver and Newton both looked at my face closely, and I knew they could tell I'd been crying. Well, I was only going to tell the story once, and then they'd know why.

Meanwhile, Stewie had tied up to the stern, and he and his passengers all lined up to step from the Zodiac onto the *Princess*'s dive platform. Stewie, Benjamin, and Dane came over without mishap. Chaun tripped and fell into the water. He sank under a few feet, then he bobbed back to the surface.

"Get him out of there. There's a biter nearby," I shouted, lurching across the deck to try to reach him.

Stewie jumped to the platform and grabbed Chaun's hand, pulling him onto the dive platform. Maddy, Stewie, and I all noticed the shark fin cresting the waves nearby. Luckily, Chaun didn't notice, or he might have had a meltdown.

Doc tied her boat to the *Sea Princess*'s other side and hopped nimbly aboard. "I hear congratulations are in order." She lifted Maddy's hand to check out the new ring.

Maddy blushed and looked over at Dane.

He turned away, keeping his face expressionless.

Stewie hadn't heard yet that my parents had remarried, and his face broke into a huge smile at the news. He shook Newton's hand. "Congratulations, Newton. You've got yourself a real prize there."

"Don't I know it," said Newton. "Maybe this time I can hold on to her."

Dane climbed up the ladder to the flying bridge.

I was confused. I'd thought my parents had only remarried to expedite Oliver's adoption, but Newton sounded like he was taking the whole marriage thing seriously. I knew he still loved Maddy, and had loved her all along, the entire time she'd been married to Ray.

In fact, I suspected the reason he'd stayed away from me while I was growing up was not to spare me the pain and confusion of his constant comings and goings for his business as Maddy had told me. No, I believed he'd stayed away to spare himself the pain of seeing Maddy happy with another man.

But we could sort that out later.

Right now, we had to rescue Gus and Theresa.

We all sat on the benches that lined the *Sea Princess*'s gunwales while I divulged how Todd had kidnapped Gus and Theresa, and had locked them in a cavern, two hundred feet below the surface.

I described how he'd kept them alive by replenishing their air supply with gas from our missing tanks. I realized then that if he'd returned the tanks instead of leaving them on the ledge, I might never have come back to the area until it was too late to save Gus and Theresa.

I told Chaun that I'd only seen the glint of the brass cage door because of his crazy dive, so their rescue was partly because of him.

"Although don't ever, ever do that again," I said.

I expressed my sadness and regret that I hadn't checked out the golden glint while Stewie and I had first gone to recover the missing tanks. If I had, Gus and Theresa would be safe by now.

Oliver looked around. "Don't beat yourself up. You're the only one in the world that would have—or could have—found them. You're a hero all over again. But where is Todd? Do you have him tied up somewhere on *Tranquility*?"

I felt my blood go cold when I remembered what had happened to Todd. I sobbed, then cleared my throat. "Todd is dead. A silky shark attacked him. Neither of us were wearing tanks, and he kept aggravating the shark. I couldn't have saved him."

Oliver looked shocked. He and Todd had been friends and they worked closely together in the dive shop. "What were you doing free diving?" he asked.

I explained about the fight, and how I'd pulled Todd down with me. "He was trying to drown me, holding me under. I thought heading deeper would surprise him into letting go, but he hung on. If I had it to do over, I wouldn't have."

"Wouldn't have what?" Newton said. "Defended yourself from a man intent on killing you? Used your skills to save your own life? Don't ever say that. You did the right thing."

"I agree," said Dane. "You did what had to be done to save your own life, and it's not like you called the shark over to finish him off. You did nothing wrong."

Benjamin had been sitting on the opposite side of the boat, but he got up and sat beside me. He rubbed my arm. "Thank God, you made it out safely." He took off his jacket and draped it over my shoulders, and it wasn't until I felt his residual warmth in the fabric that I realized how cold I was.

I smiled my thanks at him before speaking. "It's not insurmountable, but it's an added complication in the rescue plan. As it is, it's gonna be tough for way too many reasons. Gus has been unconscious all this time. Theresa has never been diving. They've been under for several days now, at around two hundred feet, breathing regular air Todd released from the tanks. They're going to have to decompress for a long time, and there's a shark in the neighborhood. And Gus's heart."

Maddy put her hand on my shoulder. "We'll figure it out. Doc knows her dive medicine, and we've got all of RIO's skills and resources to help us with the plan. Relax. Breathe like you're underwater. You'll think more clearly."

I took two long slow breaths and felt no better, but I smiled at Maddy anyway. "Let's get started on the plan."

Doc stepped forward. "I brought the other two inflatable dive bells we can use to get Gus and Theresa to the surface. I had three, but I guess Todd helped himself to one of them. They're supposed to work really well. When I told my friend I'd put them through a stress test for him, I didn't realize exactly how much stress we'd be under, but we can even do the necessary decompression stops in them. We can pump air to the dive bells from the *Omega*'s compressor."

"An inflatable dive bell?" Oliver said. "Is there really such a thing?"

"Yes, there is. The patent was only recently issued, and the ones I have are prototypes. I offered to test them for one of the inventors—a friend of mine from college. I don't think he expected me to put them through such a tough test drive though." She grinned.

"What about the shark? I asked. "You don't want to be down there in a floating plastic bag with a curious shark around."

"Easy, peasy," she said. "We'll deploy them inside the *Omega*'s shark cages. Really. We have everything we need."

"I'll go to take care of Gus and to enforce the deco protocol. Fin, I want you down there with me..."

"I've already been down there once today. Aren't you worried about decompression sickness?"

"I am," she said. "That's why I want you with me. You can decompress right now in the *Omega*'s chamber, or you can dive and decompress with Gus and Theresa in the bell. Either way, all three of you will be spending a day in RIO's chamber when we get back to be on the safe side. And you know, compared to the unit on *Omega*, the one in RIO's infirmary is positively spacious."

I remembered my last sojourn in RIO's recompression chamber with Benjamin and Chaun. It was crowded and lacked privacy, but Doc was right. *Omega*'s chamber was designed for a single person, and it was cramped even for one. Comparatively speaking, RIO's chamber was a palace.

"I choose the chamber at RIO. I'll go with you. Now can we stop talking and get moving?"

"I want to send someone down with tanks, to make sure we keep them breathing until we can launch the rescue. Stewie can go. They should be breathing Trimix, not air from regular tanks," she said

"Um, Doc. Unhappy shark in the area, remember?" I asked.

"Stewie will be in a cage. He should be fine. The only question is should he come back in case we need someone to do another technical dive, or should he stay there to keep Theresa calm? If he stays, he'll increase the air consumption…" she rolled her eyes toward the sky, performing calculations on an imaginary whiteboard she visualized.

Maddy and I had seen her do this before—performing complex calculations and applying multi-level algorithms in her head—stuff that the rest of us struggled with even with a computer in front of us.

The RIO team knew enough to keep silent while she worked her magic, but Chaun started chattering nervously. "There was a shark…"

"Hush, Chaun," I said. "Let her think."

"But I was in the water with a shark. A maneater," he said.

Stewie put an arm over Chaun's shoulder. "If you don't be quiet and let her think, I'll put you back in the water with the shark. And I'll be in no hurry to pull you out this time."

Chaun clamped his mouth shut and stared at his feet. He didn't see Stewie wink at the rest of us.

Doc finished her calculations. "Okay. We'll run the operation from the *Omega*. Stewie, I want you to bring as many tanks of Trimix as you can carry down to the cave. Theresa's been there alone for days. She probably can't handle even a few more minutes by herself, even if she knows we're coming right away. And we may need you to help get Gus into the bell. Go now."

"Wait, Stewie. Let me draw you a map." I pulled an underwater slate off one of the BCDs Maddy had stowed on board and sketched a few quick lines, showing the wall, the ledge where we'd found the missing tanks, and then the location of the cavern. "It's about a hundred feet further along the wall, and about twenty feet deeper than the tanks were. There's a small overhang, making it hard to see. Keep an eye out for the brass cage door. It's still attached on one side."

Stewie nodded and took the slate. He immediately headed for the Zodiac and ran it as fast as it could go to the *Omega*.

Doc continued outlining her plan. "Maddy, you, Newton, and everyone else stay here on *Sea Princess*."

I broke in. "Oliver should captain the *Tranquility*. He can take us to *Omega* right now, and we may need him to fish us out when we get near the surface on the way back. It'll be easier from the smaller ship than from the height of *Omega*'s main deck."

Doc nodded her agreement with my change to her plan.

"Good. You'll bring us to *Omega*, and we may need you to pick us up when we're on the surface, but don't worry. You won't be needed for hours." I smiled at my soon-to-be brother,

Oliver nodded, then made the long jump across the water to land lightly on *Tranquility*'s deck. He pulled on the rope that connected the two boats, shortening its length so the boats drew close enough for Doc and me to step aboard.

As soon as we were on the *Tranquility*'s deck, he took off for the nearby *Omega*.

We were tying up alongside the big ship when we saw Stewie getting ready to enter the water, wearing two tanks on his back and two attached to the sides of his BCD. He stepped into the shark cage, and I noticed he'd loaded it with extra tanks of Trimix.

"Look. Stewie's bringing extra tanks. And more flashlights. Smart, since we have no idea how long it will take us to get down there with the rescue equipment," I said.

"Good thinking on his part," said Doc. "Almost like he was in the olden days."

She had a dreamy look on her face, but I decided not to pry.

At least, not right now.

The *Omega*'s crew hoisted us up on rope ladders so we wouldn't get *Tranquility* tangled with Stewie's lines as we might have if we'd tied up to the rear platform.

Doc and I climbed aboard, and she led the way to the equipment room. She pulled a crowbar off the tool bench and attacked one of two identical large wooden crates. She made short work of prying off the lid.

I peered in. The crate was filled with bright yellow plastic and stainless steel bars.

"Let's get this out on deck." She looked around for a dolly.

We rolled the dolly up to the deck, where Vincent had already set up two larger shark protection cages. The cages were loaded with Trimix tanks, and a long hose from the ship's compressor was zip-tied to the cage bars.

Doc nodded. "More good thinking. Stewie must have explained to Vincent what we'd need. This will save us a few minutes."

Since we'd be underwater for hours, she and I climbed into thick neoprene wetsuits for warmth.

I packed two more wetsuits into a gear bag and tossed it into the cage. "They've been down there so long that Theresa and Gus must be frozen." I clipped a couple of spare masks to my BCD for Gus and Theresa to wear while we were swimming.

Then Doc and I went to work assembling the diving bells inside the shark cages. When we'd finished, they looked like bright yellow umbrellas, with clear plastic panels on all sides for the inhabitants to observe the undersea world.

At last, we were ready to bring Gus and Theresa home.

Vincent's team lowered the shark cages until the tops of the cages were level with the water's surface. Doc and I each climbed into one of the cages. She gave Vincent the ready signal, and he flipped the cage tops down. We were protected from predators on all sides. Vincent's crew started the flow of compressed air into the diving bells, which inflated. The cages began to descend.

Chapter 38
Rescue Attempt

My cage had descended slightly faster than the one Doc was in, and I was fine with that. We were underway, and I was quivering with the need to get there NOW. I needed Theresa and Gus out of that horrible place as soon as possible.

As usual, Vincent had anchored the *Omega* almost directly over the spot we needed to access. As the ledge where we'd found the abandoned tanks came into view, I thought how lucky RIO was to have him as *Omega*'s captain.

Now we were at the cave entrance. The dive bells were both fully inflated from the compressed air *Omega* had been supplying through the hoses, ensuring the dry opening under both domes was large enough to fit four people easily.

With traditional diving bell technology, the air space would shrink as the bell went deeper because the increasing ambient pressure of the water compressed the air inside. The beauty of these new bells was the continuous flow of compressed gas automatically adjusted to the ambient pressure, so the air pocket remained at a consistent size.

We could have released compressed gas from dive tanks as we descended and kept the air replenished—almost like Todd had done with his cave. But having surface supplied air through the hoses made much more sense because of the length of time we might have to stay in the water.

My shark cage was about twenty feet away from the cave entrance —just a short swim. I signaled to Doc that I was going to leave my cage to get Theresa, Gus and Stewie out of the cavern. She gave me the okay sign, and after a careful look around, I opened the top of my cage to head to the cave.

A frantic banging sound caused me to pause, and I looked over at Doc. She was banging with her dive knife on the cage bars to get my attention. When she saw me look at her, she pointed out into the blue, where the silky shark was passing by. He too had heard the banging, so he was headed our way at top speed for a look at what all the commotion was about.

Doc and I hovered in our cages, as still as we could be. We didn't want to create any vibrations that the silky might interpret as having come from food. He swam back and forth in front of the cages and then over the top, giving us the side eye, as sharks do. After a few passes, he took off heading up the wall and over the lip to the top of the reef.

I looked at Doc, signaling my intention to make the swim to the cave. She gave the okay sign and turned around to watch the wall in case the shark came back.

Tentatively, I pushed up the door on the top of the cage and swam out. I quickly covered the twenty feet to the cave opening. I swam inside then I turned to give Doc the okay sign.

The floor of the passageway was littered with even more clumps of the foam insulation that must have fallen from the cavern's ceiling. It was a good thing we were getting Gus and Theresa out right away. I didn't think Todd's makeshift cave waterproofing job was going to last much longer, nor was the portable diving bell which he hadn't fully inflated.

Up ahead I could see a brightening of the water, and I blessed Stewie for his foresight in bringing along the extra flashlights. His presence and the light would have gone a long way to making the wait tolerable for Theresa.

My head broke the surface and I spit out my regulator. The air pocket was definitely smaller than it had been when I left it a few hours ago. Another few hours and the cavern might be completely filled with water by the tide, leaving my friends to drown. I said a prayer of thanks to the universe that I had managed to find them in time to save them.

Gus was still stretched out on the ledge, unconscious. Near his head, Stewie was hanging onto the ledge with one hand and holding on to Theresa's hand with the other. Even though he couldn't know if Gus was able to hear him, Stewie was talking softly to Gus, letting him know everything would be okay. He was still fully immersed in the water, because between all the tanks and flashlights he'd brought in, there wasn't enough room for him to sit on the ledge.

"Are you ready to leave this place?" I asked.

"More than ready," Theresa replied.

"Then let's get you suited up." I handed her one of the spare masks I'd brought. "Put this on, then slide into the water but stay on the surface. Stewie and I will get you into your BCD. You remember how to breathe through the regulator, right?"

She nodded and put the mask over her head. After opening it to its full extent, I handed her the folding snorkel I always carried in my BCD. "You'll only need this while we're gearing up. And if your ears start to hurt, hold your nose and blow—like your mother probably always told you not to. But don't blow too hard. Just enough to make them pop a little. Okay? Got it?"

She looked terrified, but she nodded.

"Good. I'll be holding your hand all the way to the cage. And Stewie and I will each be helping Gus. He'll be fine. If I ever need both hands for a second, you hold tight onto this loop, and we'll still be connected." I turned around to let her see the lift handle of the back of my BCD. "Don't worry. I won't lose you."

While I'd been working with Theresa, Stewie had pulled Gus off the ledge and was holding him upright in the water, I swam two strokes over and pulled a BCD loaded with a tank of Trimix off the ledge. I stuffed one of Gus's arms through it, and Stewie turned him so I could reach the other arm. Once the vest was over his shoulders, Stewie cinched the shoulder straps and fastened the cummerbund while I held Gus above water.

I handed Stewie the regulator, running the hose over Gus's right shoulder. Stewie put it in his mouth, but Gus didn't clench his jaw on it to hold it in place.

Of course not. He was unconscious.

Stricken, Stewie and I looked at each other over Gus's shoulder, trying to think of a solution. If his lips weren't clamped tightly on the regulator mouthpiece, Gus would drown if he inhaled. I kicked myself for not thinking of that before we'd started the dive. I could easily have brought a full face mask that would have solved the problem, but it hadn't occurred to me.

Stewie's eyes were wide and fearful. Theresa's hand was shaking in mine. I had to think of something.

"OK," I said. "Change in plan. I will swim out backwards, holding the regulator in Gus's mouth. I can't pull him and push the regulator into his mouth at the same time. Stewie, you'll need to swim on your side next to him, pulling him along. Theresa, instead of holding my hand, you'll be holding onto the loop on the back of Stewie's vest. It'll be tight traveling through the passage, but I think we can make it. If we get stuck, let go and swim straight ahead when there's room. We'll all get back in position in the mouth of the cave, and then swim to the cages."

Stewie thought for a minute. "That'll work. I'm glad you were here, Fin. My brain froze."

"It happens to everyone sometimes," I said. "Remember how far down we are. Now, when we get outside, I don't want to scare you, Theresa, but there will be two shark cages. Doc will be in one of them, and that's the one I want you and Gus to go to. Don't worry. Stewie and I will guide you."

"Shark cages?" Theresa said. "There are sharks?"

"Just a precaution," I said, holding Stewie's gaze hoping he'd be smart enough not to mention what had happened to Todd. "Now, as I was saying, Stewie and I will guide you over to the cage that Doc is in. She'll help you get inside, and she has a diving bell that you'll stay in while we decompress. It's like the one you've had here in the cave, but it's being supplied with air from the surface. It will stay inflated. It'll be several hours before we can go all the way up, but you want Gus to be safe, right?"

She nodded, brown eyes big and wide and full of unshed tears.

"Stewie, when we get to the mouth of the cave, I'll check outside. I can't let go of Gus to use my hands to signal. When we're ready to go, I'll nod three times, really big, like this." I gave an exaggerated nod, "And then we'll swim to the cage. Doc's will be on the left as we exit the cave."

He made the okay sign that he understood.

"Theresa, Stewie and I will go to the other cage as soon as we know Doc has you settled. You'll be able to see us out the portals in the diving bells if you want to check on us or if you want to look at the scenery. Remember, I'm going to be just a few feet away, and I won't let anything happen to you. Doc has her medical kit with her, and she'll start helping Gus right away as soon as you get inside. Everything will be fine."

As soon as Theresa said she understood, I pulled my mask up over my face and adjusted the strap. Then I put the regulator in Theresa's mouth and guided her hand to the strap on Stewie's BCD. I put the regulator in Gus's mouth and held my hands around it to seal it to his lips. Stewie put in his own regulator and gave me the okay sign.

Slowly, I began swimming backwards down the passageway, keeping eye contact with Stewie as I swam. I scraped against the side of the passageway a few times because I couldn't see where I was going. But there was no harm done, and soon I felt the current of the open ocean lifting my hair. We were at the mouth of the cavern.

I stuck my head out and looked around as much as I could without letting go of the regulator in Gus's mouth or letting the group get too far into the open before I knew it was safe.

I caught Doc's eye, and she gave me the okay sign. I looked at Stewie and nodded three times.

Then we pushed out of the cave for the swim to the shark cage.

Doc had the roof door unlatched, ready to let Theresa and Gus in. We swam awkwardly, but we made good time. Stewie let go of Gus and pulled Theresa to the top of the cage. He pushed on her shoulders gently to get her inside the safety of the cage, then Doc took her hand, and led her to the bright yellow diving bell. The two women ducked under the edge and then swam up into the air pocket.

Within a few seconds, Doc was back out to take care of Gus. Stewie and I swam with him to the top of the cage, then I sank down to where

Doc could reach Gus. She took his arm and swam to the diving bell. I went with her, still holding Gus's lips closed over the regulator mouthpiece. We rose until we broke into the air pocket within the diving bell.

She gave me the okay sign, and I knew she could handle Gus from this point. I swam back out of the bell. Before exiting the shark cage, I looked around to make sure the area was clear of predators. I didn't see the shark, but I didn't see Stewie either.

My heart sank. Had the shark swooped in and taken him during the short time I'd been in the bell with Doc? Frantically, I looked around.

Right. Left.

Up. Down.

Out to the blue.

Up the wall.

No sign of him.

I blinked back tears.

Maybe he'd had to retreat into the cave to get away from the shark. I started swimming in that direction when I saw motion out of the corner of my eye. I turned to look.

Stewie was safely inside the bell, waving through the porthole and smiling broadly.

I sighed with relief and turned to swim to the cage.

A dark shadow passed overhead.

The silky was back, circling.

A silky shark's attack signature.

Circling.

Between me and the cave.

Between me and the cage.

Circling.

I froze.

Halfway between the two cages.

Halfway between the cages and the cave.

I was scarcely breathing, wondering if I should wait out the shark or make a break for it.

After a minute that felt like an eon, Stewie swam out of the diving bell. He removed his dive knife and started banging it on the shark cage bars. It made a tinny sound that carried well through the water.

The shark turned, focused on this new distraction.

He rammed the cage, shaking it and knocking Stewie backward.

Stewie crashed into the bars behind him, but he wasn't hurt.

I swam backwards, slowly, barely moving my fins, until I bumped into the bars of Doc's shark cage. I took a deep breath and let myself rise until my hands were level with the top of the cage.

Meanwhile, Stewie kept banging on the bars, and the shark kept bashing his cage.

Doc had heard the noise and emerged from the diving bell. She unfastened the hinges that held the top in place and lifted it up far enough for me to dart inside. She quickly fastened it shut again, nanoseconds before the shark bashed into the bars of our cage, shaking the whole thing.

We swam backward and ducked under the edges of the diving bell, out of the shark's view. I rose through the water, breaking the surface into the air pocket. My heart was pounding, and my mouth was dry. Doc was right behind me.

She handed me a canteen. "Drink. You need to stay hydrated."

Chapter 39
Ascent

I DIDN'T WANT to upset Theresa, so I asked the question with my eyes.

Doc said, "He'll be fine until we get him topside. I won't know anything for sure until I can examine him thoroughly." She'd put Gus on an airbed attached to the diving bell's wall. He was still unconscious, but she was monitoring his vital signs and had even started an IV line. That woman was amazing.

We stayed at this depth for about two hours before Doc flipped on the video camera that communicated directly with the crew waiting anxiously on the *Omega*. She held up a slate on which she had written the depth she wanted them to pull the cages to. Almost immediately, the cages began to ascend.

Theresa hovered near Gus, holding his hand, talking to him constantly. She stared out the portholes and described the scenery and the sea life she saw. I don't think she realized how funny her voice sounded because she'd been breathing helium. On the other hand, she was so focused on Gus that she wouldn't have cared anyway.

We made several more extended stops for decompression. Doc was taking no chances with Gus and Theresa, who'd been deep underwater for days. Whenever she wanted the *Omega* to pull us up, she turned on the video camera and wrote the new depth on her slate. Our ascent took hours.

I knew when we'd passed ninety feet, because Doc flipped on the camera and wrote Nitrox on the slate. There was a brief lull in the hiss from the surface supplied breathing gas, and then it resumed. We were breathing Nitrox.

We made another short ascent and stopped again. We were above sixty feet. Now that it was safe, Doc added an oxygen cannula to Gus's medical equipment, so he was breathing even more enriched air.

The water pressure changes more per foot as you get closer to the surface, so any gas absorbed by our bodies would expand rapidly as we rose. That made these last sixty feet critical, and excruciatingly slow.

But at last, I saw the *Omega*'s lights shining onto the water's surface and froth breaking across the top of the cage. It was night, but we were at the surface. We were all safe.

Doc's medical team helped us board the ship. They strapped Gus and Theresa to gurneys and sprinted off to sickbay. Doc ripped her gear off and trotted after them.

I smiled my admiration. Nothing stopped that woman.

Stewie and I picked up her gear and put it away. The crew was busy unloading the empty tanks we'd used during our lengthy dive and dismantling the cages and all the support equipment we'd used during the long ordeal.

"Let's go home," I said.

Chapter 40
Aftermath

DOC FINALLY AGREED to let Stewie, Theresa, and me out of RIO's recompression chamber late the next morning. She'd kept Gus in *Omega*'s chamber overnight because she didn't want to take a chance on moving him until she was sure there was no risk of making his condition worse because of decompression sickness.

Through the chamber's portholes, I could see Maddy, Newton, Oliver, and Benjamin waiting for our release. Oliver was holding Angel, and Benjamin was playing peekaboo with her. Angel laughed with a baby's lack of self-consciousness.

Theresa rushed through the door as soon as it opened and scooped Angel into her arms. "Oh, Angel. Mama's here. My baby. I missed you too much." She smothered Angel's glowing face with kisses, as the baby squirmed with pleasure.

Maddy rushed over and hugged me tight. Tears ran down her cheeks. "We could have lost you." She held on for a moment before giving me a final squeeze and stepping aside to give Newton a chance.

We hugged, tentatively, and then suddenly his arms tightened around me. "Please don't ever scare us like that again. I can't lose you." His voice was raspy and low, meant for my ears only.

Tears flowed hot against the skin of my face, and I knew for sure my father loved me. I hugged him back. He brushed his tears aside with his hands before he stepped away.

Oliver came in for a hug. "Don't do that again, okay? We need you to hold this crazy family together." He kissed my cheek and stepped aside.

Then it was Benjamin's turn. He too leaned in and kissed my cheek before he folded me into his arms. He whispered in my ear, too softly for anyone else to hear. "You are an amazing woman, Fin Fleming. I am in awe." He started to turn away, then quickly turned back. "And possibly falling in love," he whispered.

I blushed and hoped no one had heard him. His words made me uncomfortable because I'd known him less than a week, and that week had been filled with stress and anxiety on so many levels. Benjamin was coming on way too fast for me, especially considering the tortoise-like pace my previous relationship with Liam, RIO's former CFO, had taken.

Liam and I had been together over a year, taking it slow and getting to know each other. We'd sworn we loved each other, and I'd never had the slightest inkling that he had a wife back home in Australia. He'd left a year ago to "take care of the problem." Nobody had heard from him since.

I'd have to talk to Benjamin. Tell him to slow down. I needed to get to know him, better than I'd known Liam. I didn't want a repeat of that fiasco.

As I stepped back from Benjamin, I noticed Stewie had been standing off to the side, alone. I felt sorry for him that he didn't have anyone waiting to greet him with the love and concern my family and friends had shown me.

I looked over Benjamin's shoulder at Stewie. "Thank you, Stewie. You're the real hero here. Your quick thinking may have saved my life when that shark was circling."

Theresa stopped cooing at Angel long enough to say, "And you kept me sane during those last few hours while I waited to be rescued. And I'm sure Gus heard your voice while he was unconscious, and I think it helped him. In fact, I know it helped him." She smiled her thanks at him.

"Thank you both," he said, no longer looking quite as forlorn.

The sound of her clogs tapping rapidly on the tile floors heralded Doc's approach "Gus is awake and asking for you, Theresa. He's fine, by the way."

A look of joy crossed Theresa's face. She thrust Angelina into Newton's arms and flew down the hall to see her husband.

Doc crossed over to Stewie. "Good work during the rescue. You thought ahead, brought the right gear, and kept a cool head when that shark was menacing Fin. I'm sorry you had to spend all that time alone in the diving bell."

Stewie looked startled at the praise. He'd been completely undependable for years, and we'd grown used to considering him a screw-up—and he considered himself the same way. It must have been heartening to hear that many compliments, especially from someone like Doc who usually didn't offer unearned kudos.

A few minutes later, Dane Scott walked into the infirmary with Roland and Morey. "We finished interviewing Gus and Theresa about what happened. We still have a few questions to close out the case. Got time for us, Fin?" He didn't look at either of my parents.

"Sure. Let's go to my office," I said.

He made an 'after you' gesture. I set off down the hall to my office, but not before I heard Doc quietly ask Stewie if he was free for a coffee.

It took only a few minutes for Dane to wrap up the case. After all, we had the kidnap victims back safely, and the perpetrator was deceased from more-or-less natural causes. Theresa had explained how Todd had asked Gus to help him start his boat, then knocked him unconscious. Todd had gotten her on his boat by claiming Gus had asked for her. Then he'd threatened to kill Gus if she didn't do as he said, and he forced them down to the cave. He'd even bragged to her about how he'd stolen waterproof tarps and cases of waterproof foam insulation and then the new-fangled diving bell off the *Omega*, when he was supposed to be moving supplies. That answered the remaining questions. The case was open and shut.

Chapter 41
An Invitation

THE MEMBERS of the police team were snapping their briefcases closed when Newton and Maddy came by.

"I'll see you later, Fin. Thanks for all your help with this case," Dane said, turning to go.

Newton held up his hand to stop their departures. "Not so fast, Dane. We're having a formal dress party in two days. It's primarily to celebrate Gus and Theresa's safe return, but it's also to express our joy that Oliver is now our son."

"And to celebrate your recent marriage too, I imagine," Dane said. "Congratulations to you, Newton. Best wishes, Maddy. I hope you're both very happy." His voice was flat, and his eyes looked dead. He turned to go.

Maddy stepped forward. "Can I talk to you in my office please?" Her voice quavered, very unlike her usual strong and confident tone.

"Sorry," he said. "I have to get back to the station. Maybe another time." He walked stiffly away.

I glared at my father. He had been totally insensitive to Dane's feelings, and that wasn't like him at all. On the other hand, I knew he'd wanted to get back with my mother for more than twenty years. He'd loved her the whole time they'd been apart. Hopelessly.

I could understand not wanting to send her off for a heart-to-heart with his romantic rival. But then the generous and caring Newton I'd come to know won out. "Go after him, Maddy. Tell him what's going on."

She bit her lip, but then she nodded. She ran out of my office, and I could hear her sandals clopping on the floors as she chased after Dane.

"Wait, wait. Dane, I really need to talk to you right now. It's important," she called. The sound of her footsteps stopped, and we couldn't hear anything else from the corridor.

I looked at my father. "Wanna tell me what's really going on? Or will I have to hear it from Dane—assuming she caught up to him and didn't give up."

"You know her better than that. She never gives up."

I perched on the edge of my desk. "Spill."

He sighed. "Remember I told you we'd have to stay in New York for a few months while we finalized the adoption? That was a slight exaggeration. My legal residence is still New York, so we had that going for us to shorten the time we had to be away. But then our lawyer told us the judge was concerned because Maddy and I weren't married. Even though Oliver's an adult, his honor didn't want Oliver with an unmarried couple. He said we could choose who got to be his new family."

"We both knew the Russo name was important to Oliver, and he could have that legitimately if Maddy adopted him." He held out his hand to stop the protest he knew was coming. "Yes, I know he already legally changed his name. It's more about the sense of family we wanted to give him."

He sighed. "But on the other hand, he's more interested in business than in oceanography, and being my son would give him a big head start. We sat down and talked, and we offered to let Oliver make the choice."

"Maybe that wasn't fair of us, to put the burden on him. But Oliver said he wouldn't—couldn't—choose between us. He'd forget about the adoption completely rather than hurt either of us. I tell you, he's one in a million."

I nodded, biting back my jealousy. "He is one in a million," I agreed, choking on my envy.

"Yes, he is. Anyway, this whole conversation was taking place in front of my lawyer, and he said the best way to solve the judge's problem would be to get remarried. He said we could claim to the judge that our mutual love for Oliver made us realize how important it was for us to be in a strong, committed relationship."

He paused here, sounding surprised. "So, we agreed we should get married for Oliver's sake. The lawyer had a prenup done by that afternoon, and Maddy and I got married the next day at City Hall. Oliver's adoption still won't be completely final for a few months, but at least now there aren't any circumstances the judge can object to. All three of us will have to spend a couple of weeks a month in New York to give the residency claim legitimacy, but we don't have to all be there at the same time. And in a reasonable time after the adoption is final, Maddy and I will go back to being exes."

I could see the thought pained him. I reached out and gave him a hug. "I still have the best family in the world. I'm glad you're in my life."

Chapter 42
Party Time

I WAS SITTING in my office reviewing the reports Chaun had given me that showed the location and movement of all our scuba tanks. It was a lot of information to take in, but with this level of control, it was unlikely we'd ever have a problem with missing tanks again.

Benjamin walked into my office. "What time should I pick you up tonight?'

"For what?" I put down the report I'd been studying and looked up.

He blushed. "For the party tonight. I assumed we'd be going together…"

"Oh, Benjamin. I'm sorry. I never bring a date to a RIO event. I'll be working the room all night, and it's not fair…"

"Well, I'll be working too. It's no big deal. But can we at least drive in together? We can get something to eat before we have to be there."

"Sorry, again. I'm getting ready over at Newton's. He wanted to talk to me about something. We'll be driving together. Maybe afterwards?"

"Sure." He turned away.

"Before you go, I wanted to thank you for recommending Chaun. I was looking at the latest report on tank movement, and it's exactly what we need."

"Chaun…"

"What about me?" asked Chaun from the doorway.

"I was just telling Benjamin how pleased I am with the RFID tags and reports. I'm grateful for your help."

He smiled. "Grateful enough to let me be your date at the gala tonight? If we go together, then we can go back to my new place afterwards. I closed on it this afternoon. I'm dying to show it to you. It's right in your neighborhood."

Before I could say anything, Justin poked his head in. "Hey gang. I just got back. And I believe Fin and I are going to the party together, isn't that right?"

My love life was out of control. Not a single date since Liam left, and now I had a line at my door. Unfortunately, I couldn't take any of them up on their offers.

"No, sorry, Justin. Sorry, Chaun. It's a work event for me. I never bring a date to RIO events, but I'm looking forward to seeing you all there. And right now, I have to finish up a few things and then get over to see Newton."

Justin said, "I'll drive you to Newton's. I'll be in the café until you're ready to leave." He stuck his hands in his pockets and strolled off down the hall, whistling a happy tune.

Benjamin and Chaun turned and walked off in the other direction. Benjamin said, "See you tonight," as he walked away.

I finished up my paperwork and shut down my computer. Pulling the canvas tote bag I used as a purse from my bottom desk drawer, I walked down the hall to pick up Justin.

True to his word, he was sitting in the corner, working on his computer, and talking on his cellphone. When he noticed me come in, he packed up quickly and hurried over to greet me.

Once in his car, he buckled his seat belt. "Do you have time for a ride before I drop you off? It's a beautiful day. I can put the top down."

I looked at my dive watch and realized I was going to be a few minutes late for my meeting with Newton as it was. "Sorry, Justin. I need to get there as soon as possible. And by the way, how is your grandmother doing?"

"She's fine. And your grandmother said to say hello." He jammed his batmobile into gear and hit the gas.

The recoil from our takeoff pushed me back into the soft leather of the seat before I could ask about my grandmother. "I didn't mean you had to get me there quite this fast. I just meant I don't have time for a ride first." The air blasting through the open sunroof picked up my words and flung them out of the car.

But Justin must have heard them, because he slowed down to a speed that was only a little too fast instead of downright scary. I gripped the handhold above my head and gritted my teeth. Luckily, we didn't have far to go.

Justin's car screamed to a halt in front of Newton's condo. "See you tonight," he said when I'd made it out of the car.

My knees were still shaking from the adrenaline, so I simply smiled and waved.

I stepped out of the elevator outside the door to Newton's penthouse condo. I didn't even have time to ring the bell when the door burst open. Newton grabbed my arm. "Right on time," he said. "She's waiting for you. They all are."

"Who's waiting for me?" I asked.

"Whoever goes first in these things. They're all here. Masseuse. Makeup artist. Stylist. Hairdresser. It's a thank you gift for working so hard while I was away. And for getting Gus and Theresa back unharmed. Gus has really turned into a good friend as well as my right hand man at work, and I was worried sick while he was missing."

"I don't need any of that. A simple 'thank you' would have done it for me."

"Oh, I know that. But I want to spoil you, and I want to show you off tonight. Indulge me, please."

We went inside, and as he said, there was a lineup of people who couldn't wait to start primping me up. I sighed. My father meant well.

One of the crowd of people stepped forward. "Your bath is ready," she said, handing me a thick robe of some silky material lined with terry cloth. "Can I give you a hand?"

"No thanks," I said, horrified at the thought.

"Okay. Take your time. Your massage isn't scheduled for another forty-five minutes."

"Um, okay." It wasn't her fault my father didn't know me well enough to realize this was not my thing.

But I had to admit the bath was spectacular. The tub was full of scented bubbles, and a glass of champagne sat on the ledge. I eased into the steaming water before I took my first sip.

The promised forty-five minutes sped by, and there was a knock on the door.

"Ready for your massage?" said a woman's voice.

I climbed out of the tub, slipped into the robe, and walked out into my bedroom. A portable massage table was set up in the middle of the room, and racks of clothes and shoes lined the walls.

The massage went by in a blur, and then I took a warm shower. It was time for my stylist to help me choose a dress for the evening. I would have worn the same dress I wore to all the RIO galas if Newton hadn't done this.

The stylist looked me up and down. "This one," she said, pulling a beautiful long gown from the rack. It was a floor-length, dark blue silk tank-style dress, covered all over with dangling drops of silver beads that shimmered and glistened with every move of the material. I caught a glimpse of the label. Chanel.

The stylist, whose name was Marina, conferred with the hair-dresser, the manicurist, and the makeup artist. When they were satis-fied with their plan, they went to work. Two hours later, Marina held the glittering gown for me to step into. She pulled it up to my shoul-ders and zipped it up the back. "It fits you like a glove," she said. "Perfect.

Then she slipped a diamond bracelet on my wrist and a matching necklace around my throat. A diamond clip shaped like an angelfish held back my hair. She told me to step into a pair of towering heels.

"I can't wear those," I said. "My feet will be killing me."

"Nope, they won't," she said, showing me the bright red soles. "Louboutin,' she said, as if that explained everything.

I had no idea what she was talking about, but the shoes were beau-tiful. Shiny, with swirling blues and greens that looked like the ocean. It felt as though the shoes had put a spell on me, and I was powerless to resist their call.

"Oh," I said when I'd touched the impossibly soft leather with a reluctant finger.

Marina smiled. "Exactly."

Chapter 43
Final Entrance

THE TEAM GATHERED AROUND ME, patting, smoothing, buffing. This pampering and primping marathon was amazing, even though I'd been certain I'd hate it. I rarely wore anything but cargo shorts and tees, with drugstore flip flops. My hair was more likely to be sticking straight up in clumps than it was to be brushed smooth. The only lotions I used on a regular basis were for sun protection, and I knew better than to waste time polishing my nails—the constant immersion in sea water floated the enamel right off in sheets.

This degree of preparation for an event was definitely not a process I was familiar with. It was no wonder I grew fidgety with all the fussing going on. Finally, I said "Ladies—enough. Thank you all very much. You've been great, but I'm done."

Walking toward the door, I caught a glimpse of my reflection in the mirror and almost didn't recognize myself. I turned back to the team. "Wow! I had no idea. An amazing transformation. You've worked magic. Thank you."

I walked down the hall to the great room, where Newton was sitting on the big leather couch reading the Wall Street Journal. He put the paper down when I entered the room, and he smiled at me.

"The only thing I've ever seen look as beautiful as you do right now was your mother on our wedding day." He grinned a crooked grin. "Both of them. You're as beautiful as she is."

My mother is as renowned for her stunning looks as she is for her oceanography, fund raising, and management skills. This was high praise indeed.

I smiled back. "Thanks. You don't look half bad yourself."

That was an understatement. My father always looks like he'd stepped out of the pages of GQ. His silver hair, piercing blue eyes, high cheekbones, and perfect teeth make a strong impression. Today, he was wearing a bespoke Brioni tuxedo that fit him just right, and he looked totally at ease in the slim cut suit. He was the perfect exemplar of a 'silver fox."

"I love you so much I wanted to spoil you. I hope you enjoyed it." He held out his arm. "Shall we go? Maddy already left, and we don't want to leave her to greet our guests all alone."

We drove the short distance to RIO in Newton's brand new, top-of-the-line, bright red Tesla. He'd recently traded in his gas-powered Mercedes for the electric vehicle. As founder and CEO of Fleming Environmental Investments, it behooved him to do everything he could for the environment.

RIO's massive lobby was empty of guests when we arrived. The caterers were still setting up the bar and buffet, and the band was in the far corner, tuning up their instruments.

Maddy was in the other corner, wearing a long azure silk one-shoulder dress that matched the brilliant color of her eyes, which were staring up into Dane Scott's unhappy face. They broke off their conversation as soon as they saw us.

Rather than let Newton stand there looking wistful while Dane looked angry, I took Newton's arm and walked him down the hall to my office. "I want to show you the film I entered in the Underwater Conservancy competition. I'm very proud of it and I'm interested in your opinion."

When we reached my office, I queued up the file and left Newton watching the video at my desk. "I'll come back to get you before the doors open to the guests. Meanwhile, just relax here."

Benjamin and Chaun arrived together as I reached the lobby. Benjamin looked handsome in his classic tux, with a blue cummerbund that matched his eyes. Chaun was in a tux too, but he'd replaced the traditional stiff white shirt with a red RIO branded t-shirt, and instead of polished black shoes, he wore red high-top sneakers.

We were standing near the entrance, ready to greet new arrivals when Stewie entered with Doc on his arm. She was almost unrecognizable without her white coat and stethoscope, but her green silk suit brought out the color of her eyes. He wore a dark suit with an open collared shirt and sandals.

Oliver, Gus, and Theresa all came in together, Theresa holding Angelica in her arms. I knew it would be a long time before the doting mother let that baby out of her sight again.

Now that all the guests of honor were here, the invited guests began to arrive, and the entire RIO and Fleming Environmental staff was busy greeting people and introducing them to each other.

I paused near the hall to catch my breath for a minute and immediately felt a tap on my shoulder. When I turned, I was happy and surprised to see Carl Duchette, the new Editor in Chief of Quokka Media, whatever that was. He gave me a 'business hug' and then introduced me to the lovely young woman by his side. "This is Genevra Blackthorne. I believe you've spoken on the phone."

We murmured polite greetings as the band began to play. Oliver strode up and asked me to dance, but Carl claimed I'd promised him the first dance. Oliver looked at Genevra with a question in his eyes and held out his hand to her. She smiled, and they walked out on the dance floor together.

I turned my attention back to Carl. "You know I don't dance, right?"

"Me either," he said with a twinkle in his eye. He watched Oliver take Genevra in his arms. "But don't they make a handsome couple?"

I went to my office to bring Newton back to the party. He was still sitting at my desk. He stood as I entered the room, and I saw tears in his eyes. "You're so talented, you take my breath away," he said. "If that film doesn't win top honors, the judges must have hearts of stone."

I kissed his cheek. "Thanks, Dad."

We walked back to the party together.

In the short time I'd been away, the room had filled up with friends, acquaintances, business associates, and potential donors. Even the police who'd worked on the kidnapping were here. The party was in full swing.

Newton and Maddy walked across the room to the bandstand. Newton took the mic from the band's singer and began to speak.

"Tonight is about celebrations, and the many things we have to be grateful for.

First off. Maddy and I have recently remarried…" He waited for the applause to die down.

"And we've found ourselves a son. Oliver Russo, consider this your official welcome to the family." More applause, louder this time.

And most importantly, we got our beloved friends Gus and Theresa back unharmed, thanks to DS Dane Scott, his dedicated team, Stewie Belcher, Doc Warren, and my beautiful daughter Fin. Thank you all for your courage and determination."

Now the room erupted in cheers. When the noise subsided, he turned to Maddy. "Anything you'd like to add to the list?"

She took the microphone. "Usually at these galas I'm all about asking for donations to help us with the important work we do here at RIO, but tonight, I feel so blessed that I won't even ask." She lowered the mic for a second, and then brought it back to her mouth. With a laugh she said, "But you can still make a donation at any time without waiting for me to ask."

Her words were greeted with laughter. I saw several people pull out their checkbooks or hand prepared envelopes to Benjamin, even though tonight was not an official fundraising event.

Doc walked over and whispered in Newton's ear. He handed her the microphone. "I have some great news. Stanley Simmons is awake. It'll be a long time before he's back to work at RIO, but we expect him to make a full recovery." More cheers, as Doc handed the mic back to Newton and walked away.

The party was going strong when Justin Nash entered the room, his blond hair shining above the rest of the crowd. Doc and Stewie were sitting at a table along the wall, sipping coffee. Theresa and Gus were dancing in the middle of the room, holding Angel between them in a perfect family circle. Oliver and Genevra stood in a corner, ignoring their wine as they stared into each other's eyes. They did make a handsome couple. Everyone was happy and in a party mood, except me. I wanted to be alone.

I slipped away down the corridor and out the rear entrance next to Maddy's office. I walked along the crushed shell path to the dock. I removed my stiletto heels and stepped onto my boat.

I needed the *Tranquility* and the way it made me feel loved. On the boat, I felt close to my late stepfather Ray. God help me, I even felt close to Liam, after all the time we'd spent together on this boat.

It was a beautiful evening. The full moon smiled down on me, casting a silvery glow along the water. The tiny wavelets glistened and shone, and the ocean's bioluminescence was as entrancing and hypnotic as I'd ever seen it.

I sat on the *Tranquility*'s gunwale and put my bare feet up on the bench beside me. I leaned over and rested my head on my bent knees, my head turned to stare out to sea.

The sound of a soft step from the pier startled me and I turned to see who was coming to disturb my peace. A tall man walked slowly along the dock. The newly installed security lighting glinted off his blond hair but obscured his face.

It had to be either Justin Nash or my ex, Alec Stone. They were the only two blond men I could imagine following me out here when I obviously needed to be alone.

The lights made his hair and the white shirt he wore with his tuxedo glow but left his face in shadow. "Permission to come aboard, Captain," said the man, standing tall a few feet away.

"Permission denied," I said. "I came out here to be alone." I kept my face averted.

"And I came to tell you that if you'll have me, you never need to be alone again."

I heard him kick off his shoes and step down onto the *Tranquility*'s deck. I bit back my annoyance.

I heard his footsteps as he crossed the deck and then smelled the scent of the roses he placed on the bench. He knelt beside me.

I turned my head to see who it was.

He gasped when he saw my face.

"You're beautiful in the moonlight," Liam, my ex-boyfriend, said.

In one hand he held a sheaf of papers bound in a blue cover, the way legal papers often were. The light was dim, but I saw the words Certificate of Dissolution of a Marriage printed on it.

In his other hand he held a small Tiffany blue box. He snapped the lid open, and the diamond ring inside put the moon's glow and the ocean's bioluminescence to shame.

He took the ring out of the box and slipped it on my finger.

"Fin Fleming, will you marry me?"

The ring fit just right.

The ring just felt wrong.

Too easy.

Too soon.

Too late.

I admired the beauty of the ring for a moment before I handed it back to him.

Also by Sharon Ward

In Deep

Sunken Death

Dark Tide

Killer Storm

Hidden Depths

Sea Stars

Or see the entire series Fin Fleming series by following the link.

If you enjoyed Dark Tide, you can continue reading about the adventures of Fin and the gang by following the links above.

Also, nothing helps an author more than a positive review, so please give Dark Tide (and me!) a boost by leaving a review. Here's the link:

Dark Tide

And if you'd like to subscribe to my totally random and very rarely published newsletter, you can sign up here.

Acknowledgments

Nobody writes a book alone, so I am lucky to have a group of friends who are great writers in their own right, and generous enough to help me along.

Andrea Clark, your analysis is always spot on and your critiques are always brilliant. I thank my writerly stars for the day we met, and for your generosity to a friend.

C. Michele Dorsey, we've been on this journey together a long time. I always appreciate your insight and your support. Our conversations are the highlight of my week.

Mary Beth Gale, you were my first real writing buddy, and I appreciate the way you never let me get away with anything. Dang! You're always right!

Kate Hohl, my friend and confidante. You help me so much, in so many ways you can't even imagine. You're the best.

Stephanie Scott-Snyder—you're such a joy. Thank you for all you do.

Thanks also to some great writing instructors—Hallie Ephron, Steven James, Sterling Watson, Hank Phillippi Ryan. I learn something new every time.

Mila for the awesome covers.

Jack for being the most awesome husband. I don't make it easy, but you always exceed expectations.

Molly.

Erin L. Erin R. Taylor. Cameron. Scott. Pat. Collin. Anthony. Josh. Jenn. Parker. Isaac.

My three brothers and their wives.

I'm lucky to have you all.

About the Author

Sharon Ward is an avid scuba diver. She was a PADI certified divemaster and has hundreds of dives under her weight belt. Wanting to share the joy and wonder of the underwater world, she wrote In Deep.

She lives on the south coast of Massachusetts with her husband, Jack, and Molly, their long-haired miniature dachshund. Guess who's in charge?

Dark Tide is the third book in the Fin Fleming Sea Adventure Series. Killer Storm is up next.

Printed in Poland
by Amazon Fulfillment
Poland Sp. z o.o., Wrocław
21 June 2023

099c5bbb-5bff-470b-a17a-9e171e913fd3R01